BAD BEAT

A RILEY THOMPSON THRILLER

ROBIN MAHLE

HARP HOUSE PUBLISHING, LLC.

Published by HARP House Publishing
August 2019 (1st edition)

Cover design: Covermint Design

Editor: Hercules Editing and Consulting Services www.bzhercules.com

For Sgt. William Tate, 101st Airborne

Vietnam veteran

Bronze Star and Purple Heart recipient, and many more honors that would be tough to fit on this page. Your wisdom and humor guided me into adulthood. Your love for my mother showed me what love is supposed to be. Your love for this country is everlasting. Thank you for your service.

1

——————

Shafts of early morning sunlight magnified through Riley Thompson's kitchen window and induced a dull ache in the back of her eyes. She closed the sheer curtains to diffuse the intense beams and turned away to keep close watch of the coffee maker while it brewed. When the cycle finished, she raised the stainless steel carafe and tipped it into her waiting mug. Her attention was diverted when her beloved schnauzer, CJ, barked outside. With the carafe still in her hand, Riley gazed out. CJ stood in the middle of the yard, surrounded by tall green grass that skimmed his underbelly. With his teeth bared and tail pointed, he snarled at the sky.

Anguish knotted in her without warning and from a place deep-seated in her psyche. Her spine tingled and her skin crawled. As she fixed her sights on CJ's bearded face while he barked with growing intensity, a single thought exploded with white-hot energy. A mournful, agonizing wail clawed from her throat. "No!" Riley dropped the carafe into the sink, steaming coffee splattering across her police uniform shirt. She pressed her hands against her ears to mute the cries that battered her skull.

CJ fell silent and whipped his head toward the window. He trained his sights on Riley. She homed in on his stare for just a moment, then collapsed in a heap on the floor. A puddle of coffee surrounded her. "No. Please don't be dead. Please, God, don't let him be dead." But she knew he was. She'd felt the moment of his passing.

The gift that had been handed down from her grandfather had never betrayed her. The connection between Carl Boyd and Riley had formed years ago, sixteen years ago, after the EF4 that almost took her life and that of her family. That connection had just been severed with razor-sharp precision. Carl Boyd, a man who had been a stand-in father, grandfather, and mentor was dead.

She opened her heavy-lidded brown eyes and pulled away from the cabinet against which she had been slumped. Consciousness fell away for a length of time of which she was uncertain. Scratching sounded on the back door. "CJ." Riley pushed off the kitchen floor, her uniform soaked in coffee, and walked to the door leading to the backyard. As she opened it, CJ raised his eyes to her. He hurried inside, whining, and brushed against her legs. "It's okay, buddy. It's okay. I'm fine." Riley was anything but fine.

The clock mounted on her kitchen wall above the oven revealed that nearly thirty minutes had passed. The wailing in her head ceased, but her heart ached so deeply, she struggled to catch her breath. "I have to call the center." Before Riley made it to her cell phone that lay on the kitchen counter, it rang. It was the senior home where Carl had lived for the past several years. A place Riley had visited at least three times a week, bringing him food, checking in on him. Mostly, she did it for selfish reasons. Carl had so much wisdom to offer and he did so willingly.

"Hello?" She braced for the inevitable words.

"Riley, I'm so sorry, honey..."

"He's gone," she replied in a whisper.

"He passed a short while ago, after he returned to his room from breakfast."

She closed her eyes, forcing tears to spill over onto her full, pale cheeks. "Can I come see him?"

"They're on their way to take him to the mortuary. It's best if you see him there."

"Did he—suffer?" Riley asked.

"No, sweetheart. He was in his favorite chair and just—fell asleep."

"Thank you. I'll go to the mortuary." She ended the call and peered at her feet, where CJ had curled up. "I have to go see him, buddy." Riley gently moved out from under him and looked down at her uniform. "I suppose I should change first." And as if in a stupor, she walked to her bedroom.

Riley tucked a fresh shirt into her uniform pants, accentuating her curvy midsection, and returned to the kitchen when a knock sounded on her door. The hollow thump echoed in her mind, and before opening it to who she knew waited on the other side, a moment was needed to steady her emotions. Riley straightened her shoulders and gripped the door handle. She swallowed down the lump in her throat and opened the door. "Hey. Thanks for coming."

Captain Dan Ward was Riley's commanding officer at the Owensville Police Station, which employed only three other offi-cers. In the small town in southern Indiana of roughly 4,000, there wasn't much call for a large police force. Except when the Indianapolis-based mafia tried to set up operations at the old Caterpillar plant on the edge of town, but that was long over now. The court case was due to go to trial later in the year.

"Riley, I'm so sorry." Dan walked inside and embraced her. "I'm glad you called me, though. You shouldn't do this alone."

She pulled away and wiped the tears from her cheeks. "They said he went peacefully. It didn't feel that way to me."

"You—knew it?"

"I felt the pain. It took a minute for me to realize where it was coming from. I don't think he wanted to leave me."

"Of course he didn't. He loved you like a daughter. But he's in a..."

"Better place. Yeah, I know. Doesn't make it any easier."

"No. Are you ready to go?" Dan shoved his hands in his pockets and the look on his face revealed that he wasn't quite sure what to say or if his words would matter.

"I'm ready." Riley scratched CJ behind the ears. "I'll see you later, buddy. Everything's going to be all right." She waited for Dan to step outside and followed him, closing the door behind her.

"Have you talked to Jacob yet?" he asked.

"No. Not yet." She followed her captain to his police cruiser and stepped into the passenger seat.

Jacob Biggs had been Riley's high school sweetheart and her friend since she was ten. After high school, he left for college and then Indianapolis for work as an architect. Riley never held it against him. He wanted the big city life. However, that ended up biting him in the backside when he returned four months ago and brought with him the mafia, though he was an unwilling participant. It was his boss who had been corrupted. Nevertheless, trouble had followed Jacob back to Owensville and it took the entire police force with help from the big city cops to bring it to an end.

Now that it had all settled down, the two had been dating again. Riley wanted to take it slow. He'd broken her heart before, and she guarded it well this time around.

Dan rolled into the lot of the mortuary and shifted the car into park. "You sure you're ready for this? It doesn't have to be today."

"Yes, it does. I need to see him." Riley stepped out of the patrol car, adjusted her holster, and started toward the red brick building that was the town's only mortuary.

The last time she'd been here was when Carl's son, CJ, was killed. He had tried to protect her and it cost him his life. It was also the last time Riley had been to a funeral. Most of the town had shown up not because they knew CJ; they didn't. He hadn't lived in Owensville. They showed up for Carl Boyd, a man who had grown up in this town, fought for his country, lost his first wife and daughter and had lost his son. Carl had no one left except Riley.

She stood in front of the entry doors with marked hesitation.

Dan approached and placed his hands atop her shoulders. "You can do this, kid. I know you can."

Riley nodded and walked inside. The distinctive odor of bleach and flowers overwhelmed her senses, and for a moment, suppressed her grief. The moment passed when a woman in a black pencil skirt and a white button-down shirt approached. Her eyes revealed too much death and sadness. Riley wondered how one could separate themselves in this line of work.

"Good morning. I'm Shannon Goodacre. You must be Riley Thompson?" The woman offered her hand.

"Yes, I'm Riley." She returned the greeting. "This is Captain Ward. Sorry we're in uniform."

"Don't be. Times like these don't arrive at one's convenience. Please, follow me. I'll take you to see Mr. Boyd."

The thin, older woman wearing a tight bun pressed on with purpose, like she had done this many times before. Her outward appearance bore a cold detachment, but Riley knew the truth. This woman had a gift of her own. One that allowed her to push deep into her depths the sadness that accompanied grief. Riley suspected she had suffered much of it on a personal level. Her reasons for taking on a position such as this led Riley to believe it was the old adage "misery loves company."

"Here we are." Ms. Goodacre spun on her thin-heeled black pumps. "Are you ready to go inside, Officer Thompson?"

"Yes, ma'am. I'm ready."

"Very well." She turned the knob and opened the door. "He's right through here." Her heels clicked on the shiny linoleum. "Please forgive the odor. We don't usually bring family or friends down here, but we understand this is a bit of an unusual situation."

"Unusual? How?" Riley's rubber-soled shoes squeaked on the floor with her every step.

"Well, unusual in that you're an officer of the law. Please understand this isn't our normal protocol. We prefer to prepare the deceased and take them to a room to be presented to members of the family. However, it was our understanding we were to allow your visit at your convenience."

"Who asked you to allow this?" Riley tossed a glance to Dan.

"I called ahead and asked," Dan said. "I wanted to be sure he was here before we drove over. I'm sorry. I hope that's okay."

"Of course." Riley wasn't entirely sure if it was okay, but then her thoughts were so muddled right now, it was difficult to know anything for certain. What mattered was that she was about to see Carl on a table, probably beneath some white sheet. Why the hell did they always use white anyway?

Riley stopped cold and took in a breath to slow her pulse. The air was pungent, no doubt, but her emotions were about to take over and she couldn't break down here. Not here, of all places.

The woman pulled down the sheet to Carl's upper chest. The sheet outlined his body, which appeared much frailer than Riley had expected. Had he been losing weight and she didn't know it? Carl almost always wore oversized shirts. Maybe he was always this thin.

"I'm sure you would like a moment alone. Please, take as much time as you need. I'll be waiting outside."

"Thank you," Riley replied.

"Do you want me to go too?" Dan asked.

"I would like just a couple of minutes, if that's okay."

Dan nodded and followed Ms. Goodacre out the door.

Riley examined him. "Well, you've looked better, Carl." He would've appreciated the humor, even if she didn't feel like laughing. "You weren't supposed to go yet. I'm not ready to live without you. But I know you're happy now to be back with your family. You'll be sure to say hi to CJ, right?" Her eyes burned with tears as they streamed down her cheeks. Her gaze drifted to his left shoulder where she saw his tattoo. She'd only seen it once or twice before, whenever Carl felt in the mood to wear a sleeveless shirt, which over the past sixteen years, wasn't often. He had been in the Marines and served in Vietnam. The tattoo read, "Swift, Silent, Deadly."

"I'll never forget what you've done for me and my family. I

love you so much and I'm so blessed to have had you in my life." Her voice quivered and Riley felt like a child again. The same child who stood frozen before Carl when he opened the door of his trailer on that fateful day.

There was only one thing she had left to do but feared doing it above all else. Sometimes, if it was soon enough after someone's death, a touch of her hand on them would reveal a great many things. But if too much time had passed, she might pick up a few abstract images or nothing at all. Carl had died only a few hours ago. Chances were good, if she placed her hand on him, she might see his final thoughts. But was she ready to see them or would it bring too much hurt?

Riley's hand hovered over his left arm and trembled. She recalled the agonizing sensation from this morning when she sensed his death. "They said you weren't in any pain. Is that true?" She closed her eyes and lowered her hand. His skin was cool, but not cold, like he just needed a blanket. And then it happened.

Images hurled through her mind as though she stood inside a darkened wind tunnel and blurred pictures flew past her. They swirled around her like she was inside the eye of a tornado. "Stop. Please. I can't see anything. It's too fast."

In the blackness of her mind, the pictures fell to her feet. Thousands upon thousands lay around her. It was his life. Everything Carl had been through, the good and the bad, lay before her. "What do I do with this?" She peered down and a few images floated up and hovered in front of her face. Riley smiled. They were pictures of Carl and Riley, and her brother Dillon. All happiness and smiles. Then another moved to the front. Carl was on his chair. "This was when you passed?"

He hadn't been in pain. In fact, there had been a hint of a

smile on his lips as he leaned back on the recliner. "Thank God. Thank God." She felt that he hadn't suffered, at least not at that moment. Carl had had a lifetime of suffering, but this was one moment in which he hadn't.

Riley began to pull her hand away, but he stopped her, as though gravity held it down. "What? Tell me what you want to say."

As she continued to stand in the pitch black with images resting at her feet, a sense of dread fell on her shoulders. Now, instead of pictures, a deck of cards rained down on her and she raised her arms to shield her head. "What is this?"

The Queen of Hearts was the last to fall and it landed in the palm of her hand. Riley examined it. "I don't understand. Carl, what is this? What are you trying to tell me?" But that was it. Whatever had been seizing her hand had let go. She pulled it away and opened her eyes. That was all she was going to get; random images from Carl's life and a deck of cards.

The door opened and Riley swung around.

Dan walked inside. "Hey. You've been in here a while. Is everything okay? I don't mean to barge in..."

"It's okay. I've said my goodbyes." She started ahead but stopped and turned back once again. "I love you, Carl."

Dan held the door for her as she passed through. He glanced at Carl's lifeless body. "She wouldn't have made it this far without you, buddy. Rest in peace, old friend."

Riley waited in the floral-scented lobby for Dan to catch up. "If you want to drop me back at my house, I can pick up my car and head in."

Dan cocked his head and placed his hands on his narrow hips. "What are you talking about? You're not going in to work today."

"It's better if I do. Come on, Captain, you know me. I need to keep busy."

"Normally, I'd agree with you, but not this time, kid. I'll take you home. We'll talk about you coming in tomorrow."

Resigned, she followed Dan back to his car and stepped into the passenger seat, waiting for him to start the car. "Cap, please, trust me when I tell you, I'm much better off at work. I need the distraction." Surely he would understand. It was the only weapon in her arsenal right now.

"Riley, I get what you're saying and I whole-heartedly disagree —this time. Look, it's already coming up on lunch. What's the point of you coming in this late in the day? We aren't busy. Pruitt can handle whatever comes in, I promise you. Unless you don't have confidence in him."

"That's not what this is about and you know it," Riley replied.

"I think you should have Jacob head on over to your house and keep you company. You can lose your thoughts in a movie or something like that. You need the downtime, Riley. Please, just humor me, okay? I don't ask for much."

Riley turned away and peered through the passenger window. "He's at work."

"Now you're just making excuses. I ain't falling for that nonsense. You know if you ask, that boy will jump. Frankly, I'm surprised he hasn't moved in with you yet."

"Yeah, well. There's still a lot of things he and I need to work out. I guess I'm not there yet."

"You might not be, but I can tell he is." Dan made a left onto her street. "As a general rule of thumb, I know you don't like doing what I say, but most of the time, I'm right. You just hate admitting it."

"Maybe." Riley cracked a tender smile. "Fine. I'll take off the rest of the day. Maybe I'll call Jacob, I don't know."

"It'd be best if you had someone with you. Unless you want me hanging around?"

"No thanks, Cap."

He pulled to a stop and walked around her side to open the door. Riley stepped out and he followed her to the front porch. "Now if you need anything, anything at all, you just pick up the phone."

"I will. Hey, you'll tell Pruitt?"

"You know I will." Dan pulled Riley into a tight embrace. "Now go on, get your boyfriend over here to take care of you. That's what they're supposed to do."

"Okay. I'll see you tomorrow." Riley walked through the door. "Thank you, Dan." She watched as he pulled out of her driveway and then closed the door. CJ was already at her feet. "Hey, buddy. Feel like keeping me company on the couch today?" She scratched behind his ears and his tail wagged.

2

Jacob Biggs had made his unforeseen return to Owensville four months ago, amid an ongoing murder investigation in which he ended up playing a major role. Since then, in the small Indiana town, not much had happened, which was exactly the way Riley preferred it. She never was the type to seek out thrills or danger or anything of that nature. Her ability to sense the emotional turbulence of those she cast her sights upon served up enough of that to last her a lifetime. But Jacob felt differently. He thought life in the big city was the be all, end all. Turned out, it was anything but.

When he was fired from his architect job in Indianapolis and decided to return to Owensville last fall, he didn't know trouble would follow him. It was Riley, Captain Ward, and Ethan Pruitt who would stand against the mafia, with the help of some Indianapolis cops who were looking to put the bad guys behind bars.

Murders just didn't happen in Owensville, not until Jacob Biggs came back to town. Riley knew it was unfair to attribute it to him and felt guilty just for thinking it. In fact, she had faced down worse back in the days when her abilities were new and frightening, and Carl Boyd was her savior. So was Dan Ward, for that matter. She was only ten and her brother Dillon, only fourteen. They needed a strong male figure in their lives because their father, Jack, certainly wasn't one. In fact, they might have died if it had been left up to him.

Now Carl was gone and Riley was lost. From the overwhelming grief that crashed into her to the playing cards he showed her with a nameless meaning, she reeled in uncertainty.

Riley lay on her sofa with CJ in a ball beside her and the television broadcasting the evening news. She reached for her phone on the side table and made the call. "Hey. It's me. Are you still at work?"

"I'm just taking off, actually. Are you at the station?" Jacob asked.

"No. I'm at home."

"Oh. Is everything okay? Are you sick?"

"No. I'm not sick, but, um, well, it's been kind of a rough day." Her long pause would be cut short by Jacob if she didn't continue soon. This Band-Aid needed to be pulled off. "Listen, um... Carl passed away this morning."

Jacob was silent, probably absorbing the news. "Oh my God, Riley. I'm so sorry. Geez. This morning? Why didn't you call me? I would've come over."

"I didn't want you to miss work. I know you just got that job, and well, the captain helped me out. He took me to the mortuary to say goodbye. But I'm telling you now."

"Yeah. I guess so. I can be there in twenty minutes. I'll bring dinner."

"You don't have…"

"Yes I do. I'll see you soon."

THE RUMBLING FROM JACOB'S OLDER MODEL MUSTANG AS IT approached the front of Riley's house caught her attention. She stood from the sofa, forcing CJ from his comfortable spot, and walked to the door. The bright headlights lit up her living room for just a moment until he parked and turned them off. She opened the door and wore a compulsory smile at his approach. "Thanks for coming. You didn't have to…"

"Last I checked, I was your boyfriend. This is kind of my job." Jacob held two plastic bags. "I hope you're in the mood for Chinese."

"Sounds great. Come in." Riley stepped aside while he entered, and she closed the door behind him. "You can put in on the kitchen table. I'll grab some plates." Food was the last thing on her mind; regardless, Jacob had gone out of his way and made the effort. She wouldn't insult him by refusing the meal. Making others happy was what Riley did best.

Jacob set down the food and immediately advanced with open arms. "I'm so sorry about Carl, Riley. I know how much you loved him." He pulled her close to his chest.

It felt good to be in his arms. It always did. Her love for Jacob was never the problem. It was the fact that he abandoned her, regardless of whether she insisted it was what he should do. It wasn't fair to put that on him, but nothing in this life had been fair to Riley Thompson. Nothing.

He gently pushed her back. "You look like you're holding up okay, but looks are deceiving."

"I'm okay. I mean, I'm not, but I will be—in time." She walked to a cabinet and retrieved two plates. "We should eat. Don't want the food to get cold."

They sat on the sofa with their plates of Chinese food and watched the news, neither speaking of what Riley had seen when she touched Carl. Jacob was no stranger to her abilities and how her gift worked. He'd seen it when they were younger. He'd also witnessed how much stronger it had become now that she was an adult. What she'd done that day at the old plant just a few short months ago was unlike anything she had done before. Riley picked up that man as if he was nothing more than an insect and flung him across the plant floor, dangling him over a conveyor belt, ready to end his life. That was how strong she had become. Willing people to move wasn't something she could do as a child.

"I can tell you want to know what I saw." Riley placed her fork on the plate and turned to him. "With Carl."

"You don't have to tell me anything, Riley. I'm just glad you called me."

"I'm sorry. I should've told you earlier." She wiped her mouth with a napkin and tucked behind her ears her thin blonde hair. "He wasn't in pain. I know that, thank God. He showed me his life, in pictures. It was wonderful and horrible at the same time. Carl suffered a lot of terrible things in his life."

"That he did," Jacob replied. "I'm glad to know he passed peacefully. I'm sure that must be a consolation for you."

"Yes, but then it changed. I was still there, the pictures of his life were there, but then he showed me a deck of cards. They just floated down, one by one. I caught one of them, the Queen of Hearts. I don't know what any of that was supposed to mean."

"I don't know either."

Riley sighed. "I have to start making the arrangements tomorrow. I need to clean out his apartment."

"Let me help. Please. It's the least I can do, and I want to do it."

"Okay. Yeah."

RILEY PULLED HER BAG FROM THE DESK DRAWER. "I'M heading over to Carl's apartment." She looked at her partner, Officer Ethan Pruitt. "You'll be okay here for a while? I won't be but a couple of hours."

"I'll be fine. I'm sure the captain and I can hold down the fort while you're gone. Is Jacob going with you?"

"He is."

"Oh." Pruitt cast away his gaze. "Well, you shouldn't be going on your own. So. Good. Glad to see he's stepping up."

"Ethan, you know how hard Jacob's been trying. Come on. After what we all went through with the mob guys. He got shot, for Pete's sake."

"I know he did. I'm sorry. You're right. I need to cut him some slack." Pruitt returned his attention to his computer. "Still, I mean, the guy broke your heart, but whatever. Not my business."

Riley regarded him with dismay. "I'll be back later. Let Cap know?"

"Copy that." He watched as she started to leave. "Hey, Riley."

She turned back. "Yeah?"

"I know what he meant to you—Carl. If you need a shoulder, or whatever..."

"Thanks, Ethan. You've always been there for me." She smiled and pushed through the doors.

It was no secret how Ethan Pruitt felt about Riley. Not only had she seen it in his eyes and felt the emotions in his mind, but he'd said as much too. It had been hard for him to watch Jacob work his way back into her life and she tried to make it easier on him. Her efforts, however, seemed futile. No matter what Jacob did or how he helped Riley, Ethan would never forgive him for hurting her. He wasn't even there when it happened after graduation, but he knew about it. Everyone did. Riley Thompson and Jacob Biggs were supposed to be together forever. That was what the whole town thought. No one else knew of Riley's gift back then. The night of the tornado, Jacob didn't know then either. It wasn't until they started dating in high school that she revealed to him what had happened and what she could do. It nearly scared him off. Maybe she would've been better off if he had ended it then, but he didn't. He decided to wait until she was completely and utterly in love with him to cut ties.

Well, Ethan Pruitt hadn't forgiven him for that, even if Riley had. Mostly. And when Jacob returned, bringing all kinds of trouble with him, it was another reason for Ethan to dislike him. Now that a few months had passed, and she and Jacob appeared to be on the mend, Riley felt Ethan was further disenfranchised from her life. But he wasn't, not from her perspective. She never really had those feelings for him to begin with. So Jacob coming back had no bearing on what might've happened between them.

Riley pulled to a stop alongside the front of the senior facility. She stepped out of her patrol car, dressed in her brown uniform, which she begged the captain to change to blue or something less like a UPS driver. A smile stretched across her lips when she spotted Jacob walking toward her. "Thanks for coming."

He approached and kissed her on the cheek. "Of course. This isn't something you should do alone, Riley."

"Come on. Let's get this over with." She led the way inside and immediately felt grief from the two staffers who had cared for Carl on a regular basis. Riley knew them both well. "Hey."

"Oh, Riley, honey, I can't tell you how sorry I am about Carl." The older woman, slightly plump, but well put together, wrapped her arms around her. "That man was a thorn in my side, and I loved him so much."

"I know you did, Carol. He knew it too."

"And he loved you most of all. Don't you forget that, Riley Thompson. Don't you ever forget that."

"I won't. Do you think we could go up?" She peered back at Jacob, who stood with his hands in his pockets, appearing sullen. "We'd like to clear out his things."

"Of course." The woman turned to her colleague. "Hey, Rose, would you mind letting them in Carl's room?"

"Sure. I'll take you up." Rose pushed up from her chair. Dressed in pink scrubs, slim, and approaching sixty, she led them to his room. Her sneakers squeaked on the scuffed faux-marble floor and her scrubs swayed loosely around her figure. "We are really going to miss that miserable old goat."

Riley smiled because she could sense Rose truly loved Carl. He was a miserable old goat, but that didn't change the fact that he had a great big heart.

Rose inserted her key into the lock and pushed open the door.

"Take as long as you need. Anything you don't want will be donated."

"Thanks, Rose." Riley stepped inside. Her senses were bombarded. She stumbled back a few steps when Jacob reached out for her.

"Hey. It's okay. I got you. You're okay." He steadied her before turning back to Rose. "I got it from here. She'll be all right. It's just a lot to take in."

"Sure it is, honey. You let me know if you need anything at all." Her eyes shifted to Riley and began to well with tears. "You'll be okay, sugar."

Jacob waited until Rose left and shut the door behind her. "Can you stand on your own now?"

"Yeah. Sorry. It just kind of hit me all at once."

"I know. We'll take this one step at a time, okay? I'm here for you."

Riley returned her weight to her feet and smoothed down her uniform. "Okay. I'm ready." She felt his presence everywhere. It was as though he was still sitting in his favorite recliner, the one on which she now set her sights. This was going to be more difficult than she first thought. "Just suck it up," she whispered.

"What's that?" Jacob asked.

"Nothing. I just need to pull my act together. I'll start in his room. He got rid of most of his stuff before he moved in here, but anything that meant something to him will be in there."

"Sure. I'll let you go and take care of that. I'm sure you'll want the time to yourself."

Riley nodded and walked into the short hall and veered right into the only bedroom. As she gazed around the room, she realized he was a man of ordinary means. He never wanted for anything because he didn't need much. The double bed against the back wall. A couple of tattered oak nightstands with lamps. A tall-boy chest of drawers was fixed in the corner with a television on top of it. The TV had been a gift from Riley a couple of years ago when she realized he was spending more and more time in his bed as he aged. There were usually only two places one would find Carl in his apartment. His bedroom and his recliner. Unless it was meal-time, then he'd make himself go downstairs to eat in the cafeteria with the rest of the "old biddies," as he used to call them. There weren't a lot of men in this place. He often quipped how he could have had any one of them broads if he'd wanted. Pick of the litter. But he hadn't wanted that. In fact, Riley couldn't recall him with a woman in the sixteen years she'd known him. But Riley likened it to the fact that after his second wife died, he figured there wasn't much point. He might've been right.

She walked to his closet and opened the door. Several clothes hung on hangers. Mostly t-shirts and jeans. That was who he was. But as she peered up to the shelf, she spotted a shoebox. A rush of feelings pushed through her. This box meant something to Carl. She raised on her tiptoes and pulled it down, setting it on his bed.

Upon opening the lid, several photographs were stacked on top of one another. "Pictures. You showed me these." Riley tipped over the box and spread out the photos. Some were Polaroids, some were prints that had been developed at Walgreens. Most were pretty old. Riley sifted through them, recognizing several he had chosen to show her yesterday.

The image she was most drawn to, she picked up. A young woman and a child, a little girl. Riley knew instantly who they were. Carl's first wife, Rosalyn, and daughter, Mary, both killed in a car accident in 1973 when Carl was in the Marines. The one responsible for that accident was her own grandfather. It was a revelation that came by way of her gift. She hadn't recognized it as a gift in those days. It was more of a curse.

"You're with them now, Carl. And CJ. You have your family back." She pressed the photo against her chest and sobbed. She had made it through last night without succumbing to the grief, but now, seeing the picture, feeling him all around her, it was more than she could bear. Releasing the pain was her only remedy.

Jacob must've heard her cries as he rushed in. "Riley? Riley, are you okay?"

Of course she wasn't, that was obvious, but it was the usual sort of thing people said when no words could offer enough comfort.

"It's just being here, you know? Seeing all his stuff. These pictures. He kept what mattered most to him."

Jacob picked up one of the prints. "You mean, like this one?"

Riley smiled at the image. It was the day she graduated from the Police Academy. He stood next to her like a proud grandpa. Dan was on the other side. The two men who were more like a father and grandfather than her own family ever was. That wasn't entirely fair because she never knew her grandfather, not Jack's dad anyway. Though she had more in common with him than with any other member of her family.

"I remember this like it was yesterday," she said.

"It must've meant a lot to Carl to keep it with all these. You meant the world to him, Riley. But it's time to let go. He needs to rest, and he might try to stick around if he thinks you need him to. Tell him you'll be okay. That you learned all he had to teach you and you can take it from here."

Those were probably the wisest words Riley had ever heard

come from Jacob's mouth. Carl had just passed, but the strength of his soul still lived here. It was much too strong. Maybe he was right. Carl would never choose to abandon her. "You know, this guy over here," she began to speak to the room. "I think he might have you pegged. I have learned so much from you. Strength, compassion, fearlessness—forgiveness. You did your job, Carl. It's time for you to enjoy your family. I'm sure there'll be a Hoosier game on soon anyway, right? Go on. Go watch the game. I'll be just fine." She lost her voice but turned to Jacob and in a whisper began, "I'll be just fine."

3

Time heals all wounds. That was how the saying went and while that was true for most, Riley still felt the sting of losing Carl, and in the six months that had passed, she wondered when the healing would begin. Summer had arrived. However, she wasn't the same and didn't have the foresight to see if she ever would be. Still, Carl wouldn't want her to wallow in self-pity, so she worked hard to prevent that from happening. And there were great things in her life to look forward to; one of which was the fact that today was moving day.

Riley propped open her front door as the breeze had picked up with the heat of the day. Jacob walked toward her with a box in his arms. She peered around him and noticed the trailer attached to the back of his car. Everything he owned was in that trailer and it didn't appear to amount to much. All the better, though. Riley's house was a bit too cozy to add much more to it.

"You've got your hands full," Riley began. "Come on in. It may be best to stack everything in the kitchen and sort through it later."

ROBIN MAHLE

"You got it, babe." Jacob wore a broad smile and set down the box. CJ ran to him and jumped on his legs. "Hey, buddy. You want to help me unload the trailer?" He looked at Riley. "It's a good thing he likes me."

"You think you'd be moving in here if he didn't?" She chuckled and walked outside in the blistering sun. The concrete path in the front yard led her to his car and the opened trailer. It still didn't feel quite real to her that she was going to be living with Jacob. They'd gotten much closer since Carl passed. He'd been there for her every step of the way in learning to cope with the loss. Sometimes, Carl visited her in her dreams. It wasn't often, and it wasn't like a premonition, which she was prone to have on occasion. She would just see him standing underneath the great big oak outside the church where he had held his son's funeral. No words, no smile. He would only stand and look at her, then he would vanish. Riley suspected it was all part of the normal grieving process and didn't put much credence to it.

"I think he'd be happy about all this." Jacob stood behind her while she peered into the trailer.

"What's that?" She turned on her heel, beads of sweat running down the side of her face.

"Carl. I think he'd be happy we're moving in together."

"I think he would too." Riley picked up a small box and walked past him. "I'll take the light ones." As she stepped off the trailer and onto the path, a car appeared in the distance. She recognized it and stopped.

The car pulled onto her driveway and the driver's side window rolled down. "Hey. You guys need any help? I was in the area and thought I'd swing by."

"Nah, I think we got it. You want to come inside for a drink or something?" Riley asked.

"Sure. Why not?" Ethan Pruitt shifted the car into park and cut the engine. He opened the door and stepped out. "Why don't you at least let me take that for you?"

"Sure thing."

Jacob emerged and spotted the exchange. "Ethan. Hey, man, what's going on?" He offered a greeting.

"Not much. Had to run some errands and found myself nearby. Thought I'd see if you guys need any help, but Riley, here, says you got it under control."

"Hey, far be it from me to refuse help. There isn't much, but this heat's a bitch. Wouldn't mind an extra set of hands, if you got the time."

"I do." Ethan walked toward the trailer and grabbed a couple more boxes before making his way back toward Riley. "You got that one there, right?"

"Yeah. I got it." She watched as he and Jacob walked side by side into the house.

Ethan seemed accepting of the idea that Riley and Jacob were moving in together. Things had been awkward between them for a while, but that, too, changed after Carl died. She figured Ethan didn't want to make things worse for her by pushing back on the relationship and instead embraced it, though there were still indications he wasn't entirely over her. She pushed those aside and hoped that, in time, those feelings would dissipate. For now, Riley wouldn't look a gift horse in the mouth. She would accept this at face value and move on. It was time to move on.

CAPTAIN DAN WARD HAD CLOSE TO TWENTY YEARS ON RILEY. She remembered how he looked at their first meeting all those years ago. He was in his late twenties and she was just ten, but she remembered his smooth face and light brown hair. His eyes held more innocence in those days. Today, his hair was a little thinner and a little greyer, but his face showed only a few lines and most anyone would guess him to be forty at the most. He kept himself in shape, still worked out three times a week. But his eyes still held sorrow and loneliness, and there was nothing Riley could do about that. He wasn't interested in dating anyone after Melissa died eight years ago and still had no interest.

Riley blamed herself for not knowing, not seeing that Melissa would get sick so soon after she and Dan married. She was in her teens when Melissa died, and Dan pulled deeply into himself. Riley couldn't pull him out. It took several more years and now here they were. Dan was still alone, Riley had Jacob again, and there was nothing she wanted more than for Dan to find happiness. Right now, that was outside her purview, if it was there at all.

Captain Ward walked into the bullpen where Riley and Ethan sat at their desks. "Hey, did either of you take a look at last night's calls for service?"

"No. Should we have?" Riley asked. "I figured Abrams or Decker would've made mention of any issues."

"They didn't encounter any problems, but they did get a call about an illegal card game. Some folks set up shop at the back of the Crooked Horse near Montrose Street."

"Did they bust it up?" Ethan asked.

"Didn't have to. The boys got there and nothing was going on. I have to assume they got advanced warning and broke it up themselves."

"What do you want us to do?" Riley asked.

"Keep an ear out. Maybe make a visit to the bar in the next few days or so. Just to let them know we're watching. Last thing we need is people gambling away their paychecks around here."

"Right. They can go to the casino in South Bend to do that," Riley replied.

"Just don't want that stuff going on here. You think drunk folks are a pain in the ass? Just wait till they're drunk and lost all their money. It'll be fun times around here." Ward returned to his office.

"Captain's in a good mood," Ethan said.

"You know what Abrams is like. Probably blew it out of proportion trying to make himself look good. You want to know what happened last night, it's better to ask Decker."

"I won't argue with you there." He peered at her.

"You look like you want to say something," Riley began. "Everything okay?"

"Yeah. Of course." Ethan cast away his gaze. "Well, now that you mention it, there was something I wanted to talk about. I was going to mention it on Saturday when I was helping you guys unload the trailer, but..."

"What is it?" Riley felt an urge to look behind his eyes to figure out what he wanted to say before he said it. It wasn't the right thing to do, using her gift that way, and it wasn't something she often did, but intrigue captured her imagination because the look in his eyes wasn't one she'd noticed before.

"I hear Gracie's coming home from college soon."

"That's right. She's graduating next week. Dillon and I are taking Mom up there for the ceremony and then she'll hang with us for a while. How did you know?"

"I saw that Gracie posted something on Facebook," he replied.

"Oh. Okay, right."

"I haven't seen her in a long time. She's all grown up now," Ethan said.

"Yes, she is. I don't know how long she'll be staying here in town. She's already had offers for internships with a few marketing firms."

"That's great," Ethan replied.

There was something else. She could feel it and it was starting to take shape. "Have you been talking to Gracie lately? I mean, on Facebook or whatever?"

"Um, yeah. Like a couple of times. I don't remember exactly."

There it was. She felt it emanating from him. "Are you and Gracie together?"

"What? No. I mean, no. She's your baby sister."

"Ethan, she's an adult now. Old enough to drink. She can date whoever she wants. If you're going out with her, it'd be nice if you told me."

"You can already see it, can't you? I was surprised you didn't say anything on Saturday. Thought you might be slipping. I've been wanting to say something for a while now. I mean, not that long, but you know. We've been talking a lot lately. She was pretty broken up about Carl."

"I know she was." Riley peered at him. It felt strange to think Ethan and Gracie were an item. His feelings for her had been pretty strong for a long time and now, well, he was over her. He was with Gracie, her little sister. "Look, I'm happy for you. And for Gracie. I'm going to kick her butt for not saying anything to me, but it's her life. And yours. You both deserve to be happy. I just hope you realize she's got a bright future ahead of her."

Ethan turned defensive. "What's that supposed to mean?"

"Like I said, she's got offers. I wouldn't count on her staying in Owensville for long. She wants to spend time with Mom and then, who knows? I just want you to be prepared."

"Why? You don't want me to get my heart broken?"

Riley felt the bite in his tone. "As a matter of fact, I don't."

"Well, you're too late for that." Ethan returned to his computer and pretended to punch in a bunch of keys as if he suddenly got very busy.

Riley wanted to say more, but what was the point? Maybe things would work out between Gracie and him. She didn't see otherwise—not yet.

JACOB WAS HVM's NEWEST IN-HOUSE ARCHITECT. THE small homebuilder who specialized in entry-level houses had recently opened a branch office in Owensville. In fact, construction on the business park where the office was located was very near the old Shady Acres mobile home park. That was where Carl lived for far too long and it had finally been demolished a few years back. New businesses came to town to set up shop and HVM was one of them. Owensville was growing, even if a little slowly.

No one had the nerve to take on the Caterpillar plant that had become a dog food manufacturing facility until it got shut down because it was being run by the mafia. People died in that place. Everyone figured it had bad karma.

The business park was given state funding and off it went. HVM was the only builder in town and employed about thirty people, not including the contractors who were put to work. They were good-paying jobs and Jacob was lucky to get one. There wasn't much call for architects in Owensville, and especially not one who had been entangled with the mob and the old plant.

Jacob walked into the breakroom for an afternoon iced coffee. It had been a hot summer and didn't appear to want to let up anytime soon. "What are you guys up to?"

Three of his colleagues sat at a small round table eating chips and playing cards. One of the guys, and Jacob's contemporary, went by the name of Alex. The structural engineer was roughly the same age but was married and had two kids.

Alex looked back at him. "Got a game of Texas Hold-em going. Care to join in?"

"Aren't you guys supposed to be working?" Jacob replied.

"Took a late lunch. Come on, jump in. The water's fine."

"No thanks. Just came in for a coffee. I have a crap-ton of plans on my desk." Jacob walked toward the fancy coffee machine and punched in the code for iced coffee.

"Your loss, man." Alex waited for the next player to make his move.

Jacob watched for a few minutes and returned to his desk with his coffee. He never had been much of a gambler. He didn't like losing money and the pressure of a game was too much for him. And after facing down mafia hitmen, he figured he'd spent all his luck already since he made it out of that situation by the skin of his teeth.

ALEX LAUGHLIN HAD BEEN PLAYING CARDS SINCE HE WAS A teenager. He played mostly online before the Feds made it too difficult to win any money. If only they'd been smart enough to figure out how to tax the winnings, the government could've made a killing. Instead, they took down just about every website they could to stop people.

So Alex would play every now and again when the opportunity struck. Usually a few guys who would gather at one another's homes. Small money, nothing major, but it was fun. Of course, his wife didn't care for it when the boys would be at their house. His two young kids, a boy and a girl, four and six respectively, were a handful and the last thing she wanted was to have to cater to a bunch of guys getting rowdy and drinking beer over a poker game.

"I hear the cops were about to bust up that game last night at the bar," Alex said. "Looks like I left before all the excitement. Any of you there to see it?"

"Nah, man." A file clerk named Craig, not more than twenty-two, spoke up. "I bailed early, even before you. Not worth the trouble."

"I agree." Billy Flores, HVM's accountant-extraordinaire and the smartest guy in the building, nodded. "This is okay for fun, but it isn't worth getting in trouble for it. It was hard enough finding a job here. I'm not doing anything to jeopardize it."

"Christ, I didn't realize I was working with a bunch of pansies." Alex dropped his cards to the table. "Fold. I'm out of here. Got to get back to work." He pushed up from his chair. "Catch you losers later."

Alex made his way through the corridor and stopped at Jacob's cubicle. "Hey, man."

"What's up?" Jacob turned to him.

"We should grab a beer sometime. We're about the same age, right?"

"I guess so."

"Kids?" Alex asked.

"No. I just moved in with my girlfriend actually."

"Lucky you. No wife. No kids. Life of Reilly over here, yeah?"

Jacob couldn't help but smile. "You have no idea. I'd like to hang out sometime. Thanks for the offer."

"Sweet. Catch up with you later?"

"Sure." Jacob was feeling pretty good about the offer. He'd been employed here since just before Carl passed and was finally starting to make friends. Riley would be happy. "Life of Reilly." He chuckled.

DINNER WAS ON THE TABLE AND RILEY'S OLDER BROTHER, Dillon, secured little Danny into his high-chair. Marjorie brought in a pitcher of tea and finally sat down. The little family had grown, and Riley regretted not spending more time with them. Dillon's wife, Marjorie, wasn't exactly Riley's type, but they got along well enough. She was a little too Type A for her liking. And the kids, Danny, who was almost four, and Ella, who had just turned one, well, they were almost unrecognizable.

"Thanks for having us over," Riley began. "It's been a busy week and Jacob hasn't finished unpacking yet." She glared at him, though mostly in jest.

"Of course. We're glad you both could make it." Marjorie poured herself a glass of tea. "Anyone else?" She held the pitcher.

"I'll take some." Dillon waited for her to fill his glass and then turned to Riley. "Gracie's graduation ceremony is next week?"

"Yep. Mom's getting excited. Did you get the time off?"

"I did. It's finals week, so it was tough, but they got a substitute lined up. It's only a day."

"You're not staying the night? I thought we were planning on visiting Jack."

"I don't know, Riley. It's bad enough I'm leaving Marjorie here to deal with the kids. I don't want to make it harder. And Mom, I mean, what are we going to do? Leave her at the hotel while we visit ol' Pops and his new family?"

"He's going to the graduation. You know that, right?" Riley said.

"I know. But there'll be a lot of people there. It's not like we have to sit next to him. Mom won't stand for that."

"Well, here's a little tidbit of news I picked up today." Riley quickly shoved a small piece of grilled chicken into her mouth. "Gracie's got a boyfriend."

"Oh, she does? And who is this guy?" Dillon asked.

Riley swallowed down her food and wore a smirk on her face. "You won't believe it."

"Don't keep me in suspense. You know the guy, or what?"

"Um, yeah. You could say that." She paused a little longer to prolong Dillon's agony. "It's Ethan."

"What? Ethan Pruitt? Your partner, Officer Ethan Pruitt?" Dillon said.

Jacob turned to Riley with a mouth full of food. "What? Are you serious?"

"Oh yeah, I'm serious." Riley peered again at Dillon. "I guess they've been talking on Facebook. I don't know if they've officially gone out on a date, but it sure sounds like they're going to. At least, that's what Ethan told me today."

"The same Ethan who's had a crush on you since, I don't

know, since forever?" Jacob appeared hot under the collar. "Now, what, he's going to date your younger sister?"

"Why are you so pissed off about this?" Riley asked.

"Language, please." Marjorie shot her a scornful gaze.

"Sorry. Why are you angry?"

"Come on, are you serious? You of all people should see through this. I can't believe you don't."

"You know what, I'm sorry I brought it up at all. This clearly isn't the time or place to get into it. I see that now. Geez. Didn't realize it would be a sore point."

Dillon peered at Riley, seemingly siding with Jacob. "Well, anyway, we can figure out the logistics next week. I just want to watch Gracie walk across that stage and get her degree. After all, it cost us both a hell of a lot of money." He smiled.

Marjorie slapped the edge of the table. "Language!"

"Sorry, hon."

4

The impression of a backroom poker game sparked images of cigars and smoke hovering in the air. Middle-aged men with beer bellies and bald heads, laughing and shoveling potato chips in their mouths. However, the game had evolved. The money was serious and most of the players were millennials and the occasional Gen X'er who had cut their teeth with online poker, just like Alex Laughlin. He'd raked in a fair bit of cash in online tournaments. Even found himself winning an entry into the World Series of Poker in Las Vegas a few years back.

So when he heard about the games held every Tuesday and Thursday at the Crooked Horse bar, he thought, why not? As long as the wife didn't mind looking after the kids on those nights, what was the harm? He rarely lost, and if he did, it wasn't enough to be concerned about.

He'd convinced a couple of the guys at work to join in, but they weren't serious players and got pissy when they lost. If there was one thing Alex hated, it was a sore loser. So tonight, he was heading down there on his own. It had been a concern the other night when the cops dropped in and the owner got antsy. His solution was to move the time to later in the evening and so far, so good. A couple of games and no more cops. Alex had soon learned there weren't a lot of them here in Owensville anyway, and from where he'd originated, that was a pleasant change.

After some trouble with the Feds because of his online gaming habits, he'd lost his job with the City of Indianapolis. Too bad. It had been a cushy gig, but they caught wind of his troubles and that was that. He'd uprooted his family and headed south to Owensville when he'd been offered a position with HVM. It wasn't great money, but it was work—and health insurance. Besides, he thought it would be good for the kids to move to a small town. He'd never lived in one and figured it was a positive thing. His wife was still getting used to the idea, and she didn't work, so it was an easier decision.

"Adios, muchachos!" Alex waved to his colleagues. "See you mañana." He pushed through the doors and made his way to the parking lot. "Hey, Jacob! You heading home too?"

Jacob pressed the remote to unlock his car and opened the door. "Yep. Girlfriend and I are driving up to Indianapolis to see her little sister graduate from Purdue."

"That's awesome, man. Must be a smart kid."

"She is. We're all proud of her. Where are you off to? Figured you'd be working late tonight since we got the comments back from the review board."

"Bugging out on time tonight. I have to get home and have dinner with the fam. I'm heading out after that to go have some fun with the boys."

"Oh yeah? What kind of fun? What, did a strip club open up here?"

"I wish. That's what this town needs. No, just joining a friendly game of cards."

"That's right. You're into poker." Jacob slipped into his car. "Cool. Have fun. I'll catch up with you on Monday. Won't be here tomorrow."

"Right. See you Monday. Safe trip." Alex approached his Toyota 4Runner and stepped inside, starting up the engine. He watched Jacob drive away and felt mild relief. "Well, guess your girlfriend won't be around to cause any trouble at the bar tonight." He knew Jacob lived with one of the four cops in this town. "One less to worry about."

THE CROOKED HORSE BAR AND GRILL APPEARED IN THE distance. It had recently been refurbished after it was taken over by new owners. A lot of things were under renovation in downtown Owensville. The place was starting to shape up in the face of growing jobs and wages. One thing hadn't changed, and that was the old diner. It was looking worse for wear and needed a facelift. But it was a fixture in town and people still flocked to it in droves. Mostly, it was known for its Sunday brunch that catered to the church-going crowd. This was still God-fearing country, after all. But not for Alex Laughlin. He feared nothing and no one—an arrogant position to take for someone with a family.

Most of the stores and restaurants along this strip of downtown were closed for the night. It was 11pm, and on a Thursday, most folks were tucked up in their beds resting up for another day of work. Alex didn't need a lot of sleep, never did.

He walked inside the bar and was enveloped in the muted amber light of the pendants hanging above. Shadows landed across his face and warped his features, producing a malicious canvas. The crimson tufted booths and bar-height tables with a single LED candle burning atop each one added to the sultry vibe of the trendy establishment. Almost too trendy for this backwater town.

"I'm starting to dig this place." Alex continued inside and hoisted himself onto a black leather barstool. He caught the attention of the bartender, a hipster-looking twenty-something who was trying too hard to appear cool. "Hey, man. I'll take a Stella."

The bartender nodded and retrieved the upscale cold brew and poured it into its signature chalice. "$7.50."

"Can I start a tab?"

"Sure."

Alex retrieved his credit card and laid it on the table. "Hey, um, I'm here for the game. You know if they're getting started yet?"

The bartender turned to his right at a door marked "office." "Back there. You invited?"

"I was, yes."

"Feel free to go back, then."

Alex returned his card to his wallet and grabbed his glass. He sipped on the frothy top and headed to the room for the invitation-only game of Texas Hold-em. "Evening, boys. Got room for one more?"

Six men sat around a card table and their eyes landed on Alex. An older gentleman with rakish salt and pepper hair and a relaxed blue polo shirt smiled. "I was wondering if you would show up, since you bailed early during the last game. And your friends followed."

"Yeah, um. Sorry about that. Kid was sick. Won't happen again."

That wasn't the real reason, of course, and it seemed the handsome man, who also happened to be the owner, had caught on.

With his previous exploits, Alex didn't feel the need to take chances with the authorities. He pulled out a chair and sat down. "What's the buy-in?"

"One thousand," another man replied.

"No problemo." Alex dropped the bills on the table. "Let's get this party started."

RILEY SQUIRMED IN HER SEAT AT THE HALL OF MUSIC AT Purdue University. "I'm so nervous."

"You're nervous?" Jacob began. "Gracie should be the nervous one. She has to get up on that stage."

"I know. It's just, well, I wasn't sure she would get here. Lord knows, we have enough baggage, and even though Dillon and I shielded her as best we could, you just don't know."

"You look like a proud parent." He peered beyond her and spotted Riley's mother. "Ellen's coming."

"Hey, Mom. Did you find the restrooms okay?" Riley asked.

"I did. It's busy, though. Probably best you don't try to go until the ceremony's over." Ellen sat down.

"Okay, Mom. I won't." She noticed Ellen gazing around the hall. "Who are you looking for?"

"Your father. I expected him to be here by now, assuming he plans on showing up."

"He'll be here, Mom. He's not going to let Gracie down."

"Sure. Because he's never let any of us down before," Ellen replied.

Riley rolled her eyes at Jacob before turning back to her. "I know this isn't ideal, but it's just for a couple of hours, tops. Jack has every right to be here, same as you."

"You've given him the benefit of the doubt your entire life, Riley."

"I've learned to forgive, that's all." An announcement sounded over the loudspeakers. "Looks like they're about to start."

Ethan walked through the row of seats and sat down next to Jacob. "Gracie's a little nervous, but she's doing fine."

"Glad to see you're an expert on Riley's little sister," Jacob said.

"I can't win with you, can I, man? After the shit you've pulled, you'd figure it'd be the other way around."

"Okay, that's enough. I'm not dealing with this right now. My sister is about to go on stage, and I don't want to hear a peep from any of you."

Ethan glared at Jacob. "Good job pissing her off."

The graduating class at Purdue University was enormous and the ceremony took over two hours. But Riley had watched Gracie receive her degree and felt a sweeping sense of relief. Her little sister would be okay. She could go out into the world and make her own way now and Riley played a big part in that. So had Dillon, who also beamed with pride at the sight of his sister. If not for the both of them, it wouldn't have been possible.

By the end of the ceremony, Riley stood and noticed Jack two rows below and peering at her. At least he'd made it. Now the real fun of this little family reunion was about to begin.

Jack had stopped drinking shortly after the EF4 when Riley was a kid, but the marriage couldn't be salvaged. Too much had happened and Ellen couldn't forgive him. Riley never held it against her. Ellen had been abused verbally and physically by Jack, and while Riley was grateful her father had found a way out, there was reason for Ellen to still be angry, even if she herself wasn't—anymore. Part of that had to do with Carl.

"We should go say hi to Jack," Riley said to Dillon.

"I suppose you're right. What about her?" He gestured to Ellen.

"Jacob, would you and Ethan mind taking Mom out into the reception area? I'm sure she'll want to find Gracie."

"Sure thing, babe." Jacob reached for Ellen's arm. "We'll work our way down to the reception, Ellen. Come on."

Ellen peered at Riley, knowing exactly what she was doing, but she didn't object.

"Better to get this out of the way." Riley led the way into the aisle and Dillon followed. Jack and his wife and two children were headed up to meet them. She had only met his new family twice before and it was awkward both times. They didn't know anything about who Jack had been and she wasn't going to tell them. "Hey, Dad." Riley walked into a distant embrace. "Barbara, nice to see you again." She peered at the boy and girl. "Nate, Sydney, how are you guys? You got so big."

"Hi, Riley." Nate was twelve and already pushing five feet nine.

"Hi." Sydney was only nine and appeared to be a very shy little girl.

"I'm so glad you all could make it. I know Gracie's excited to see you guys." Riley knew that was a little bit of a stretch, but Gracie didn't have the same animosity toward Jack as she once had. The advantage of being the youngest.

"Should we go down and try to find her?" Jack asked.

"Sounds like a good idea." Riley took Dillon's hand, and both navigated through the throngs of elated parents and grandparents.

Upon arriving at the reception area, Riley spotted Jacob. "I see them. Looks like they found Gracie." They walked several more feet when Riley opened her arms and pulled in her sister, embracing her fully. "I'm so proud of you, Gracie!"

"Thanks, Riley. I'm so happy all of you could come. I've just been catching up with Mom."

Gracie had become a beautiful woman. A little on the short side at only five feet four, but with light brown hair in curls that rested comfortably on her shoulders. Her round eyes were big and bright and full of promise. She had the luxury of not knowing or feeling the pain of others. Riley was grateful for that.

Gracie's attention was diverted at the sight of Jack. "Dad! You made it." She hugged him with the intensity of a child whose father had been away at sea.

"I wouldn't have missed this for the world, kiddo." He turned to his wife. "You remember Barbara, and Nate and Sydney."

"Of course. Thank you, guys, for coming. I know it's totally crazy around here right now."

"Your father's right. We wouldn't have missed this," Barbara replied.

In any other situation, Riley would've probably liked Barbara. She appeared kind, friendly, and motherly. But she wasn't there quite yet. She'd forgiven Jack, for the most part, but allowing Barbara into her life, into her heart, wasn't in the cards.

"Well, look," Riley began. "I think we had plans to take you to dinner. You still up for that?"

Gracie regarded her with some concern. "All of us?"

"Um, sure, if you want." Riley turned to Jack. "If you guys can, you're more than welcome."

Ellen folded her arms as a tsk rolled off her tongue.

Jack shot a glance to her before turning back to Riley. "You know, we should probably head back. These guys have sports practice early in the morning. I don't want to keep them out too late. Maybe another time?"

"Sure. Of course, Dad," Gracie said. "Guess it'll just be us, then." She eyed Ethan and smiled.

"Okay, well, we should probably go." Jack squeezed Gracie once again. "I'm real proud of you, kiddo."

She smiled in return. "Thanks for coming, Dad. I mean that. All of you."

Jack nodded to Riley and gathered up his troops to leave.

Riley watched as they started away and noticed Nate turn back and capture her gaze.

"I know what you can do."

She creased her brow and her lips parted slightly. He hadn't spoken that out loud; it was in her head. And when she held his gaze again, the corner of his mouth raised into a half-smile. They disappeared from view. Her face felt drained of color and she looked at Jacob with noted alarm.

"Are you okay, Riley?" he asked.

"Um, yeah. It's nothing. Come on. We should head out or we'll never get a table."

It was Friday and five o'clock was fast approaching. Alex had already shut down his computer and was rolling up his blueprints. A little light weekend work never hurt anyone. And it would make him look good in the eyes of upper management.

Billy Flores, who worked in Accounting, appeared in Alex's doorway. "Hey, man, you taking off for the weekend?"

"You know it. Got some celebrating to do with the wife. Got us a babysitter and all."

"Sounds like you cleaned up at that game last night. Kind of wish I had been there to see that."

"You didn't miss much. Just a bunch of assholes whining 'cause I took their money. Even the owner gave me the stink eye when I completely cleaned house." He laughed. "Not sure they'll want me back after that."

"Cool deal. Well, you have a great weekend. Maybe if you do get another invite, I'll join you. Could stand to learn and thing or two about the game." Billy slapped the doorframe and headed into the hall.

Alex was feeling pretty full of himself because he'd had a good night last night. Better than he expected, in fact. It would help pay the bills, that was one thing for sure. Since his wife didn't work, he could use the extra cash. And he did make plans to celebrate with a dinner out. It had been a long time since they'd had date night. This was long overdue.

With his arms wrapped around several sets of house plans, Alex shut off his office light and started toward the front exit. "Night, guys." He waved to a few stragglers who were shooting the breeze on a Friday afternoon.

"See ya, Alex," one of them replied.

He pushed through the glass doors and squinted in the late afternoon sun. The air felt sticky on his skin, like the clouds were sitting on the ground. Rain must've been coming. The bugs were out and the leaves on the trees were still.

His 4Runner was in sight as he strode through the parking lot. On approach to the driver's side door, Alex reached into his pocket for the keys. "Damn it." He grabbed them, but they'd snagged on something in his pocket.

"Having a little trouble there, Alex?"

He whipped around to see the owner of the bar where he'd taken money from several people last night. "Silas. Hey, man, how's it going?" Alex felt the hair on his neck stand on end. "What are you doing here?"

"I thought you might be leaving work. Hey, what you did last night, that was something else."

"Um, thanks," Alex replied.

"I was thinking the fair thing to do would be for you to come back on Tuesday and give us fellas a chance to earn our money back. You think you might be up for that?"

Alex picked up on his tone and the question didn't sound like a question at all, more like a demand. "I—sure. I guess I can do that." He peered up as if thinking on the matter. "Oh, you know what? My kid has soccer practice that night. I promised him I'd be there. You know how it goes."

"Sure. Sure. I'm a father. Course, my kids are adults now, but sure, I get it." Silas started to walk away then stopped and turned on his heel. "But you know what, I bet your wife could probably take the little tyke to practice, couldn't she? She's a stay-at-home mom, right? And the card game is pretty late."

"She is. Yeah." Alex couldn't recall mentioning that fact to anyone at the game. "I'll run it by her. See if that'll be okay. Just the one time."

"Just the one time." A smile played on his lips, though his blue eyes were empty. "So we'll see you Tuesday night, yeah?"

"Yeah. I'll be there."

"Good. Glad to hear it. I knew you were a stand-up guy, Alex." Silas patted his shoulder. "Have a good night. Enjoy dinner with your wife." He walked away.

5

The home in which Riley, Dillon, and Gracie had grown up was in view as Dillon parked the car in front of the house. Ellen still lived there and Dillon had helped maintain it for his mother. Gracie would be staying there for a week or so before heading back to Indianapolis for the internship she was awarded upon graduation.

She opted to stay at the old house because Riley had Jacob now, and while Riley insisted it was okay, she didn't want to feel like a third wheel. And Ellen needed the company.

Ellen unlocked the door and opened it to the scent of mildly stale air due to her absence for the past few days. It soon cleared when she opened the windows.

"Mom, it's pretty warm in here. You should turn on the air conditioner," Riley said.

"That's what fans are for," she replied. "Do you think I'm made of money?"

"That's okay. It's not that bad in here," Gracie said. "I'll go put my things upstairs."

"I'll give you a hand." Ethan followed her up the staircase, the treads popping with each step.

"I need to take a look at those stairs," Dillon said. "Hey, Mom, I'm going to take off. Marjorie's got her hands full. But if you and Gracie need anything, just give me a call and I'll come over." He walked to Ellen and kissed her cheek. "Love you."

"Love you too." Ellen placed her hand on his shoulder. "Thank you for driving, sweetheart. I'm grateful to have been able to be there."

"I know. You did good, Mom."

The underlying meaning wasn't lost on Ellen. It had been tough for all of them to see the life Jack had chosen. He seemed to be a much better father to those kids than he was to any of them. It was a bitter pill to swallow.

"Riley." Dillon gestured for her to approach.

"Yeah?"

"Are you going to be okay here with Jacob and Ethan?"

"I'm fine. It's those two who keep pissing on each other."

"You know why that is, right?" Dillon asked.

"I know what you're thinking. Ethan had a thing for me and now he's dating Gracie. Maybe he finally got over it. Did you ever think of that? A lot's changed in the past few months. I think Ethan realized it was a lost cause, and frankly, I'm glad he did. It was getting in the way of our friendship."

"If you say so, Riley. Look, I have to head out. Just get Gracie settled in. I'm sure Mom will be grateful for the company." Dillon started out the door. "I'll give you a call later."

The notion that Ethan Pruitt was seeing Gracie for the sole

objective of making Riley jealous was absurd. He was a kind and caring person and would not, for one second, intentionally hurt Gracie or use her in any way. Dillon was wrong. Jacob was wrong. And in time, they would see it too.

Riley closed the door behind Dillon and walked into the family room. "I need to go into the station, Mom. I can come back later this evening. Do you need me to pick up anything?"

"I have Gracie here with me now. She can take my car and run to the store if need be. You go on. I know you have work." Ellen approached her. "None of this would have been possible without you—and Dillon. Don't think I don't appreciate that."

"I know you do, Mom." Riley smiled before turning her attention up the stairs. "Hey, Gracie, I need to take off."

At the top of the staircase, Gracie, who stood only slightly shorter than Riley, but was much slimmer, peered at her. "I have things under control, Sis. See you later."

Ethan approached and stood behind Gracie. "Are you going into the station?"

"Yeah. I figured I should check in and see how things were going since we missed Friday."

Ethan turned to Gracie. "I should go too, but I can come back later."

"Okay. No problem. It'll give me time to get settled in and catch up with Mom."

"I'll come with." Ethan trotted down the steps and met Riley at the bottom. He shot a gaze to Jacob. "Is he coming with us?"

"I'll drop him off at home," Riley said. "Is that okay?" She turned to Jacob.

"Sure. I can catch up on my emails at home."

"Then it's settled." Riley again opened the front door. "See you guys later. Have fun." She led the way to her car that had been left at the house and walked to the driver's side.

Ethan and Jacob appeared to be at a standoff as to who would sit in the front seat. Finally, Riley interjected, "Ethan, why don't you jump in up front. Jacob's getting out at the house anyway and it's only a short drive there."

A triumphant smile appeared on Ethan's lips as he opened the passenger door. "Sounds like a plan."

Jacob slipped into the back seat.

RILEY AVOIDED ANY MANNER OF DISCUSSION ABOUT GRACIE as she and Ethan returned to the stationhouse. It was late afternoon and the day had proven long with the drive back from Indianapolis.

Perhaps what weighed more heavily on her mind was what Nate had said, or rather, thought. The boy of twelve had the gift and showed off his skills the day of Gracie's graduation. He was only slightly older than Riley had been at the lowest point in her life when the gift was still uncontrollable. The idea that someone else in Jack's family would have been bestowed such a life-altering and terrifying ability had haunted Riley for some time. Neither of her full siblings had it, but Nate, the youngest son of Jack Thompson, appeared to. She wondered if Jack knew, and if he did, what had he been prepared to do to help the boy? He could not go through it alone. Riley had Carl and Dan Ward, but who did Nate have?

"Riley?" Ethan peered at her. "What's wrong? Why are we just sitting here in the parking lot?"

"What's that?" She was pulled back into the moment. "Oh. Sorry." Riley turned off the engine. "I guess I got lost in thought."

"Anything you want to talk about?"

"No. We should go in." Riley stepped out of the car and started toward the entrance to the station.

Lowell Abrams and Chris Decker, the night shift cops, had just arrived. And as usual, it was Abrams who was prepared with the quip. "Look who decided to show up for work today." He sat at his desk and threw his feet on top of it. "A little late, don't you think?"

"You know we were scheduled to have yesterday and today off. The captain gave us permission, so if you have a problem with that, maybe you should take it up with him," Riley said.

"Geez, Riley. Take it easy. I'm just giving you shit." Abrams was a couple of years older than Riley. While he was easy to look at with short wavy brown hair, a strong chin, and deep brown eyes, his personality left little to be desired. He fancied himself a man's man, which really meant he spouted off sexist jokes and was a jerk most of the time. His only redeeming quality was that he was a hell of a good cop and would have Riley's back without hesitation.

She tried to look beyond his false bravado but was in no mood to deal with him today. Riley had enough machismo between Ethan and Jacob and didn't need Lowell Abrams to add to it. "Speaking of the captain, is he here? I thought I saw his car outside."

"In the john, last I checked." Chris Decker was at the opposite end of the spectrum to his partner. The same age as Riley, he was slightly pudgy with dark hair, decent-looking, but not handsome in the Hollywood sense. But it was his heart that Riley adored most of all. He was the type of man to give the shirt off his back and he would defend Riley, or any of them, without question.

Riley hadn't developed much of a friendship with either of them until the day at the warehouse ten months ago. They'd witnessed, first-hand, Riley's abilities. And while frightening for anyone, they remained loyal to her regardless. They'd all become closer since that day and their loyalty to her was genuine, not because of fear. She could sense that in each of them and it put her at ease. It put all of them at ease. But the friendly rivalry between the day shift and the night shift would survive.

"Did I hear my name?" Captain Ward appeared from the hall. "Hey, I wasn't expecting to see you two here today."

"We got in a few hours earlier than expected and thought it best to stop in and see how things were going," Riley said.

"No trouble, right, boys?" Ward peered at Abrams and Decker.

"Nope. No trouble, Boss," Abrams replied.

Riley wanted to take Ward aside and tell him about her half-brother, but there were times when she had to remind herself that she was his subordinate and there was protocol in place. He would never see it that way, but it was her way of becoming more reliant upon herself. Ward had been more of a father to her than Jack ever was, but she was an adult now. Carl was gone and it was time Riley figured things out on her own.

"Good. Well, I'll just get caught up on some paperwork." Riley sat down at her desk. She peered at Ethan. "Might be a good idea to check in on the Crooked Horse soon." She returned her attention to Ward. "Has anyone stopped in recently, like we talked about?"

"Not since you left on Thursday. Decker here dropped in on what, Wednesday night around midnight?"

"That's right. Nothing unusual that I could see or get a sense that anyone was trying to hide anything. I agree though, might be a good idea to stop in again in the next day or so just to keep those guys on their toes," Decker replied.

"I couldn't agree more," Ward added. "Owensville's got some new folks in town and let's just say we need to keep them informed as to the rules around here." He started toward his office. "Let me know if anyone needs anything. I'll be in my office." He turned briefly and eyed Riley.

He knew something was up. He usually did. But Riley didn't take him up on the offer. First and foremost, with Abrams and Decker on hand, she didn't want to draw the attention. And then there was Ethan, who'd already felt slighted by their close bond.

Instead, Riley opted to catch up on her work and go home to Jacob. The time had come for Riley to be dependent on only herself. Ward needed to let her out from under his wing. She was ready.

RILEY WAS GREETED AT HOME BY CJ, HIS TONGUE AND TAIL wagging with delight. "Hey, CJ! Who's a good boy?" One could never understate the importance of the unconditional love of a pet. It was Riley's salvation on those days when her thoughts turned to Carl, or when a particularly terrible crime had been committed. Thankfully, that didn't happen often.

However, this wasn't the only warm welcome Riley would receive tonight. The pleasant aroma of grilled chicken passed her senses. She continued inside and made her way into the kitchen. "Look at you."

Jacob stood at the stove with his back to her and spun around. "Welcome home. I figured I should whip up some dinner. I know it's been a tough few days."

Jacob didn't possess Riley's gift for insight, but he had known her since the age of ten and had become familiar with just about every facet of her personality, including the gift, and still loved her.

"What a nice surprise. Thank you. And thanks for picking up CJ from the kennel." She slid her hand across his back and leaned in to kiss him. "This is exactly what I needed." Riley peered at the table, which was already set, and noticed the candles and flowers. "Maybe my skills have rubbed off on you."

"Go and get changed. You have a few minutes. I'll pour you a glass of wine."

Riley paused for a moment, thinking of the buttery chardonnay as it would swirl on her tongue. She didn't drink for a good many reasons. One of which was her father and the other, well, it tended to open her mind to receive the thoughts and images from others she tried so hard to stave off. But no one was around tonight. It was just the two of them. Maybe it would be okay. Just one glass. "Sounds perfect."

She started into the hall and toward the master bedroom of her small cottage-style home. The day was beginning to fall from her shoulders. Gracie was looking after their mother. Ethan had Gracie and Riley's life with Jacob seemed like a fairytale, if one's fairytale included the ability to see the worst in people. Okay, maybe fairytale was a stretch, but she was feeling normal again.

Riley returned to the kitchen wearing shorts and a t-shirt. Her gun was stowed away, her boots under her bed, and her thin blonde hair pulled back in a messy bun. "This smells delicious. I'm starving." She spotted Jacob at the stove, switching off the burners.

He turned to her.

Her eyes widened and she screamed. "Jacob!" Riley rushed toward him. "What happened? You're bleeding!" She ripped several paper towels from the roll under the cabinet and doused them in water from the kitchen faucet. "Oh my God. What happened?" She began wiping away the blood on his face and neck with speed in search of the origin of the spillage that dripped onto the tile floor.

"Riley! Riley, stop!" Jacob pulled away her hands. "What are you doing? I'm fine. See? I'm fine. I'm okay."

Riley pulled back and shook her head as if to clear it. Her eyes landed on him again, only this time, there was no blood. No sign of any injury at all. "What? I don't understand. You were bleeding."

"Baby, I wasn't bleeding. I'm okay. Look." He wiped at his face and showed her his palms. "No blood." He held her gaze. "What did you see?"

"I—I don't know. You turned around and..." She couldn't finish and could only stare at his face to be sure this wasn't a trick. But a trick had been played on her. Her mind had shown her something horrific.

He regarded her with worry. "You had a vision. Your forehead is sweaty." He rubbed her palms. "Your hands are sweaty too.

"Riley, is something going to happen to me?"

THE NOTION OF RILEY GETTING ANY SORT OF REST LAST night was laughable. She put at ease Jacob's concerns and insisted the vision was nothing more than a result of the stressful weekend. She was pretty sure he bought it. Either that, or he didn't want to admit how frightened he was.

The wonderful and thoughtful dinner Jacob had cooked was spoiled by the grotesque interruption. Riley had refused the wine, though it would have helped take off the edge. The risk of another terrifying vision was enough to put her off the idea altogether. So they lingered in silence and went to bed in silence.

Today was a new day, however, and Riley had to push back the misfire in her mind and do the job she was supposed to do. Jacob was at work and today needed to be like any other day.

"Morning, Riley." Ethan sipped on his coffee as he sat at his desk. "You look tired. Everything all right?"

"Fine. Just one of those nights. How was your night? Did you go back to my mom's place to see Gracie?"

"Actually, no. She wanted to spend some time with Ellen, which I can understand. I'll see her tonight. I'm taking dinner over there."

"Thank you. That's kind of you to do that," Riley said.

"What can I say? I'm a thoughtful individual." He smiled.

"Have you seen last night's service call log yet?"

Ethan nodded. "Yep. No news. Guess that's supposed to be good news, right?"

"Did Abrams and Decker pay another visit to the bar?" she pressed on, no longer in the mood for small talk.

"No. I thought you said you wanted to take a trip down there today. I assume they held off because of that. It's not like we can harass the owner. Technically, they've done nothing wrong."

"I suppose you're right. Yeah, maybe we'll run out there later today, say around happy hour time?"

"Sure. Sounds good."

Riley's speakerphone came to life. "Riley, you mind coming in here for a moment?"

"Sure, Captain." She stood and peered at Ethan. "Anything I should know about before going inside?"

"Not that I'm aware of."

Riley nodded and walked into Ward's office. "Hey, Captain. What's going on?"

"I heard you had an incident last night. Care to talk about it?"

As she sat down in the chair opposite him, she began, "Who told you that?" Though she already knew.

"Jacob called me a little while ago. Said you had a pretty bad vision. Are you doing okay? It's been a while since you experienced something like that. Not since, what, not since Carl died, right?"

"It was nothing. A misfire, which was exactly what I told Jacob. To be honest, I'm a little ticked off he told you."

"Don't be mad at the kid. He was concerned, and rightly so. But you're doing okay? Didn't see anything else that bothered you?"

"No. That was plenty, believe me. But I'm fine. And I really think it's best if we don't have these types of conversations anymore."

Ward appeared taken aback. "What do you mean?"

"I mean the rest of the guys. I don't want them to see me as a freak or someone who needs to be looked after because she might just lose it. Dan, it can't be like that. Not anymore. I need to handle things on my own. You've done your job. You taught me how to channel feelings and I appreciate that more than you know. But the time's come for me to figure out this stuff on my own."

Ward raised his hands in surrender. "Okay. I won't ask how you're doing. Far be it from me to overstep."

"You're not. It's just..."

"I know, Riley. I get it. I'll pull back. Maybe you're right. I've been too much like a helicopter parent and, well, you're not my kid. Not that I don't love you like you are, but that's beside the point."

"Thank you. That doesn't mean I don't need you. I just need to handle things on my own, as best I can anyway." She pushed up from the chair. "Ethan and I are going to run out to the Crooked Horse later today. I'd like to chat with the owner and just make sure he knows we're only looking out for the safety of his patrons."

"Okay. You let me know how that goes."

6

When Alex Laughlin arrived at the offices of HVM Builders, his stomach was already in knots. A gambler he was, but tonight's so-called friendly game of poker was going to be anything but friendly. Silas had made it crystal clear he was to lose so the others could win back their money. That wasn't how things worked, but in Silas' world, that was exactly the way it was going to be.

The one thing working in Alex's favor was that he hadn't spent the money. Silas approached him only a day after he raked in the $3000, and while he'd had big plans for the extra dough, it was a good thing he hadn't followed through on any of it. To go back there tonight and essentially return the money wasn't something he relished. Then again, he didn't relish the wrath of Silas Levin, the man who owned the Crooked Horse and, as legend had it, was prone to taking out his aggressions at random.

What was worse was that the heat had been on the bar thanks to a scuffle the previous week in which Alex hadn't been involved.

Regardless, it now seemed the cops in this backwater town were always stopping in just to make their presence known. What would happen if they were there tonight? It was an illegal game with fairly high stakes, at least for Owensville.

"Morning." Jacob walked by Alex in the hall as he held a cup of coffee. "Hey, man, are you all right?"

"Huh? Yeah, I'm fine. Sorry. I was just thinking about something." Alex returned a pleasant smile and tried to play off his distraction. "Welcome back. How was the graduation ceremony?"

"Good. Went off without a hitch," Jacob replied. "Looks like I didn't miss too much. How's the resubmittal going for Woodmill Estates?"

"On schedule. I'll catch up with you later? Got a million things to jump on this morning." Alex continued along the hall.

"Sure thing." Jacob peered back at him with noted concern.

Alex entered his closet-sized office and sat down at his desk. He was feeling off his game and the guys around here would notice, no doubt. Jacob had; he was certain. Maybe he was part of the problem. Alex knew Jacob was living with one of the cops, a woman named Riley. He'd heard stories about her but never asked if they were true. Alex hadn't lived here long enough to stir up anything, so he figured if Jacob wanted to share, he would. Alex was in Owensville because he had to be. Indianapolis wasn't a solution any longer. The other larger cities, Terra Haute and South Bend, well, they just didn't appeal to him. And he'd heard good things about Owensville. How it was growing, and jobs and houses were sprouting up everywhere. It was a great place for a fresh start. He needed that if he wanted his marriage to heal and his kids to be happy. He'd learned a tough lesson back in the big city. One he wouldn't want to repeat.

SILAS LEVIN, A FIFTY-SOMETHING MAN WITH A HIGH-STYLED coif of salt and pepper hair and a stubbled gray beard, stood behind the bar and wiped down the counter. His dynamic personality matched his looks and it helped him to draw in a healthy crowd. The Happy Hour regulars arrived, and even for a Tuesday, it was decent. He'd learned to temper his expectations in the small town. Having come from Chicago, and before that, Pittsburgh, it was an adjustment coming here. But he enjoyed the peace and quiet of Owensville. There were enough people to keep his bar afloat, but not enough to get rich off of. These were to be his golden years. His kids were grown and finishing college and starting their own lives. He'd matured from his younger days and didn't look for trouble anymore. The only problem was that the tight-ass cops around here were verging on harassment with their recent drop-ins. Oh, they played it off like it was all cool and they were just making sure things were going well, but Silas knew the truth. The God-fearing folk around Owensville didn't care for his friendly card games and made sure the cops were aware of them. So far, they hadn't done much but to remind him he was under their watchful eye. It was the one place he didn't want to be, so he moved things around, shifted them so as not to draw too much attention.

There were a few people here in town who enjoyed a bit of gambling and some who had the money to make it interesting. Those were the folks he wanted to attract. So the goal was to keep the cops off his scent. After all, compared to where he'd been, this was nothing. These cops didn't know what a real setup was like.

Silas cast his sights on the front door, which opened to reveal precisely who he'd been thinking about. "Your ears must've been burning," he said to himself.

Two of Owensville's finest entered the establishment. A young female who looked like she didn't take shit from anyone and a young male who was clearly the one who took orders from her. And they were walking right toward him.

"Evening, officers. Can I get you something to drink, on the house, of course."

"No thanks. Still on duty," the female officer replied. "I'm Officer Thompson, this is Officer Pruitt. We just wanted to check in on things. We heard there was a scuffle the other night and just making sure you don't need us for anything."

"I appreciate the gesture, Officer Thompson, but I've been around long enough to know how to handle these things. There's no need to get the law involved. In fact, it tends to set my patrons on edge, if you catch my meaning."

"Sure. We understand," Officer Pruitt replied. "But like my partner suggested, if we can be of any assistance at all, don't hesitate to call on us."

Silas wore a smile uniquely disingenuous. "I'm quite sure that won't be necessary." He peered at the female officer. "Well, as you can see, I'm a little busy, so if there's nothing else?"

"Nothing else, but we thank you for your time." Officer Thompson turned on her heel and started back toward the entrance. She stopped and peered back at Silas. "You've done a lot with the place. I remember when it was the old Moose Head."

"You grow up around here, then?" Silas asked.

"Yes, sir. My dad spent a lot of time bellied up to that bar there. You have yourself a good evening, Mr. Levin." She pushed through the doors.

Riley waited at the curb outside the Crooked Horse for Ethan to catch up.

"What the hell was that?" he asked. "You didn't ask to have a look around or anything. Just walked right on out of there."

"I saw everything I needed to see." She folded her arms and leaned back against the patrol car. "He's hiding a few things, or at least, he thinks he is. I think we need to learn a little more about Silas Levin."

"What'd you see?"

Riley pulled off the car and walked around to the driver's side. "Trouble."

It seemed the air was especially sticky tonight as Alex stepped out of his Toyota 4Runner in the parking lot of the Crooked Horse. The hour was approaching 11pm, which for a Tuesday and for a working man such as he was, this was late. But then again, he hadn't planned on being out tonight. That was, not until Silas Levin insisted he participate in a friendly game of poker to allow his buddies a chance to earn back their money. And if Alex was under the impression this was anything but coercion, he wasn't as smart as he thought he was.

He entered the darkened bar where less than a handful of patrons remained. Silas was behind the bar and the two locked eyes immediately. With a slight clearing of his throat, Alex approached him. "Hey, man. I'm ready to get this party started."

Silas held his gaze and chuckled. "No need to be nervous,

Alex. We're just here to have a little bit of fun. What can I get you to drink?"

"I'll take a beer, thanks."

"I'll get you your favorite. Stella. You had luck drinking that the other night. Wouldn't want to throw you off your game." He pulled on the tap and filled a glass with the beverage, leaving just a hint of foam on the top. "Here you are. Let's go back. The boys are waiting."

Alex grabbed his glass and followed Silas to the backroom where he'd been only a few short days ago under much different circumstances.

"All right, fellas. The man of the hour has arrived." Silas held open the door.

Alex peered inside at the faces that appeared much less friendly than they had last week. "Hey." He raised his hand in a sheepish manner. "Good to see you guys again." He skulked to the table and pulled out a chair.

"Where're your friends?" one of the men asked. "Couldn't hack it, could they? Pussies."

"Yeah, they don't have the balls to hang with serious players like yourselves." Alex studied the men in search of a friendly face but didn't spot one. "Okay, so what's the buy-in tonight?"

Silas leaned in his ear and whispered, "All you have to do—is lose." He stood upright again and patted Alex on his back. "Let's get this ball rolling, fellas."

The only empty chair at the table was where Silas sat down, and it just so happened to be next to Alex. And as Silas' words reverberated in his mind, he stared at the cards that lay in front of him. It was an easy ask, losing. Nothing to it. Alex was reminded of the wad of cash in his pocket and how it would soon be returned to its rightful owners, whether they deserved it or not. As far as he was concerned, they should've been man enough to accept defeat and this whole thing would never have come to pass. What kind of men were they anyway?

Heat began to rise under his collar the more he considered the notion of being strong-armed into throwing in the towel. What did he really have to fear from this guy? Who the hell was he? After all, Alex had Jacob. And Jacob's girlfriend was an Owensville cop. He could have this guy arrested, if he wanted to.

But as he peered at his hand and cast a brief glance to Silas, he realized there was something about him that said Silas wasn't messing around. Alex could feel it in his bones, and to defy him, well, that could bring more trouble than this three grand was worth. He had a family to consider; a job. A gambling man by nature, Alex couldn't bring himself to fight this time. "Fold."

The room filled with grunts and growls. Silas cocked his head and peered at Alex. "What the fuck, man? Don't puss out like that. We just started."

Confusion swept over Alex. Hadn't the man just told him to lose? And he did, so what the hell was going on? He shrugged his shoulders and returned a sheepish grin. "What can I say? Luck wasn't on my side with this one."

The hand continued until it was Silas' turn. He peered at his cards. "Call. Let's see those cards, boys."

The hands were laid on the table. Alex couldn't believe the round ended so quickly, but the interesting thing was who ended up winning the pot.

Silas pulled in the chips. "There's always the next hand, fellas."

Alex peered at him, wondering why he wanted his buddies to

get an opportunity to win back their money when it was he who had won that pot. Maybe it was still early, and Silas didn't want it to look set up, which of course, it was.

Riley hadn't filled in the captain on what transpired at the Crooked Horse earlier this evening. There wasn't much to say on the matter and thought it best to wait until tomorrow to give him the low down. But that wasn't really how she felt about Silas Levin, that there wasn't much to say about him. She just didn't know what that was at present.

"Can I get you some water or anything, Riley?" Jacob stood from the sofa and started into the kitchen.

"Thanks. No, I'm okay."

He retrieved a glass from the cabinet and placed it under the sink. "You haven't said much tonight. Are you feeling okay?"

"Fine." Her voice carried through the small house into the kitchen.

Jacob shook his head and returned with a glass of water and sat back down. "You've been on your laptop for the past two hours. Are you looking for something?"

Riley set her sights on him and folded down the lid of the laptop. "Not really. Maybe just doing a little bit of recon before I talk to Ward tomorrow, but I haven't come up with anything."

"Recon? For what?" Jacob sipped on his water.

"I just got a funny feeling when I met the owner of the Crooked Horse."

"No one should feel good when you get a funny feeling." He used air quotes around the words.

"It's nothing. I mean, I didn't see anything significant, so either the guy is really good at hiding his emotions or he doesn't have any, which could also be true. He didn't exactly strike me as a man full of feelings."

"So what about him has your hackles raised?" Jacob asked.

"I don't know. I thought if I tried to root around his history, I might find something. But the thing is, he doesn't seem to have one. Not that I could find and I have access to a few different databases. He's just not there."

"Did you think that maybe he's never committed a crime?"

She peered at him. "Or he's just never been caught. Point being, I'm just trying to cover my bases."

"Hey, far be it from me to stand in the way of your job. If you need to do this, then by all means, go for it. I do know that one of the guys I work with, Alex Laughlin, he was there the other night when the bar had that fight or whatever."

"He was there?"

"Yep. Said he bailed early, but I don't know. He's a pretty big poker player. Even played in the World Series of Poker in Las Vegas a couple of years ago. Maybe you should talk to him. He might know something."

"That's not a bad idea. Thanks. Of course, it's not legal to gamble here, so Captain wanted to put a stop to that before it got out of hand, which, by the sounds of it, it had, at least that night. Anyway, that's why I was there earlier with Ethan. Ward wants us to be sure the owner knows we're here and looking out for the place."

"Did you and Ethan talk about Gracie at all?"

"No. It's not my business, Jacob. And it's not yours either. I'm glad Gracie has Ethan, if that's what this turns out to be.

She's a good person. He's a good person. I don't see the problem."

"That's because you're not letting yourself see the problem," Jacob replied.

"I don't want to fight about this." Riley stood from the couch. "It's getting late. I'm going to bed. Are you coming?"

"Sure."

MIDNIGHT HAD ARRIVED AND ALEX REMAINED IN THE GAME, down almost two grand. The guys he was playing against weren't good players and he'd actually won a few hands without trying. Silas took in a fair chunk of the winnings, which still confused him. It seemed all that would accomplish was to ensure the players didn't return. He knew the deal. The game would go under if people didn't feel good about it at least some of the time. Just like anything in life. One could take a beating once in a while, but if it happened all the time, the answer was to remove oneself from the situation.

"I don't know about you fellas, but I'm feeling worse for wear. Who's ready to call it after this hand?" Silas peered around. "Glad we're all on the same page. Tonight's been a good night and I think we have Alex to thank for that. He gave us a shot at earning back our losses from the other night. And by the look of things, you fellas did your level best."

"Better than before, that is a fact," one of the men said. "However, it does seem ol' Alex here might've been playing us for fools."

"I'm sorry?" Alex asked.

"Boy, after the way you played the other night, I'm just

supposed to sit here and believe that was some sort of dumb luck? I may be slow, but I ain't stupid. Silas, I think we was getting played the other night and I think we got played tonight. This boy here just wants to keep us on the hook, I suspect. Ready to pounce on us again the next time around. Lull us into a sense of complacency."

"Is that true, kid?" Silas turned to him with furrowed brows. "You weren't playing us, were you?"

Alex's mouth might as well have fallen to the floor. What the hell was going on? What was Silas playing anyway? "No, sir. I enjoyed playing with you guys last week, had a run of good luck, and figured I could duplicate that, but it turns out, I overestimated my own skills. I hope there are no hard feelings 'cause I'd like to try my luck with you bunch another time."

Silas returned to the other man. "See? The boy's just wanting to join in with us. That's all it is. Sometimes you win, sometimes you lose." He pushed up from the table. "And I think we all came out a little better this go-round."

Alex waited in the room for the men to leave and Silas walked them out. He wasn't sure if he was allowed to go just yet, and when Silas finally returned, it was a good thing he stayed put. "Hey, I had fun tonight. Thanks." He took a step.

"Whoa now." Silas jutted his hand and smacked Alex in his chest. "We aren't done here. I covered for you with Jim over there because I think you were being obvious to try and fuck me over. Is that true?"

"No, sir—Silas. I wasn't. You asked me to go easy on them and I did. Just like you said. I didn't lose it all, but you know I can come back. I got no problem with that."

"Okay then. We'll do this again on Thursday." Silas started out the door. "But there's something you should know." He stopped dead in the doorway. "We're going to have to come together on a solution here."

"A solution for what?" Alex asked.

"If you and me are going to work together, we'll have to come up with a plan of action. I can't afford for those boys to turn on me. You'll play like you do and we'll split the winnings. If they see me losing too, well, they'll believe we're copacetic. After all, I'm the owner of this establishment."

"Wait, you want me to take their money and split it with you?"

"Did I not make myself clear, kid?"

"Um, yeah. Perfectly clear." Alex felt the weight on his shoulders.

"And just so we're on the same page, you'll need to make sure your boys are here too. We gotta go big or go home, so we'll need to step up the game. Bring in some fresh meat. You can do that, right?"

"Sure."

"You're a good kid, Alex. I knew that the moment I met you. Now go home to your family."

Alex walked past him in a daze until he made it out the door. The fresh air pulled him back and he realized what he'd just done. He was going to be working for Silas Levin and there wasn't going to be a choice in the matter. And worst of all, he would have to drag his friends in with him.

7

The clock showed midnight and Ethan turned to Gracie as they both rested on the sofa, the television airing a late-night talk show. Her head lay against his chest and her curly brown hair lay in reedy strands against her cheek. He pushed them away with the tip of his index finger. "I should probably go home. It's getting late and I have work in the morning."

Gracie pulled upright. "Sure. It is getting late. Thank you for coming over tonight." She held his gaze for a moment too long until leaning in to kiss his lips.

Her mouth pressed gently against his and he felt her warmth and tenderness. Gracie was young, barely 21, and he dangled between his mid and late twenties. He knew she hadn't had a serious boyfriend before but had dated in college as one does. But he also knew she would be leaving for the city in a matter of days and wondered where that would leave him. His fondness for her had grown over the past few months since they'd been in contact, usually through texting and a weekly video chat. She desired him and the feeling was mutual, though they hadn't yet crossed that line, mainly because she had been at school and he was here.

However, the idea that might happen tonight was not in play. This was Ellen's house and Ethan wasn't going to cross that line, regardless of how much he wanted to.

Gracie pulled away from the kiss and smiled. "I'll walk you out."

And the answer had arrived without the question being asked. Ethan couldn't bring himself to inquire what the future for them might hold. It seemed premature and a little on the needy side. He was left with no choice but to let her drive the ship.

She started toward the door and Ethan followed. He watched her gentle stride, her hips sway with each step. Gracie wasn't like Riley in any way. Not with her personality or her physical appearance. In fact, it surprised him how different they really were. But she was no less beautiful than Riley.

Gracie pulled open the door and raised on her tiptoes. "Goodnight, Ethan. I'll see you tomorrow?" She kissed his lips only briefly this time.

"I hope so. Maybe we can go out for dinner or something?"

"I'd like that." She peered over her shoulder at the staircase, then turned back. "I know it's tough with my mom here. Maybe we can go to your place?"

"If that's what you want."

She cocked her head. "Don't you?"

"You'll get no argument from me." He crossed the threshold and stepped onto the front porch. "I'll talk to you tomorrow. Goodnight." Ethan walked to his car parked along the front of the home and stepped inside. He peered at Gracie and smiled while she returned the same and closed the door.

Riley had always kept him at a fair distance and especially as it related to her childhood in this very home. He knew things had happened—bad things. But he didn't know her then. It wasn't until high school and then they never really hung out in the same circles.

Over the past few years since they'd worked together, he'd come to realize who Riley truly was and what she was capable of doing. It was something he was sure she'd hidden as best she could from Gracie. The younger sibling had been protected by both her brother and sister from the worst of the family secrets and tragedies.

There was conflict in him about his feelings for Gracie. Jacob could see it, no doubt, and he assumed Riley could as well, but refused to acknowledge them. She was good at that—denying the truth when it stared her in the face. Who could blame her? Seeing what she had seen and still saw would turn off anyone to true feelings.

Jacob was a permanent fixture in Riley's life now, whether Ethan wanted it or not. She'd made her choice. But what would happen if Ethan moved forward with Gracie? Would it force Riley to confront her feelings for him? He knew they were there. Somewhere deep inside, because he could feel them. He didn't possess her gift, but he wasn't blind. There had been an attraction there once, until Jacob returned.

Perhaps that was the real line he shouldn't cross. It wouldn't be fair to Gracie and he would not hurt her. He loved this family. His heart, however, was holding on to something that just wasn't going to be possible. The question was, could he let go?

THE PERCEPTION THAT THERE WAS SOMETHING DUPLICITOUS about Silas Levin prickled the back of Riley's mind. While she hadn't felt anything in particular, it left her unsettled as she arrived at the stationhouse.

Upon entering, she noticed Ethan emerge from the kitchen with a cup of coffee. "How is it that you always beat me here?"

He stopped and smiled. "Face it, Riley, I'm the better cop. What more can I say?"

"Well, considering how late you were out last night, it's quite a feat." Riley continued toward her desk.

"Someone say something about me?" Ethan returned to his desk appearing mildly concerned and possibly gratified at her interest.

"I got a text from Gracie this morning saying you were there until about midnight. You must be tired."

"I'm a young, virile man, Riley. You're going to have to get used to it."

She laughed. "Okay. Slow your roll there, pal." Riley peered at Ward's office. "I'd like to sit down with the captain this morning and talk about Silas Levin. Do you have some time?"

"Yeah, of course. He's not in yet, though."

"I figured as much since I didn't see his car outside. Any idea where he's at?"

"No. He doesn't tell me his schedule." Ethan sifted through some paperwork on his desk. "I did hear that Abrams and Decker got a call last night about a domestic disturbance. I haven't checked the logs yet, but I assume it's on there."

"Really?" She paused to think on the matter. "Yesterday was the first of the month."

"Oh, that's right. Probably what it was. That's usually when we get the calls. I have to say, though, I'm a little surprised it was just the one. Could mean things are getting better here, right? More jobs? Fewer people on the rolls. I don't know, Riley. Owensville is on its way up."

The beginning of the month usually brought in more than a few domestic disturbance calls thanks to the stamps and checks arriving. Fights between spouses or partners often ensued because money problems always seemed to do that to people. Maybe things were getting better.

"I'm going give the captain a call and see..." Riley's attention was diverted to the door. "There you are. I was just about to call you." She immediately noticed something in his eyes. It would only take another moment to realize what that was, but she tried hard not to see too deeply anymore and especially not with those she cared about. "Is everything okay, Cap?"

Captain Ward continued inside and perched atop Abrams' desk. "I was out on a call. Came in around 3am."

Riley and Ethan traded glances.

"If you've seen the service call logs, then you know what I'm talking about."

Riley's heart sank. She could see it so clearly in Ward's eyes that it was practically screaming out at her. "The domestic disturbance call. The wife is dead."

Ward didn't reply, only lowered his head. "Decker went out there. She was already gone when he arrived. The husband is in the back, in lockup. He'll be transferred to County today. I stayed until the coroner picked up the body."

"Captain, maybe you should go home and get some rest. Pruitt and I can handle the paperwork. I'll call Decker and have him come in."

"No. I'm staying here. I'll be all right." He pushed off the desk. "Goddamn it."

After he disappeared into his office, Riley looked at Ethan. "We need to take off some of the load."

"Already on it." Ethan typed on his keyboard. "I'm pulling up the report now."

Riley picked up her phone. "I'll call Decker. I'm sure he didn't sleep."

Ethan retrieved the report and pulled it off the printer, walking to Riley's desk to hand her a copy. He sat down opposite her and began perusing the document while she spoke to the night shift officer, Chris Decker.

"Chris, it's Riley. How you holding up? I didn't wake you, did I?" She felt confident she hadn't. Chris was the type of guy to be pretty broken up about something like this.

"You know you didn't wake me, Riley. I'm just sitting here on my couch in my skivvies trying to forget what I saw this morning. I guess Cap told you what happened?"

"Didn't give us the details. Ethan just pulled up the report and we're about to take a look at it. Is there anything I can do?"

"You mean, with the gift?"

"Yeah." She disliked using it in anything but extreme cases. Murder, in her eyes, was pretty extreme. And of course, it didn't mean she'd get anything, but if it could help, there was a reason God and her grandfather bestowed on her the gift.

"I know you don't talk about it, Riley, and I completely understand," Decker began. "What I saw that day..."

"I know. And I appreciate you letting me keep that to myself. But if there's something I can do..."

"The guy's in custody. You'll see in the report that he says he was drinking. Surprise, surprise. And that he'd gotten upset at his wife over money or some shit, but it was enough that he decided to take out his aggressions on her. Only he took it too far. Preliminary suggests blunt force trauma to her skull. You'll have to speak to the coroner for more details and when his final report will be available."

"Ward said this guy was going to County today," she continued.

"That's right. We can't hang on to him for long here. We don't have the facilities. Our cells usually get filled up with the drunks and junkies."

"Right. What did Abrams have to say about all this?"

"Come on, Riley. What do you think? The man's got no internal filter."

"Okay. Well, look. I'll review this thing with Ethan. Ward's in his office and I'd like to take some of the paperwork off his plate, if you're good with that. This was your collar."

"It don't matter to me who brought in this asshole. Just do what you gotta do, Riley. I'll be in tonight as usual. Just do me a favor?"

"What's that?"

"Let me know when that prick is getting transferred? The sooner he's out of our custody, the better I'll feel."

"Will do. Go and get some rest. I'll see you tonight." Riley ended the call and peered at Ethan.

"Let me guess, he's not doing real well," Ethan said.

"No. He's not. What have you read so far?" She picked up the report he'd placed on her desk and began to read it.

"I don't know if you want to talk to this guy or not," he began. "Probably ought to get Ward's okay, but maybe we can ask him about the money troubles. According to this, the guy works a steady job. The wife worked too."

"Kids?" She almost hesitated to ask.

"One. He's with CPS now. I hope he has other family who can take the kid," Ethan replied.

"So they both worked and yet the argument, according to Decker, was about money," Riley pressed on.

"Right. People can still need money even if they have jobs. But it wasn't what I thought. I assumed it was the welfare checks. Timing and all that," he replied.

"Same here. Does he have a record?" She flipped through the report in search of the answer. "No priors." Riley regarded Ethan. "How does a guy with no priors end up killing his wife? No other domestic calls. Nothing."

"He must've snapped. That's all I can figure."

"For God's sake. That's one hell of a snap." Riley peered at Ward's office. "Should I ask if we can chat with the guy?"

"You can ask, but he's got no lawyer here. I doubt, even if Ward allowed it, that'd he'd say one damn word to us."

"You're probably right."

"Of course, you don't need to talk to people to get what you need from them, do you, Riley?"

"No, I suppose not." She peered into the corridor that led to the holding cells. "I mean, the guy's guilty, so what's the point in seeing what he did to her? You know that's what'll happen. I'm not sure I want to go through that."

"Well, he is guilty and the reason you do what you do is to find the guilty parties. Maybe you're right. Maybe in this instance, it's unnecessary. He'll go to prison with or without your insight in his reasons why. Unless..."

"Unless he had motives. Did the wife's family have money? Was there an insurance policy? Was this premeditated?"

"Those are questions to which I do not have the answers, Officer Thompson. But answers might help determine how long he'll serve. Premeditated will be a hell of a lot longer sentence than second-degree or even involuntary manslaughter. And if you think his attorney won't push for the lesser of those, especially with no witnesses..."

'Okay, okay. I get what you're saying. But you're forgetting, there is a witness. The son. How old is he?"

Ethan searched the report and peered back at her. "Five."

"Damn."

"What do you want to do, Riley? It's your call."

She held his gaze, then shifted her sights to Ward's office. And without another word, Riley stood from her desk and approached Ward's door, knocking on it.

"Come in." His voice sounded on the other side.

Riley opened the door. "Hey, Cap, I was thinking I should pay a visit to our detainee before he's transferred. If that's okay with you?"

"For what purpose? He won't talk, not without a lawyer."

"I know. But maybe I can get to the bottom of his motives."

Ward leaned back in his chair and studied her. "Motives. He admitted to killing her."

"Yes, but as I was discussing with—well, it doesn't matter. But what if it'll help determine the charges? Whatever murder charges he might face?"

"Riley, even if you could see whatever it is you wanted to see, you can't exactly use that in court. Why put yourself through that? You know what it does to you."

"I know. But if I get why he did it, there could be evidence to corroborate and if there is, then there you go."

"It's Decker's collar. Have you talked to him about this?"

"I did. He's on board with whatever I need to do."

"And I assume Pruitt's behind you one hundred percent, as usual."

Ethan appeared in the doorway. "Yes, sir. You know I am."

"Okay. Go pay him a visit. But do not, under any circumstances, do anything that could jeopardize the County's case. You understand?"

"I understand," she replied.

"Pruitt, go with her. Make sure this guy doesn't get out of hand."

Riley eyed Ward. "Really?"

"Yeah, I know. Just humor me, would you?"

She turned on her heel and started back. "Pruitt, are you coming or what?"

Ethan looked at Ward. "Thanks for that. Now she's going to be mad at me."

"Hey, she'll never admit it, but it's harder on her than she lets on. Riley needs you whether or not she realizes it."

Ethan turned and followed her down the hall toward the holding cells. "Do you have the report?"

"I do." Riley's shoes squeaked on the vinyl flooring as she walked. The stationhouse had only three holding cells, which were usually empty or mostly empty, except maybe on a weekend when people would drink too much. And today, it was just the one occupant. "Wyatt Sims. Thirty-nine years old, employed by the high school. That's interesting."

"Doing what?"

Riley glanced back at him. "Phys. Ed."

"Yikes. He wasn't one of our coaches, was he? The name doesn't ring a bell," Ethan asked.

"I don't think so. Looks like he and his family moved to Owensville about four years ago from South Bend."

"Oh, thank God. I do not want to see one of my high school coaches in jail for murdering his wife."

"You and me both." Riley unlocked the door to enter the holding cell area. "You ready to do this?"

"Oh, I am. It's you who has to be ready. But I'm here for you, Riley. Always have been."

She revealed a demure smile and pushed inside. "Mr. Sims. I'm Officer Thompson. This is Officer Pruitt."

"I'm not talking to you folks until my lawyer gets here."

"That's okay. We're only here to check in and see how you're doing. See if you need anything. Have you eaten or had any water?"

"I'm fine. I don't need nothing." His face was marred with scratches and his stocky frame donned a t-shirt that was ripped at the bottom hem.

"Did the paramedics take a look at you?" Riley asked.

"I don't need no paramedics either. What do you want, officer?"

Riley stepped closer to the cell while using her palm to prevent Ethan from doing the same. "I got this," she whispered.

Ethan held his ground, appearing reluctant.

"You're due to be transferred this afternoon to County. Is there anyone here you'd like us to get in contact with?"

"I don't have family here." He wouldn't look at her.

Riley inhaled deeply. "What about your son? Who's looking after him?"

Sims shot her a look and that was all she needed.

8

In a barrage of memories that drilled into Riley's mind, she stumbled back from the jail cell where Wyatt Sims held her gaze. The brutal attack against his wife, the boy in the background watching with not just tears in his eyes, but rage. She was helpless to do anything about it but stand there and witness the event.

Ethan lurched forward and placed his hand against her back to steady her.

Sims scowled at Riley. "What the hell's wrong with you? You having some kind of seizure or some shit?" He looked at Ethan. "Boy, you better do something about her. Something ain't right."

"She's fine!" Ethan's voice raised but his eyes never left Riley.

She continued to stand inside the home and watch as Sims beat his wife, screaming and yelling at her. "Why are you doing this?" Riley shouted at him, but he didn't stop because he couldn't hear her. She wasn't there. Saving this poor woman wasn't possible and all Riley could do was find a reason for the heinous act.

The woman was on the floor now, her arms shielded her face from the blows. "I'm sorry. I didn't mean to get mad at you," she wailed in pain.

The little boy screamed at his father with clenched fists and a red face. "Stop hurting my mommy!"

Riley's eyes filled with tears, impotent to stop any of it. She watched Sims walk toward the boy. "Please don't hurt him."

"Go to your room!" Sims yelled and the boy ran. He turned back to his wife. "I'll do whatever the fuck I want to do with my money. You think you're the boss around here, huh?"

"No. No," she whimpered. "We just—we needed that money."

"You think I don't know that, bitch?" With the back of his hand, he struck her cheek while she lay on the floor of the living room. "I'll get it back, okay? I'll get it fucking back and I don't need you telling me what a piece of shit I am."

The final blow came and she was out cold. As Riley looked on in horror, she knew the woman would not awaken again.

Riley's back shot straight, her eyes widened, and she inhaled a great deep breath as though she'd been underwater the entire time.

"Riley? Riley, are you okay?" Ethan stood in front of her to block Sims' view. He gripped her shoulders and peered into her eyes. "You're back. Christ All Mighty, I wasn't sure when you were coming back."

Riley regained focus on the present. She held on to Ethan's gaze as though he were the only person in the world. It was how she remembered the when and where. Time lost all meaning when she was submerged in a vision. But her wits returned. "I'm okay. I'm back." She studied her clammy palms and wiped the sweat from her brow.

She stepped aside to lock eyes with Sims.

"Jesus H. Christ, lady, the hell is wrong with you? You sick or something?"

"You lost money that your family needed, and you got mad at her for being upset about it."

Bewilderment masked his face. "What did you just say?" Sims gripped the bars of the cell. "What did you just say to me?"

"That's why you killed her. You lost your temper and couldn't stop." Riley moved toward him, close enough to smell his fear. "I think you would've killed your son too if he hadn't run from you."

Sims released the bars and his eyes exposed his remorse. He stepped back. "I would never hurt my kid. You don't know what the hell you're talking about." He looked at Ethan. "You better get this crazy bitch away from me. I'm not saying another goddamn word."

"Riley, let's go. It's over." Ethan tried to move her, but she wouldn't budge.

"I'm not going anywhere until he tells me about the money." She stood firm and fixed her sights on Sims. "How much and how did you lose it?" Riley waited for a response but felt the walls tower around him. He wasn't going to say anything else and the trauma of the event made it too difficult for her to see beyond his crime. She couldn't see the source behind it.

"That's enough now. We're leaving." Ethan squeezed her shoulder. "Now."

She broke away from Sims' stare and returned her sights to Ethan. And without another word, she started back out into the corridor, the door to the holding cells slamming behind them.

As Riley and Ethan stood in the hall, Ward appeared and walked toward them. He looked at Riley, then to the door and back at her again. "Was it worth it? Did you get what you wanted?"

"It was about money," Riley said.

"It usually is." Ward folded his arms. "Anything else that might be useful at all?"

"I know you don't agree with it, but I..."

"I don't agree with it this time because I'm not sure it was necessary. Look, Riley, I get that, yeah, sometimes the things you see are invaluable. But we have the culprit in our custody. We might not know why, but we know how, and it's going to put him away. The rest will come out in the trial. I just hate seeing what it does to you. It changes you, whittles away at your soul. I see it. So while it might help put him away for longer, I'm not sure it's worth the price. Are you?"

THE COMMERCIAL STRIP WHERE HVM's OFFICE BUILDING dwelled also housed two other office buildings and a café that served breakfast and lunch only. Jacob ate lunch there at least three times a week, and today, he opted to sit outside on a rare cooler day this summer.

As he bit down on the tuna salad sandwich, a shadow crossed his table. With the afternoon sun shining down, he gazed up to see Alex in front of him. "Hey, man. Finally taking your lunch break?"

"Yeah."

"Have a seat. Did you order already?" Jacob asked.

"I did." Alex pulled out the metal chair and dropped down. He removed his sunglasses and set them on the table.

"What's wrong? You looked bummed out." Jacob wiped his mouth with his napkin. "Is the resubmittal going okay?"

"Sure. Yeah. Sorry, I'm just a little tired. How's things with you?"

"No complaints. Man, are you sure everything's okay? You don't look well. Maybe you're coming down with something."

"I said I was fine."

"Here's your food, sir." The waiter set down the plate in front of him. "Can I get you anything else?"

"No." Alex took a mouthful of hotdog and washed it down with a Coke. "I don't mean to be an asshole. I guess I'm a little stressed."

"About what? Anything I can help with?"

"Nah. It's on my shoulders. I have to deal with it." Alex took another bite and appeared to reconsider. "Well, actually, there is one thing."

"Oh yeah? What's that?"

"You feel like joining me for a friendly game of poker on Thursday night?"

"Don't tell me you're in on that deal at the Crooked Horse?" Jacob asked. "Dude, my girlfriend's a cop. She's been in there making sure the owner knows the drill. Shit's illegal, man."

Alex peered down at his plate of food and took in a deep breath. He gazed back up at Jacob. "Look, I'm in a bind. I just need you to come with me and throw some games. I'll cut you in so you aren't actually losing any money."

Jacob held up his hands. "Wait. Cut me in? To what? Alex, what the hell's going on?"

"I'm trying to tell you. The owner of the bar, Silas Levin, he's a shady character and I didn't realize it at first, but I went in there last week, took all his guys for a shit ton of cash. Next thing I know, Silas is paying me a visit insisting I come back. Well, I did. I let those guys win back their money, except it was Silas who kept the majority of it. Now he wants to set up some con or something. Hell, I don't know."

"Should I get Riley involved? This sounds bad, Alex. Like really, dangerously bad, for you."

"Are you kidding me? This guy has already unleashed threats against my family..."

"What? That's it. I'm calling Riley." Jacob retrieved his cell phone.

Alex slapped it down. "Dude! Are you serious? Do you hear what I'm telling you? He knows where I live, and that my wife stays home. How the hell do you think he found that shit out, huh?"

"There has to be a way. I mean, you can't go through with this. You'll be the one to get busted. If this guy is smart, he'll figure a way to put the blame on you."

"Look, I think if I just play the game, maybe once or twice more, lose my shirt, he'll move on. I have a feeling he must rotate his favorites and keeps the game fresh with new people. Otherwise, he'd have no one to play. I just need you to come with me. Just this once. I have to bring in people or, well, I don't know what'll happen, but I don't want to find out. Will you help me or are you going to puss out and call your girlfriend?"

Jacob held his phone and eyed Alex. He considered for a moment that this might help Riley and Ward if they had an inside track on Silas Levin. Riley already had a feeling this guy wasn't on the straight and narrow. Although it would mean he would have to lie to her, or rather, keep the truth from her. Either way, that was always a challenge when faced with a woman who could literally see through you.

"Well?" Alex asked. "If I came to the wrong person, then so be it. But I'd appreciate it if you keep this to yourself." He began to rise. "Otherwise, you might've just signed my death warrant."

"Hang on, Alex. Sit down." Jacob waited until he returned to his seat. "If you think you're in real danger, then maybe you have come to the wrong person. I won't sit back and watch something bad go down around here. Been there, done that, my friend. But if what you said before is true, that this is just a means to an end—a short end, then you can count on me. But if I think it's going south or either or both of us are in real danger, you'd better believe I'll take it to Riley. I'm not an idiot and I don't think you are either. Unless I'm wrong?"

"You're not wrong. I appreciate it, man. Let's see how Thursday plays out and we'll go from there." He took a drink of his Coke. "I'm glad to know you've got my back."

TWO DEPUTIES FROM THE COUNTY SHERIFF'S DEPARTMENT arrived to take custody of Wyatt Sims, the man who had beaten his wife to death because she questioned him over money. And all of this in front of their young son, who was now with Child Protective Services.

Ward directed them to the holding cell. "He's back here and he's all yours." He unlocked the door and allowed them entry before following behind to unlock the cell. "It's time for you to get the hell out of my town, Mr. Sims."

Wyatt Sims stood up and brushed off his clothes as if he needed to impress the deputies. "I still haven't seen my lawyer."

"He'll be waiting for you at County," one of the deputies

replied.

"Good. There are some crazy-ass cops in this town. I'm better off someplace else." He was led in cuffs past Ward. "Safer someplace else."

"Whatever you say, Sims." Ward closed the door behind them and led them back to the main bullpen area where Riley, Ethan, and Chris Decker waited.

The three officers stood in a line as Sims was pulled along.

"That one there," Sims eyed Riley. "You folks better watch out for her. She's bad news."

Decker shot a sideways glance to Riley, then quickly looked away.

She felt his gaze and knew exactly what it meant. Decker was still afraid of her, at least, a little. He'd been at the warehouse when the mafia attempted to destroy the evidence about the murder and hide the real reason behind their arrival in Owensville. She'd lost control that day and it almost cost the lives of the criminals. Those there at the time had no idea what she was capable of. Not her colleagues and not the bad guys. And now it was clear Decker wasn't going to forget anytime soon.

"You're the one who's bad news and you'll pay for what you did." Ethan pulled open the front door. "Good riddance, asshole."

"That's enough, Pruitt," Ward chided. "Thank you, deputies, for doing us a favor. Don't let him out of your sight."

"Not a chance, Captain." The first deputy walked through the door and waited for the prisoner to follow. "Let's get you loaded up."

Sims turned back again and peered through the window directly at Riley. She returned a menacing smile and he looked away.

"He is an asshole." Riley returned to her desk. "But I know he did what he did for a reason. Now I just need to find out what that reason was."

Decker approached her desk. "What do have in mind?"

"I'd like to run a background check on him."

"This isn't our case anymore." Ward approached Riley's desk. "Decker here will likely be called to testify, but as far as anything else goes, there'll be minimal input from us. I can see you want to say something there, Thompson."

"What if I can prove this is part of something bigger?"

"You mean that Sims killed others?" he replied.

"No. I mean I think Wyatt Sims is involved in some sort of money scheme. Laundering, I don't know yet, but I'd like the opportunity to find out. A man doesn't just kill his wife for asking about money. At least, I don't think he does. I think there's something hiding below the surface."

"You have a hunch about this, do you?" Ward asked.

"I do, Captain. I think it'd be a shame to have let that woman die for nothing."

Ward looked at the other officers. "You two agree with your colleague?"

"I can't disagree," Ethan replied.

"Uh-huh." Ward turned to Decker. "And what about you? You think there could be more to this than meets the eye?"

"If Riley thinks so, then who am I to disagree?"

"Well, I can see I'm outnumbered here." He started toward his office. "Fine. But you best not let any of this get in the way of your day to day, you understand me?"

Riley revealed a victorious smile. "Understood, Captain."

9

For the most part, Owensville was a sleepy town, which meant the police department was only called upon to investigate petty crimes. Sometimes a residential break-in, the occasional traffic violation, but rarely anything more serious. Not like today, when they'd arrested a man for beating his wife to death. Not since the mob attempted to infiltrate the quiet town had anything so horrifying transpired. And none of this was sitting well with Riley as she emptied her dishwasher, her mind pondering the reasons behind Wyatt Sims' actions. He was a high school coach, for Pete's sake. "He must've been in something deep," she whispered.

"Did you say something?" Jacob walked into the kitchen holding a glass and plate. "I brought in the dishes from the living room. Thought I heard you talking."

"Just to myself." She returned a glass to its rightful home. "I'm struggling with Sims. The captain said I could root around and see if something pops up, but I can see he's not keen on the idea."

"Can you blame him? The County's taken over the case and you want to keep it going. It's not your problem anymore, Riley."

"I know it isn't, but somehow I feel like it's going to bite us in the ass, you know?"

"Look, I'm the last one to question your instincts, but maybe Dan's right on this count. The man who killed that poor woman is in jail and he won't be getting out anytime soon. Isn't that what's really important here?" Jacob walked behind the breakfast counter and helped her reload the dishwasher.

"Yeah, but I'll see what comes up." Riley's attention was diverted by the knock on the front door. Her brow furrowed. "Are you expecting company?"

"No." He appeared just as curious.

Riley made her way to the entry and peeked through the security lens. "Oh." She unlocked the door and pulled it open. "Hey. What are you doing here?"

"I heard about what happened." Dillon walked inside. "You know Sims worked at the school, right?"

"I do. Can I get you something to drink?" Riley returned to the kitchen.

Dillon trailed behind. "I'll take a beer, if you have one."

"Hey, man. Course we do." Jacob opened the refrigerator and retrieved two bottles of Bud. He popped off the tops and handed one to Dillon. "I assume you must've known this guy, huh?"

Dillon dropped to the barstool and took a swig of beer. "I know him. We're all shocked by what happened. It just seems so out of character. No one would ever believe he could harm anyone, let alone kill his wife."

"So word's already reached the school?" Riley leaned over the bar top, resting her elbows against it.

"Are you kidding? It's like that game, Telephone, except nothing was lost in translation. The principal is going to make an announcement tomorrow to the students. Sims was the coach for junior varsity basketball."

"Well, he'll get what's coming to him. County took him to lockup today." Riley pulled up again. "What can you tell me about him?"

"What do you mean?" Dillon tossed back another gulp.

"I mean, did you know him well? Are you aware of any bad habits he had?"

"Bad habits? Like smoking or drinking?" he replied.

"Drinking, maybe. Although he wasn't drunk when Decker brought him in. I'm thinking more along the lines of illicit activities."

"What did you see, Riley?" Dillon peered at her. "What was Sims into?"

"I don't know for sure. I saw something that was troubling, aside from the fact that he beat his wife to death in front of their child."

"Jesus, Riley." Jacob turned to her.

"What? It's true. Dillon has a right to know. He worked with the man." Riley peered at Dillon again. "He needed money, or he lost some money, something like that. Would you know anything about that?"

"No. We didn't hang out in the same circles. The counselors and admin generally stay together. The teachers do too, but Phys. Ed..."

"You can find out?" Riley asked.

"I can ask around for you."

"And you won't get into any trouble, right?" she added.

"I don't think so. I'm just asking a few questions."

Riley folded her arms. "Good. Thanks. Is that why you came by? You wanted in on the action?"

Dillon raised the corner of his lips in a half-cocked smiled. "Maybe. No, but, in all seriousness, I'm concerned. And if I can help, then you know you can count on me." He pushed off the barstool. "Thanks for the beer. I should get back home. Marjorie will be pissed if she has to put down the kids without any help." He started toward the door.

"Thanks, big brother." Riley walked with him to the door. "Just be careful, okay?"

"Always." He turned to Jacob. "See you later, brother."

"Oh, and one more thing," Riley added. "Gracie's due to head back to the city in a couple of days. Let's put something together for her."

"Sounds good." Dillon kissed her cheek. "Night, little sister."

Riley closed the door as he left and engaged the deadbolt. She noticed an uncomfortable look on Jacob's face. "What's wrong?"

"Nothing. I'm just not sure Dillon should get involved. He's not a cop."

"I know that. I'm not asking him to do anything that would get him into trouble. Besides, I think he enjoys feeling a part of what I do. Reminds him of the good 'ol days."

"The good 'ol days?" Jacob began. "Like when you two were running from crazy gun-running militia? Those good 'ol days?"

Riley stepped closer and placed her hands against his chest. "Relax, Jacob. It's fine. He's just asking his colleagues a few questions about a man they thought was someone else. That's all this is." As she held his gaze, blood dripped from his forehead, first in small streams, then poured down him as though it had been spilled atop his head. She released his shoulders and gasped.

"Babe, what's wrong?" Jacob spoke with the blood trailing over his lips and into his mouth.

Her eyes widened and her mouth fell. Her pulse raced and she closed her eyes. When she opened them again, Jacob was fine. His face had returned to normal.

"Oh no. What did you see? It must've been bad by the look on your face. Riley, please tell me what's happening here? Is it the same as the other day?"

She shook her head wildly, trying to oust the image from her mind. Her vision cleared again and she peered at his frightened face. "It's nothing. Just another misfire."

"For Christ's sake, Riley, a misfire—again? I don't think so. You have to tell me what this is. I'm freaking out over here."

"I don't know. I don't know what it is."

JACOB WAS LEFT TO HIS OWN THOUGHTS AS HE LAY NEXT TO Riley and stared at the ceiling. It appeared as though she was asleep, but he never knew when she was pretending. Sometimes she did it to make him believe she wasn't worried about anything. Perhaps it was her way of protecting him and he hated it.

He supposed she held back things from him, either with work or her visions. Whatever it was, she didn't have the faith in him that he could handle it. What worried him most was that he feared she would sense what he was hiding. She wasn't the only one with a secret. And maybe that secret was the reason for her vision earlier tonight. Her misfire, as she called it. *Misfire my ass,* he thought.

There was no telling what her visions meant. Sometimes they were a warning, sometimes they were inevitable. It was up to Jacob now to decipher this newest apparition. His first thought was Alex Laughlin and how he'd convinced Jacob to take part in the high-stakes poker game on Thursday. Sure, it seemed innocuous enough, but according to Alex, Silas Levin was anything but. And now Jacob was embroiled in this thing, whatever it was, and with Riley suffering terrifying visions, it was adding up to trouble. She was protecting him as she did with everyone in her life. Without Carl Boyd to temper her, who could give her the level-headedness she needed?

Jacob had hoped he could fill the void, but so far, Riley was refusing to let him in. What then could he do to help her? Maybe not get involved with the likes of Silas Levin, for starters, but he was committed now. There was no turning back. Visions be damned, Jacob was all-in.

THE DINER WHERE RILEY HAD SPENT MUCH OF HER YOUTH, and where her mother was currently employed, had cleared out its breakfast crowd. Although, on a Wednesday, it hadn't been much of a crowd, except for the construction workers who were building the new housing community near the edge of town. The model homes were under construction and HVM Builders was the owner.

"You mind if we stop in for a coffee? I'd like to check in with

Mom to see how she's doing with Gracie." Riley slowed the cruiser as she entered the row of stores where the diner was located.

"Sure. No problem. I could use a coffee." Ethan was in the passenger seat thumbing through his phone. "But as far as I know, Gracie says it's been a really good visit."

Riley parked in a spot fronting the diner and pulled the gear shift into park. "Speaking of...How's things going with you two?"

"Good, yeah. I mean, she's leaving soon, but it's been really nice spending the time with her," he replied.

"You're not upset she's moving to the city for that internship?"

"How could I be upset by that? It's a great opportunity for her."

"Yes, it is. And I wouldn't want her to squander it any more than you."

"Exactly. So, yeah. I've accepted it." He opened the car door. "Are we going inside or what?"

Riley stepped out of the car and walked toward the sidewalk. She peered through the diner's window. "There she is." A quick wave to Ellen and she walked inside.

Ellen approached her daughter with a smile. "Well, good morning. I wasn't expecting to see you two in here. Come on in and have a seat." She directed them to a table. "Coffee?"

"Yes, please," Ethan replied.

"That'd be great. Thanks, Mom." Riley watched as Ellen returned to the counter and retrieved the carafe of freshly brewed coffee. "Listen, I'm sorry about grilling you over Gracie. It's really none of my business."

"It's okay," Ethan began. "She's your sister." He peered up at Ellen as she returned with the mugs and coffee. "Thanks, Ellen."

"You got it." She poured the coffee. "Either of you care for some food?"

"No thanks. Just looking for a caffeine boost, if that's all right." Riley sipped on her coffee.

"Of course it is. Any opportunity I get to see my girl, I'm happy about." Ellen turned to Ethan. "You too, Ethan." She peered over her shoulder. "Shoot. I need to get back up there. If you two need anything else, just holler."

Riley nodded as Ellen left them alone again. "She seems happy. In fact, I don't think I've seen her so happy in a long time."

"I think having Gracie there has given her purpose again, like her kid needs her." Ethan drew a ring around his cup. "Look, Riley, I know this whole thing is kind of weird with me and Gracie, but I do care a lot about your sister. And I think she feels the same. I kinda like that too."

Riley cast away her glance for a moment. The dig wasn't intentional, but it was there, nonetheless. His implication that he'd had feelings for her that were unrequited wasn't lost on her. She wore the guilt around her neck like a noose ever since Jacob returned. "I'm glad you two are getting along so well. I mean that. And who knows what the future will hold? Long distance relationships work sometimes."

"Sometimes." Ethan sipped again on his coffee. "Is this the only reason you wanted to come here this morning? To see Ellen?"

Riley studied him for a moment. "There might be something else. Something I wanted to talk about away from the station."

"I'm listening." He pulled up at attention.

"I didn't want to say anything around the captain, but last night, I had a terrible vision. And it wasn't the first time."

"What about?"

"Jacob. Ethan, he—he was all bloody and his face—it was horrifying. The first time I experienced it was just before we left to see Gracie graduate. And then it happened again last night. He's upset."

"No doubt. You can't see anything else? A cause or reason behind it? A feeling?"

"No. Nothing. I'm afraid of what it might mean." She held up her palms. "Now I know that I've had similar visions and they've turned out to be false. And maybe that's all this is." She held his gaze. "But what if it's more?"

"What can I do to help, Riley?"

"This is something that has to do with Jacob. Something he's doing or going to do. I don't know yet."

"I don't suppose he's come out and said he's doing something dangerous or that you wouldn't approve of?"

"No. Maybe if he is, he doesn't know it's a problem or that it could be dangerous and so he doesn't think to say anything. He's not a liar, Ethan."

"I didn't say he was. I'm looking for an explanation, same as you."

"Yeah. Sorry. I just wish I could see it. Whatever 'it' is." She held Ethan's gaze once again. "I guess what I'm asking you is that maybe you can get him to talk."

He chuckled. "Get him to talk? You mean like an interrogation?"

"No. I mean like get him to open up to you. I don't know. Go have a beer with him or something."

"Why me? Why can't you do that?"

"Because he tries to shield me from everything. If he thinks it'll bother me or set me off or any reaction really, he'll avoid the topic.

Like I said, he might not know what he's doing or that it could bring him closer to danger. But I'd like to leave that up to you to be the judge."

"Riley, this might be a better task for your brother. Jacob doesn't like me, and honestly, he's not my favorite person. Do you know what you're asking me to do here?"

Riley finished her coffee and set down the cup. "I'm asking you to snoop. I get that. And you're the best one for the job. Dillon's his pal, his buddy. He won't think anything about whatever it is Jacob could be up against."

"I'll go along with it, but there's no guarantees Jacob will. I think the moment I ask him to go and have a beer with me, he'll zip up. He won't say or do anything that might put him in a bad light because he won't want me to go and tell you."

"What can I do then, Ethan? Maybe you're right. Maybe Jacob will do exactly that. If that's the case, I have no one else to turn to. Can't you just play it off that you're trying to overcome the history between you two? Come on. I wouldn't ask if I didn't need the help. I need you, Ethan." She was treading dangerous waters now, using Ethan's feelings for her to get what she wanted. But her back was up against a wall. She needed information to determine if Jacob was currently or was going to be in any kind of trouble. The idea harm could come to him wasn't going to happen on her watch. She'd lost Carl. There wasn't a chance in hell she would lose Jacob. Riley waited for Ethan's response.

"I'll try, Riley. That's all I can do. But make no mistake, this is for you. I don't want anything bad to happen to Jacob, but I'm doing this for you."

"Thank you."

THE OFFICE OF HVM BUILDERS WAS BUSTLING WITH administrative staff, plan reviewers, accountants, and everyone in between, including the in-house architect, Jacob Biggs. He walked into his office with a Starbucks in hand and sat down. It was about time the town got a Starbucks. He hated going into the diner or to the McDonalds for a coffee. And today, he was especially tired and in need of the caffeine. Riley's visions, which she refused to share or explain to him, still had his nerves on end. It was part and parcel of being involved with a woman who could feel others' emotions and see what the future might bring, even if that future was unclear. It was usually given to her in fragments and up to her to piece together. That was what her visions about him had been —fragments.

He peered up from his laptop and noticed Alex in his doorway. "Morning. What's up?"

Alex moseyed inside. "Not much. Just getting started for the day. I just wanted to double check with you that you're good for tomorrow night? It'll be late. I hope that's okay."

"I'm not sure any of this is okay, but I said I'd help, and I will. So yeah, I'm on board."

Alex smiled. "Thanks, man, I appreciate it. We should grab some lunch today."

"Sure thing." Jacob returned a pleasant smile and waited for Alex to leave. His smile faded. "It's just a game of poker. No big deal," he whispered.

Still, the whole thing had put Alex off a little and that left Jacob feeling somewhat uncertain. But really, there was nothing to worry about. Playing an illegal poker game when your girlfriend was a cop, no big deal. He must've been getting pretty good at hiding at least certain things from her. She could see a lot, but she couldn't see how he really felt about Ethan, or how he was a little nervous about this game. There was a spot in the back of his mind where he kept those things from her. Perhaps he'd learned a thing or two from being around Riley Thompson. He was sure Carl kept things from her too and he watched their conversations at times. He noticed Carl's shifty gaze or his empty eyes, like he was trying to clear out everything in his head so she couldn't see it. She didn't see when he was going to die and Jacob was pretty sure Carl knew about when it would happen. He'd grown weak, wasn't eating as much as he should. He knew, but she didn't. And all Jacob had to do was mimic that. So far, so good.

10

Having a good sense of timing was a skill that required cultivation. Knowing when to speak and when to keep quiet. Inserting a punch line at the appropriate moment. And cooking. This was perhaps the greatest test of one's ability to master the art of timing. Too long and it would be ruined, too soon and it would turn cold.

For Ethan Pruitt, timing was a skill he did not possess. The end result was often foot-in-mouth syndrome, not to be confused with foot and mouth, a terrible disease. Or smoke rising from an oven signaling he'd waited too long to take out the garlic bread.

He pulled open the oven door to a wall of white smoke and heat and waved it away with a gloved pot-holder. When the smoke cleared, he pulled out the cookie sheet and peered at the charred bread. "Damn."

The scream of the smoke alarm pierced his ears and he ripped off the gloves and rushed to open the back door, then the front. "Oh. Uh, hi."

On the other side of the door stood Gracie, for whom he was cooking this extravagant meal of spaghetti and garlic bread, the latter of which was now wrecked. "Hey." She cringed at the wailing alarm. "You need some help or something?"

"No. Come in." His voice raised above the noise. "I'm just going to leave this open for a minute until the smoke clears." He returned to the kitchen. "Sorry about this. I forgot about the bread, and well." He presented the blackened slices.

"Don't worry about it. It's sweet you're cooking for me."

Finally, the commotion of the alarms silenced. "That's better." Ethan smiled. "Can I get you a glass of wine?"

"I'd love one, thank you." Gracie placed her palm atop the kitchen counter and leaned over. "Looks delicious. Spaghetti, I see."

Ethan popped open the cork and poured the mild pinot noir into a glass meant for white wine. A wine aficionado, he wasn't. Luckily, he was an attractive man with an admirable job who also happened to possess a kind heart. "The good news is that you identified the meal. That bodes well for my confidence as a chef, who apparently can't make garlic bread."

She laughed. "It's fine. I'm just glad to be here." Gracie raised her glass. "Cheers."

"Cheers," Ethan responded in kind and took a sip. "So, shall we eat?"

"Yes, please. I'm starving."

He dished out the plates and put them on the kitchen table that was set with candles and cloth napkins. And as quickly as he could, he rushed to her chair before she could sit and pulled it out for her.

"Oh, thank you." Gracie sat down. "You're a lot different from the college boys I've dated. Their idea of romance usually involved fast food and Netflix on their laptop in their dorm room."

Ethan recalled in that moment just how young she was by comparison. While it was really only a few years, it seemed much more. He was well beyond that life and in fact had never experienced it in the first place. Ethan went straight into the academy after high school. "Well, this is what a man is supposed to do for a lady."

They each piled a heap of noodles on their forks and tucked into the meal. An awkward silence ensued and Ethan began to feel the pressure to engage in witty conversation. None of this was coming as naturally as he had hoped. Sure, they'd spent time together since her stay with Ellen, but it was usually on the sofa watching, well, Netflix. It wasn't like with Riley. Their conversations flowed with the ease of water over river rock. However, he had to remind himself that they had shared a greater history and he really didn't know Gracie all that well. She rarely came home to visit, except for Christmas, because she worked. But he had expected her to be more like her sister. It was becoming quite clear Gracie was not Riley. And Riley was not his.

Gracie swallowed down her food. "This is really delicious, Ethan."

"Thanks. I'm glad you like it. I don't cook often and even less for others. I hope to improve." He sipped on his wine. "Listen, um, I know you're leaving for Indianapolis soon and I was wondering, you know, if you wanted to maybe still see each other. When it's convenient, of course."

"I'd like that very much. In fact, I was hoping you'd ask. I know we haven't really talked about the future and we haven't been going out for that long and all that, but I'd like to try. I like you a lot, Ethan. And I feel like I've known you for a long time because you work with Riley and she's told me how you've had her back. Nothing's been easy for her, you know. And with losing Carl, that hit her hard, and if she didn't have you to lean on..."

"She has Jacob for that."

"Right. Of course. He's a big part of her life, but so are you. She needs you probably more than you know."

"Well, that's where I'll have to disagree with you, but thanks." He began to understand where this was headed and wasn't sure he was ready for it. There was a line, and if he crossed it with Gracie, there would be no turning back.

"You know, I mentioned to my mom that I'd probably be home pretty late. I didn't want her to worry."

He directed his gaze to her. "Oh. Good."

"Just wanted to let you know I'm not in any rush to get home." Gracie averted her eyes and shuffled around the food on her plate.

Ethan picked up on her meaning and the time had come to decide. Riley was with Jacob now. She had made it clear for a number of years that she wasn't interested in him that way. Perhaps the time had come for him to move on, though he tried to avoid the fact that it would be with Riley's sister. There might have been a hidden meaning that he hadn't wished to explore. "Great. That's great." He tucked into his food once again.

THE CALL SERVICE LOGS FROM THE PREVIOUS NIGHT WERE few and far between. And none so bad as the other night when Wyatt Sims killed his wife. Riley was glad to be spared another event such as that when she arrived at the station this morning.

Decker and Abrams were packing up and readying themselves for a day's sleep at her arrival.

She appeared from the corridor into the bullpen. "Morning. I stopped in to view the logs from last night. Must've been pretty quiet for you two."

"We were still out there, hitting the pavement and doing our jobs." Abrams immediately replied, as if she was testing his mettle.

"Okay. I wasn't questioning your skills as an officer, Lowell." She continued toward her desk. "I'm surprised Ethan's not here. He always arrives before me."

"Heard he had a hot date last night," Decker replied. "Someone by the name of Gracie Thompson." He winked at Riley.

"I know they're dating, Chris. It's no secret." She sat down. "Hey, have you made progress on poking around into Sims' history?"

"Not much. I was hoping you could jump on it today. I managed to pull his employment history, then we had to hit the streets," Decker replied.

"Anything special there?"

"No. He'd been with the high school for four years. Before that, same type of job in Fort Wayne. It's like the man just went off the edge, you know?"

"Yeah. Maybe. I'll see what I can find today. You two go get some rest and I'll see you on my way out tonight."

"See ya, Riley. Wouldn't want to be ya," Abrams replied.

She furrowed her brow and peered at Decker.

He raised his palms and shrugged. "Night, Riley." He approached Ward's office. "Hey, Cap, Abrams and I are clocking out. Riley's here."

"Thanks, Decker. See you tonight." Ward stood from his desk and walked into the bullpen. "Where's Pruitt?"

"I don't know. He must be running late today." Riley knew he was scheduled to have a dinner date with Gracie and wasn't particularly interested in learning the details. "Decker mentioned he ran an employment background on Sims but didn't come up with much. Dillon said he'd ask around for me."

"I love your brother like a son, you know that, Riley, but he can't run interference. He's not a cop. You want to ask questions, fine. I said do what you need to do. But that means you do it. Not Dillon."

"Okay. I'll tell him to forget it."

"Uh-huh. Knowing him, he's probably already got the goods." Ward's attention was diverted to the hall. "Well, good morning, sunshine. Glad to see you decided to join us."

"Sorry, Cap. I overslept." Ethan shot a glance to Riley. "I saw the guys leave. Anything we need to follow up on?"

"No, sir. Pretty quiet night from what I gather. Same for you?"

"What's that now?" Ethan pressed his hands against the back of his chair, digging in his nails.

"Nothing, son. Go on and get yourself settled in." He started back toward his office. "You never know what'll come up in a small town. Best to be prepared." He closed the door to his office.

Riley watched Ethan boot up his computer and organize his desk. It was as though he was doing everything in his power to avoid eye contact or to talk to her. This was a troubling sign. "I take it you didn't make the call to Jacob about meeting up?"

Ethan turned his sights to her, appearing somewhat relieved. "Oh, no. I'm sorry, Riley. I was actually planning on doing that this morning. Maybe seeing if he wanted to grab a beer at the end of shift today. If that's okay with you?"

"Of course, yeah. That'd be great. Thanks." She couldn't bring herself to ask about Gracie because she was still her sister and the idea that Gracie had slept with Ethan, regardless of the fact that Riley didn't have feelings for him, it just felt weirdly inappropriate. And maybe there was a small part of her that mourned the idea that there could never ever be anything between them now as a result.

"In fact, I'll call him right now." Ethan retrieved his cell phone and pressed on Jacob's contact information. He peered at her with the phone to his ear. "Jacob. Hey, man, it's Ethan. I didn't catch you at a bad time, did I?"

"No. Not at all. Is Riley okay?" Jacob asked.

"Of course. Yeah, in fact, she's at her desk right now. Listen, I was wondering, you know, maybe you and I could grab a beer after work this evening?"

A silence lingered between them that someone was going to have to break. Turned out, it was going to be Ethan.

"Unless you're busy, of course. It's just, well, I thought we could iron out a few things, you know? Make sure we're all on the same page." *On the same page?* he mouthed to himself.

"I guess that'd be okay. I'd need to check with Riley and make sure we don't have any plans tonight..."

"I already did. She's happy to turn you over to me for an hour or so." Ethan shook his head at his own awkwardness.

"Okay, then. Yeah. I guess that'd be fine. You want to meet at the diner?"

"I was thinking maybe the Crooked Horse?" Ethan replied.

"Sure, great. Okay, so I'll see you what, around 5:30-6:00 tonight?"

"I can be there by 6," Ethan replied. "See you then, buddy."

Jacob listened as the line went dead. "Buddy?" He peered at his phone. "What the hell was that about?" As he sat at his desk and considered the meaning behind this unusual request, he peered into the hall and spotted Alex. "Oh shit."

"Hey, man." Alex walked inside. "You still up for tonight? Like I said, a couple of hands should do it. No big deal. No reason to stress."

"That's tonight, isn't it?" Jacob asked.

"Yeah. It's tonight." Alex's turned worried. "You're not bailing on me, are you?"

"No. I'm not going to bail. I just made plans for earlier in the evening and I almost forgot. Actually, it should work out okay."

"The game doesn't start until 11pm."

"That's fine. I'll figure out something. No worries. I'll see you tonight," Jacob replied.

"You're a lifesaver, man. I mean that." Alex slapped the door jamb and walked back into the hall.

Jacob smiled at Alex as he left, before it quickly faded. "Now what the hell am I going to tell Riley?"

DILLON ENTERED THE STATIONHOUSE AND WALKED TOWARD Riley, who was at her desk. "Hey."

"Dillon. What are you doing here? Shouldn't you be at school?"

"There's an assembly and it's the last week of school, so I

thought I'd use the time to come see you." He peered at Ethan. "Hey, Ethan."

"Dillon."

He pulled up a chair and sat across from Riley. "So I didn't want to call and talk about this over the phone because there's always someone eavesdropping."

"What is it?" Riley asked.

"I asked around about Wyatt Sims. Everyone's in major shock over what happened. Most everybody knew his wife too. It's a real shame." He turned away for a moment. "Anyway, so I guess Wyatt's been in some financial straits for a while. Not sure how long exactly, but I was talking to one of the other coaches and he said that there'd been a problem with gambling. Dogs, horses, whatever. Wyatt got into some serious debt. And he's a high school coach. It's not like he was raking in the dough."

"No. I'm sure he wasn't," Riley replied. "What about alcohol? Any talk of a problem there?"

"No. Not really. Didn't you guys do a breathalyzer on him?"

"Decker did. Came back below legal, but that doesn't mean he didn't have a problem. But, good to hear no one at school seemed to think so."

"Right, so anyway, he did okay with the betting for a while, I guess. Actually bringing in some money, from what I gather. But it didn't last long. Never does."

"House always wins," Riley said. "Go on."

"I don't know much more than that. I didn't want to keep prying because they'd want to know why."

"Sure. Hey, this is great for us. This is helpful." Riley shot a glance to Ethan. "We can probably do something with this, right?"

"Of course," Ethan replied. "We can go to the track, talk to some of the folks around there, and see if anyone knew him on a personal level."

"Exactly." Riley returned her attention to Dillon. "You should get back to the school. Probably don't want anyone knowing you left campus."

Dillon pushed up from the chair. "Probably not. But I'm glad I could be of some help anyway. And you know I'll keep my ears open if I hear anything else." He started back toward the door. "Catch up with you later, Ethan. Riley."

After he left, Riley turned back to Ethan. "What do you think? Gambling? You think this whole poker thing at the Crooked Horse could be something he was into?"

"I don't know. Maybe. Still, Riley, just because the guy had a gambling problem, doesn't mean he committed premeditated murder for some insurance policy or something. I don't know where you want to go with this. It's like you're looking for a connection to the bar owner. Why?"

"I wish I could say exactly, but I just don't know for sure. It's just a hunch. Ever since we caught wind there was a backroom game going on, I just feel like maybe it's something we need to be in on. And with Sims' killing his wife over lost money? If we don't find records at the race tracks that he lost a ton of money, I'm not sure we'll have another choice but to look into the poker game more closely."

"If you say so. I'll follow your lead," Ethan replied. "Just like always."

JACOB SAT AT THE BAR OF THE CROOKED HORSE WAITING FOR

Ethan to show. He checked the time. Ten minutes late. But then a tap on his shoulder forced him to peer over and he spotted Ethan. "I thought you might've reconsidered." He patted the barstool next to him. "Have a seat."

"I wanted to get changed. I hate going out in uniform when I'm off-duty. Puts people off." Ethan shoved his hands in his pockets and gazed around the upscale bar. "I was actually hoping we could grab a table, if that's okay with you? Maybe get a bite to eat?"

Jacob picked up his glass of beer. "Sounds good to me. Lead the way."

Ethan approached one of the waiters. "Is it okay if we grab a table?"

"Sure thing. Anywhere is fine. We're not busy tonight," the waiter replied. "I'll send someone over to take your order."

"Thanks." Ethan slid into the high-back crimson-tufted leather booth. "I've never actually been in here other than for work. It's a nice place."

Jacob slid in across from him. 'Probably the nicest place in town. So how's Riley?"

"You'd know better than me," Ethan replied.

"I haven't seen her since this morning. I assume she went home after her shift?"

"That's what she said she was doing. I don't keep tabs on her," Ethan replied.

"Neither do I." Jacob held his gaze for a moment. "How's Gracie doing? You sleep with her yet?"

11

The awkward interactions between the two men who so clearly loved Riley dwindled as the beers arrived and the wings disappeared from the plates. The question of Gracie and her relationship with Ethan evaporated just the same.

"Listen, man, I'm sorry about prying earlier," Jacob said. "It's none of my business nor is it Riley's, no matter what she might believe."

"I get it and it's fine. But the reason I'm here is to try to get back to a place where you and I can be friends."

"Friends?" Jacob smiled.

"Okay, how about better than acquaintances, not quite friends? It's taken a toll on Riley and I'm sure I'm not the only one to see that," Ethan replied.

"No. I know it has. So how about this, you and I table all discussions of Riley and look for common ground?"

"I can agree to that. You've sacrificed for her and for this town, and I'm grateful. So we'll leave it at that." Ethan tossed back a swig of his beer. "I am curious about one thing."

"What's that?"

"Why do you think she's having visions about you?"

"She told you?" Jacob added.

"She did. Any idea where they might be coming from, because I'll tell you, she's pretty freaked out and can't see beyond them. It scares her. Not since Carl died have I seen her so beside herself about something. Why do you think it's happening?"

"How should I know? It scares me just as much. I know there are times when she gets warnings, and other times, it's just a sign of something more. In all honesty, I couldn't tell you which one this is, if any. Is that the real reason you're here? You see she's upset and you want to find out why?"

"I am here for her, yes," Ethan began. "Regardless of our history, I'd never want to see anything happen to you. So if there's something you want to say, maybe now's the time before it's too late."

"Before it's too late? I got nothing, man, I'm telling you." Jacob wiped away the wing sauce from his mouth. "I'll be riding this one out, same as you, until she sees more. I'm minding my p's and q's. That's all I can do."

Ethan nodded. "Copy that." He checked the time. "I should be heading out. You ready to take off?"

Jacob surveyed the bar with some uncertainty. "Um, actually, I think I'll stick around for a while longer. I'm meeting up with a work friend in a little bit. He's got some family issues and just wanted someone to vent to and I mentioned I would be here with you."

"Okay." Ethan stood up and retrieved his wallet.

Jacob raised a pre-emptive hand. "I got it, man. Really."

"Thanks. I'll catch up with you later. Have a good night." Ethan walked through the bar, where the patrons had swelled as the hours passed. He pushed through the door and returned to his own car. A conscious effort had been made when leaving his shift tonight. The idea was to return home to change into plain-clothes and drive his own vehicle, an older-model Chevy Tahoe, dark blue. And as he stepped inside, he peered through the windshield at the Crooked Horse. Ethan wasn't going home. While not part of his initial plan, the fact that Jacob was staying set his nerves on end. Riley had said nothing of this, which meant perhaps she wasn't aware. He was going to find out why Jacob was staying put and for how long.

It was 9:45pm when Alex Laughlin pulled into the parking lot of the Crooked Horse bar. He cut the engine of his Toyota 4Runner and surveyed the lot in search of Jacob's car. While he'd texted his imminent arrival only minutes ago, certainty that his friend and now co-conspirator was there would put his mind at ease.

The smile that formed on his lips indicated his friend and colleague had not let him down. Considering that he might be forced to abandon the planned con weighed heavily on his mind, but relief swelled inside him and he felt renewed confidence.

Alex stepped outside his SUV and locked the doors. With an intake of breath, he started into the bar. As he opened the doors and walked inside, he searched for Jacob. A raised hand from a nearby booth came into view and he approached. "Hey. Thanks for coming."

Jacob remained seated at the booth where he and Ethan shared wings and drank beer only a short while ago. Now there were two more empty beer glasses in front of him. "Was there a choice?" He paused a moment. "Sit down."

Alex slid into the booth. "A couple of hours, at the most. Then we both go home and that will be that."

"How do you know Levin won't ask you to participate again?"

"I fully expect he will. However, it doesn't need to include you. He wants fresh meat and so I'll ask another, and then another. And hopefully, by then, he'll tire of me and find some other flunky."

Jacob studied him. "You're not afraid the cops will bust this thing and you'll be arrested?"

"Why? Did you tell your girlfriend?" Alex fidgeted in his seat.

"No, man. I said I'd keep it quiet and I did—I am. But that doesn't mean they won't catch wind of what's going on. What then?"

"I'll get fined or something. Jesus, it's not like I'll be put away for life for playing cards and gambling a few bucks."

"It's more than a few bucks or else I wouldn't be here." Jacob's shoulders appeared to drop and his face smoothed from the concerned wrinkles that had formed. "When do we go back?"

"I'll go find Silas." Alex pulled out from the booth. "Hey, order me a Bud?"

"Sure."

Alex approached the bar where the owner and organizer of the illicit game stood behind it with his bartender.

"Laughlin. Glad you could make it." Silas surveyed the bar. "Not alone, I hope."

"I have a friend with me. Good poker player."

"But not too good, I trust?" Silas replied.

Alex returned a polite nod. "Are we about ready to get started?"

"A few more minutes. Why don't you and your friend sit tight with a beer on the house? I'll call you back soon."

"Thanks." He slapped the bar top and turned back toward the booth. When he arrived, Jacob had two more beers in front of him.

"Got you a beer," Jacob said.

"Appreciate it. Silas is picking up the tab on these two here. He says to give him a few minutes and we'll head back." Alex tossed back half the glass of beer. "I'm hoping to take off the edge a little."

"I'm way ahead of you," Jacob replied. "I had a few beers with my girlfriend's partner earlier. That was a treat."

"You two don't get along?"

"It's tenuous, I'll say that much. He's had a big-time crush on her for who knows how long. And since I've been back in her life..."

"He's not happy about it," Alex said.

"Bingo."

"Why did you hang out with him then?"

"Because she asked him to. She's rooting around for something she won't find, not if I can help it. A guy's gotta have some secrets, right?"

"Depends on the secret. You have a little on the side or something?"

"No. Nothing like that. It's a long and complicated story that I won't bore you with. Anyway, I just want to get this going so I can go home."

"Same here. I have to see this through and hope that it ends better for me than I expect it to."

"Listen, Alex." Jacob rested his elbows on the table and leaned over. The pendant light cast a dubious shadow atop his head. "This shit gets too real, I'll help you out, okay? You need to know that. I don't know what Silas has power over, but we have more. This is our town. Not his."

"I hope you're right."

Jacob spotted Silas approach.

"Gentlemen, it's time. Feel free to bring your drinks." Silas turned on his heel, and with a slow and purposeful gait, made his way to the backroom.

The man wore a salmon-colored button-down and white pants and reminded Alex of a Miami drug dealer. The hair on Silas' head, thick, and the perfect mix of grey and black, was slicked back. It reflected the downlighting and gave him a sort of halo-effect, but there was no mistaking that Silas Levin wasn't an angel. He followed Silas and continued to peer over his shoulder to make sure Jacob hadn't deserted him.

Silas opened the door to the now-familiar space where six other men, only two of which Alex recalled from the previous game, sat at the table. "Our final guests have arrived. This is Alex and this is...I'm sorry, I didn't catch your name earlier."

"Jacob."

"Jacob. Please, have a seat gentlemen, and we'll get started."

JACOB PULLED OUT THE FOLDING CHAIR AND SAT DOWN NEXT to Alex and another man to which he had yet to be introduced. It was immediately apparent that these men had money. Jacob noticed a Rolex, a Tag Hauer, and Omega watches. This was no good ol' boy game of poker either. These men were well-dressed in high-end labels, and their haircuts likely had a price tag higher than Jacob spent on his hair in a year. His first thought was mafia because he'd seen this type before. But it wouldn't be the same ones. No way would the Indianapolis thugs come back here, those who hadn't already been arrested. No this looked like something else, something of which Jacob couldn't quite be sure, but they had to be involved in organized crime. And it probably had a lot to do with Silas Levin.

Riley was right to be concerned about this guy. As Jacob eyeballed the players, his sights turned to Levin, who stood only feet away, leaning against a post with his arms folded, like he was posing for a magazine cover. *GQ*, no doubt. He sized up these men in a manner of seconds and the results weren't looking good for him or his pal, Alex. The idea this was a one-off for him seemed implausible as it now stood. Still, time would tell and now he had to play poker and lose, which wouldn't be difficult for him since he wasn't much of a card player in any case. Alex promised Silas would front the buy-in, and when the chips were placed in front of him, at least that much was true. But this money wasn't his, not by a long shot. These chips would end up back in Silas' hands, so he'd better do his best to lose.

"Two grand buy-in." The dealer waited for everyone to ante up and then dealt the hands.

Jacob knew just enough about the game and in fact had watched poker videos on YouTube for the past couple of days in order to get a handle on the rules. But the idea was to lose without being too obvious. He peered at Alex, who seemed much calmer than he'd expected. Calmer than he was sitting in the booth. Maybe he knew what was at stake should he fail and get called out by the other players as some sort of plant.

After the cards were dealt, Jacob peered at his hand. A good start; he held pocket tens. He was in second-to-last position with Alex ahead of him. The question was, how was Alex going to play this? They hadn't discussed the logistics of making this scheme plausible. Would he fold immediately or would he try to at least put up a fight?

"Fold." Alex laid down his cards.

An indiscernible groan escaped him. Jacob couldn't understand why Alex had given in so quickly, unless he simply hadn't had a good hand, which was possible. Only turning over the cards would reveal that. But for now, all he could do was play the hand he'd been dealt.

Jacob kept his eyes on the cards and occasionally glanced at the other players, not wanting to give away anything. He hadn't practiced his poker face and was never good at hiding his emotions as they paraded across his features.

When eyes were on him, Jacob knew what he had to do in order to make a good show of it. He raised 3 times the big blind, indicating he had a good hand, and shoved his chips into the pot.

"Fold," said the man in last position.

Of the six players in this round, only two were left standing, Jacob and another man he didn't know. Silas hadn't made any introductions.

The dealer dealt the flop. Jacob prepared for another round of betting between himself and the other guy. He would need to be a little more aggressive this time. Make a real show of it to prove he knew what the hell he was doing, even if he didn't. In a bold move, Jacob bet half the pot.

"Son of a bitch." The other man tossed his cards onto the table. "I'm out. Fold."

"The young buck takes the pot." Silas smiled and walked around to Jacob, appearing ready to congratulate him. Instead, he placed his hand on Jacob's shoulder and squeezed.

The pressure was enough to make Jacob uncomfortable but wasn't enough to cause pain. It was a warning shot and Jacob heard it loud and clear.

ETHAN PRESSED THE BUTTON ON HIS PHONE TO CHECK THE time. "Midnight. Shit." He was hunched down in the driver's seat of his Tahoe still parked in the lot of the Crooked Horse. "How long are you staying, bro?"

Noting the time of Jacob's departure and who, if anyone, would accompany him was Ethan's sole purpose. He suspected this co-worker friend of his might be the root cause of Riley's troubling visions of Jacob. There was no way to be certain, but he was the only variable Ethan could think of. The only thing in Jacob's life that had changed most recently. While Jacob hadn't revealed anything that would give rise to an answer, Ethan was going another way, looking into whoever Jacob was hanging around.

Still, the bar would close by 1am, and if he didn't see Jacob roll out of the place by then, he'd start to worry. His purpose was to protect Riley whether she wanted him to or not. And if that meant keeping tabs on her live-in boyfriend, then that was what he would do.

He unleashed a wide yawn before cutting it short and instinctively lowering himself deeper into the seat. The door to the bar opened and two men walked outside. "Jacob." He didn't know the other one but assumed it was the co-worker. Both appeared, at this distance, to be sober. Good thing. And neither looked as though they'd been harmed in any way. Another good thing. So what had they been doing?

Maybe Jacob was being straight with him and he was just talking with this friend. He almost went with that until two more men appeared. They stood out and not in a good way. More like in a way that made it seem they were there for purposes that were perhaps less than legal. These guys, if Ethan didn't know any better, looked like the mob. But how could that have been? They'd already chased the mob out of town last year. So who were they?

They caught up to Jacob and his friend and all four stopped in the parking lot several feet away from his Tahoe. For a moment, he realized Jacob would see his car, but it didn't appear that Jacob was paying attention. In fact, his attention was wholly on those two men.

Ethan pressed the camera button on his phone and started taking pictures of the four of them, focusing in on the two he was certain didn't belong in Owensville. When they started off again, the two gentlemen walking away with smiles on their faces, he began to feel more at ease. It seemed the meeting wasn't a confrontational one. Good thing because he wasn't prepared to jump out and brandish his weapon to stop a fight. His cover would be blown, and Jacob would never trust him again, if he trusted him now. Which he might not after he showed these pictures to Riley.

Sometimes, all it took was seeing a picture and she would see all she needed to know. It didn't always work that way, as he'd noticed in the past, but if it did, then problem solved. And his covert activities could cease.

The man Jacob walked out with, likely his co-worker, entered his car and pulled away. Jacob had reached his, which was parked two rows away, and was stopped by one of the other men. His buddy had also left in his car.

"Oh, hell," Ethan said. There was no way to know what was being said, but he did see the look on Jacob's face. It appeared to be a fusion of unease and cordiality. And now his hackles raised.

Ethan waited for one wrong move, however, it seemed that would not come to pass. The man standing next to Jacob slapped him on the arm and wore a broad smile. Jacob wasn't smiling. The moment the man walked away, his smile faded, and he slipped into his sedan.

Ethan appeared even more perplexed. "Okay. What the hell was that?"

There was only one thing Ethan could do to assuage Riley's concerns and help Jacob out of what appeared to be a potential situation. He would need to find out who those two men were.

12
———————

When the headlights of a car shone through Riley's front window, she knew it was Jacob. A sense of relief swept through her that he had returned. She listened as the car's engine died and the lights flickered off. Riley waited for him to enter with the sound of a key manipulating the lock. The door opened and she peered at Jacob as he walked in. "You look tired."

He turned to her with some surprise. "What are you still doing up?" He raised his hand. "Never mind." Jacob set down his keys in the bowl on the foyer table and walked into the living room.

CJ ran to him and jumped on his legs.

"Hey, buddy." Jacob scratched behind his ears. "I bet you're tired too."

"Did everything go okay? With your friend, I mean?" Riley asked.

"Sure. He just needed a shoulder. Look, I'm beat. Can we just go to bed?"

She peered at him in search of meaning behind his words—a vision or a feeling—but nothing came. "That's a good idea." Riley uncurled from the sofa and padded toward him, rising to her tiptoes for a kiss. "I'm glad you were able to help out your friend. And I'm glad you're home." She started into the hall and that was when Riley sensed something in Jacob she had not sensed before. At least, not in a very long time. It was guilt. When he decided to leave Owensville for college, she'd sensed it then, but this felt more intense somehow. Riley stopped near the entrance to their bedroom to face him.

"What?" he asked in a whisper.

She held his gaze and he must've known what she was doing because he looked away for a moment. "Nothing. Let's just get some rest. It's late."

THE NAME SILAS LEVIN STILL HAD NO MEANING TO IT, OTHER than the fact that he was the owner of the Crooked Horse. As Riley peered at her monitor in search of some insight into this man, nothing materialized. No criminal record. No bankruptcies or foreclosures. Nothing to suggest he was a man who had lived a secret life in the criminal underground. Her probe into him was on the sly because the only one the captain had given her permission to look into was Wyatt Sims and he had committed murder, so there was something worth digging into. This was for her own purposes and had skirted around insubordination.

It was the look on Jacob's face last night when he returned home. The guilt she felt inside him, like he was hiding something from her, and yet, she couldn't see what it was, if there was anything there to see in the first place. Fairness never entered into the equation when it came to her gift and how she used it, and unfortunately for Jacob, he was the recipient on that occasion.

Riley often wondered how she would feel if he could see her thoughts and feelings. No doubt, it would be an unacceptable intrusion. So could she blame him if he tried to hide things from her? One's thoughts shouldn't be subjected to search and seizure and yet she was doing that very thing. However, she did recognize this and it was the reason she didn't pursue a line of inquiry last night. Now all she could do was discover for herself why he would have felt that way with her and if it meant he was involved in something he shouldn't be.

Her attention was sidetracked when Ethan approached her desk. He held two cups of coffee and placed one on the corner of her desk. "Sugar and cream, just the way you like it."

"Thanks." She reached for the paper cup.

He lowered himself into the seat across from her. "I suppose you want to know how last night went."

"It had crossed my mind," she replied.

Ethan appeared to want to prolong the suspense as he sipped ever so slowly on his coffee. "Well, I can't say I learned much from my conversation with him. We drank beer and ate wings and talked about a lot of things. You were the topic of conversation for the early portion, but then we moved on."

"So?" She leaned back and folded her arms in anticipation. "Do I have anything to worry about?"

"Frankly, Riley, I don't know. You know me and you know I'm pretty good at reading people. Not as good as you, of course, but since I don't share your God-given talents, I believe myself to be good at it. That said, I didn't get anything from him."

"Damn. I suppose I should be happy about that, but somehow, I'm not."

"I didn't get anything from him while we were together, however..."

At this, Riley's interest piqued. "However?"

"I decided I was going to hang out for a while because Jacob mentioned he was meeting a friend later on. I assume he told you this?"

"He did."

"Okay. Good. So I waited. And waited. And waited. By about midnight, he emerged with who I assume was his friend. I didn't recognize him. Only less than a minute later, two men also walked out and approached them. These guys, Riley. These guys were not from here. I'll stake my life on it."

"What happened after that?" she pressed on.

"Jacob's friend took off. I can't even say for sure if the men said much to him. They might've but of course it's not like I had wires on anyone. But when Jacob reached his car, one of the men caught up to him. It was like they were in the clear, and all of a sudden, one of the guys moves in on Jacob. I thought they were going to throw blows, and I was ready for that, but whatever the man said, Jacob didn't seem upset by it or pleased or anything really. The man smiled, patted him on the back and left. Then Jacob left. That's when I figured it was safe for me to take off."

Ethan retrieved his cell phone. "Oh, I did manage to get a couple of shots of the men." He opened the images and handed his phone to Riley. "Any idea who the hell they are?"

Riley peered at the images, zooming in for a better look.

"It was dark, and I wasn't about to use my flash, so they're pretty grainy."

She shook her head. "I have no idea who they are. I'm not seeing anything either. Good, bad, or indifferent." Riley returned the phone to him. "But we need to find out who they are."

"I couldn't agree more. What about talking to the bar owner?"

"Silas Levin? He's squeaky clean," she replied.

"Doesn't mean he doesn't know who frequents his bar," Ethan replied.

"He already thinks we're harassing him, and right now, I can see no good reason for us to make another visit. I think that ship has sailed. What about talking to Jacob's friend?"

"That would have to be up to you to broach that topic with Jacob. But like I said, his friend took off. The man talked to Jacob alone, from where I stood."

Riley peered at the captain's office. "You think Ward would let us try out the facial recognition software they're using in Indianapolis? We could ask Lieutenant Moody for some help."

A wide smile played on Ethan's lips. "I knew you'd come up with something. I think that's our best bet, at least, to start. If we still don't get answers after that, well, maybe we talk to Jacob. But I know you don't want to go there right now, so I'll stand behind you on that count."

"I'll still talk to him and find out who his friend is. That might give us something without looking like I'm sticking my nose where it doesn't belong. He hates it when I do that."

"Can you blame him?"

"No. No, I cannot."

Jacob entered the HVM office and hoisted his carrier

bag atop his shoulder. The air-conditioned building brought relief from an overly warm and muggy June morning and he continued toward his cubicle. "Morning." He nodded to a passing colleague.

It was Friday, and by the look of things, several of the staff were enjoying the day off. He wondered if he had missed the memo. After the late night, he would've been more than happy to grab an extra few hours of sleep this morning. But no such luck.

"Morning, Jacob. Hey, I was looking for Alex. Don't suppose you've seen him yet?"

Jacob's department manager, Ty Henry, rested his elbow on the short wall of the cubicle. His white button-down Oxford pulled tight across his plump midsection. "I heard you two were hanging out last night."

"Who mentioned that?" Jacob set down his bag and regarded Ty once again.

"A couple of the guys. I asked if anyone had seen Alex and they said to come talk to you."

"Oh. Right. Yeah, we had a couple beers last night. I figured he would be here already. Did you try his cell?"

"Went to voicemail. Okay, I'm sure he'll be in soon enough. But if you see him, do me a favor and send him my way. I wanted to talk to him about the revised structural drawings he resubmitted last week."

"You got it, Boss." Jacob sat down at his desk and turned on his computer. He peered at his phone and opened Alex's contact information. *"Hey man. You coming in today, or what? Boss is looking for you."* He sent the text message and returned to his email as his inbox loaded the far-too-many messages from just the night before. "Geez, do people ever sleep?"

Jacob was already in need of a fresh brew while he waited for the heap of messages to pile onto him. He pushed up from his chair and started into the corridor and toward the breakroom.

"Hey, man." Craig brushed past him in the hall and stopped on a dime. "You see Alex yet this morning?"

Jacob came to a stop and turned back. "Not yet. I texted him but haven't gotten a response. We had kind of a late night. He probably overslept."

"That's right. You went with him to that," he cleared his throat and surveyed the area for eavesdroppers, "that poker game."

"Yep."

"How'd it go?" Craig peered at him as if he already knew.

"Fine. Why?"

"No reason. Just..." He swatted away the remainder of the sentence.

"No. What? Just what?" Jacob pressed on.

"It's just a shady deal, that game, you know? I told Alex I wasn't interested in going back. He asked me to join him yesterday too, but I took a hard pass."

"Really?"

"Yeah. It was fun the first time, but things got too real, you know what I'm saying?"

"Yeah. I get it. I'll let you know if I hear back from him." Jacob continued on his path to the kitchen.

He walked inside the small breakroom with a round table in the center, a sink flanked by cabinets and a full-sized refrigerator. The fancy coffee maker rested atop the counter next to the sink. Jacob reached for a mug in the cabinet and inserted the pod, waiting for it to brew. He poured in a touch of flavored creamer and waited until it finished before pouring it into the mug.

As he turned to head back to his desk, another of his co-workers entered. "Morning," he said after taking a sip from the steaming mug.

"Hi, Jacob."

Steven Anderson worked in Human Resources and no one was ever really happy to see him, although as Jacob peered at him, he considered that the guy was okay, just maybe a little intense.

"How's it going? There's still water in the reservoir," Jacob said.

"Good, thanks. Hey, um, I hear Alex was with you last night?"

Jacob furrowed his brow at the sudden interest in his extracurricular activities with a co-worker. "Yeah. We had a few beers last night. Why?"

"I got a call a few minutes ago from his wife. Actually, Ty got the call and he came to me and asked me to ask around. Anyway, she said he didn't come home last night. Do you know anything about that?"

An awkward smile teased along Jacob's lips as though the question in and of itself was farcical. "Uh, no. We parted ways, oh, I don't know, about midnight or something. I saw him get into his car and drive away. I have no idea why he wouldn't have gone straight home."

"Well, I had to ask. I'm sure he'll turn up. Probably slept it off somewhere in his car and hasn't made it home yet."

"He wasn't drunk," Jacob replied. "I'm certain of that."

"Okay, well, look, if you hear from him..."

"I'll let you know." Jacob walked by him and into the hall. His mind raced with concern for his friend, who wasn't really a friend, but was now more than just a colleague.

The men who approached them in the parking lot of the Crooked Horse offered their condolences because they knew

Jacob and Alex had lost their asses in the game. Of course, they didn't know that it was done on purpose. And in fact, Silas Levin was the big winner of the night. Was it possible one of them scared off Alex? He didn't know how that could've happened. Sure, they were scary dudes and their words had an underlying meaning. The meaning was that they wanted to be sure Jacob and Alex weren't plants. He thought they'd done a decent job defending their losses. But now?

Jacob returned to his desk with renewed concern for Alex, who still had not replied to his text. He had to assume his wife would've tried to reach him as well and only called work as a last resort. Things were not looking good.

"Hey, Cap." Riley approached Ward's office where he sat at his desk. "Pruitt and I are heading out for patrol."

"Sounds good. Check in with dispatch," Ward replied.

"Got it." Riley returned to her desk and grabbed her keys. "Mind if I drive?"

"You're the boss," Ethan said.

"No, I'm not," she sneered at him and started out the door. "I just like to drive. You have a problem with that?"

Ethan followed her into the parking lot and toward her cruiser. "No problem. You like to be the one in control, Riley. This is no secret and I've made my peace with it."

"Gee, thanks." She pressed the remote to unlock the door and stepped into the driver's side of the cross-over SUV. The black and white Ford Explorer was an older model, but still had some get-up and go to it. Their department was too small and underfunded and there wasn't a chance in hell she'd ever get to drive one of the new models with all the bells and whistles like the ones they had in the city.

After Ethan buckled himself into the passenger seat, Riley turned over the engine. "Where do you want to start?"

"Oh, I don't know. Main Street, then branch out from there."

She reversed out of the lot. "See? I don't always have to be the one in control."

"Uh-huh."

The radio crackled and the dispatcher's voice sounded over the speaker. "Car 319, be advised, an abandoned vehicle was spotted around the 500 block of East Hillcrest Road."

Ethan picked up the receiver. "Car 319. We'll head over there now and check it out."

"Thanks, Ethan," the dispatcher replied.

Riley turned the steering wheel and headed in the direction of Hillcrest Road. "You know, I think she has a thing for you."

Ethan wrinkled his nose. "Who? Our dispatcher? Lisa?"

"Yeah."

"Riley, the woman's in her fifties."

"What? She can't have a crush on a younger man?"

"Please. Just drive, would you?" He gripped the handle above his door and peered through the windshield. "Someone must've broken down and left the vehicle for help or something."

"Probably. We'll find out here shortly." Riley continued through the streets of the small town and drove past the new housing development. "They're making progress up there. The models in the second phase look almost finished."

"It's good for the town, I know, but I kind of wish it could stay small, you know? Everyone knows everyone. Now we're going to have more new people moving in."

"If we didn't have people moving here, we'd soon be out of a job. The town would dry up and wither away. We need to keep bringing in jobs and houses. Otherwise, the place is going to look like it did when we were kids, after Caterpillar shut down. I don't want to go through that again."

"I suppose not." Ethan pulled upright and focused ahead. "Hang on. Is that the car?"

Riley veered toward the shoulder. "I'd say so. Let's go check it out and run the plates, see if we can track down the owner." She shifted the gear into park and opened her door. "I don't recognize the vehicle off the bat, do you?"

Ethan's face turned deadpan and he opened his door without a reply.

Riley regarded him with concern. "Everything okay?" she started toward the abandoned car.

"Yeah. Fine."

His curt reply brought her greater concern. She homed in on the car as it straddled the shoulder and the road. Her hand pressed against the butt of her gun, but it remained holstered. So far, she wasn't picking up on anything unusual. "I'll take the driver's side. Go around to the other."

"Copy that." Ethan cautiously approached the passenger side and eyed Riley as she neared the driver's side.

"Anyone in there?" Riley announced before she stood too near. "It's the police." She tossed a glance to Ethan as they remained in lockstep on the opposite sides of the car. The time had come to brandish her gun and she did, aiming it at the closed window on the driver's side.

Ethan followed her lead.

Riley now stood squarely in front of the driver's window; weapon trained on the car's interior. "It's empty." Her shoulders dropped and the tension in her face evaporated. She grinned and looked at Ethan. "Let's run the plates."

Ethan appeared relieved but didn't turn back until he retrieved his flashlight and shone it inside just to be sure. "Yeah, okay." He returned to the patrol car and opened the laptop to enter the plate number.

Riley made a final sweep of the abandoned vehicle before returning to find out who owned the car. She sat down in the driver's seat, half in and half-out, and waited for his reply.

"I'm just getting it now. One second." Ethan peered at the screen and creased his brow. He shot a glance to Riley. "Alex Laughlin."

"He's the co-worker, isn't he?" Riley held his gaze, reading him like a book. "You already knew who it belonged to. It's Jacob's work friend he was with last night."

Ethan cast down his gaze. "I'm sorry. I had to be sure. It was dark and I thought, yeah, maybe that's his car. But I can see you already saw through me."

"Well, it was written all over your face. Didn't need any special powers to see it. So what do you think?"

"I don't know. I saw him drive off last night. I didn't think he was drunk, but it's not like I followed him."

"Okay. I guess we'll have to track him down. In the meantime, let's get a tow truck out here." She stopped for a moment and peered back at him. "Before we do that." She reached for her cell phone. "Let me call Jacob. I'll ask him if Alex is at work today."

She made the call and Jacob's line answered.

"Hey, hon, what's up?" Jacob asked.

"Hey, um, I don't suppose your friend Alex Laughlin is at work today, is he?"

The silence on the other end lingered for too long and raised the hackles on Riley's neck.

"Actually, no. How did you..." He trailed off, but then added, "I haven't seen him here today. And...his wife called into the boss because she hasn't seen him since yesterday."

"Oh no." Riley closed her eyes. "We just found his car on the side of Hillcrest Road."

13

It hadn't fully registered. The suggestion that Alex Laughlin had gone missing when Jacob had spent several hours with him only the night before seemed implausible. But Riley's insistence that Alex's car had been found on the side of the road challenged that assumption. Now Jacob was faced with a decision. Was it time to tell the boss or wait until the police found him? Assuming they would find him.

Jacob scrolled through the messages he'd received from Alex last night, searching for any clue that might suggest he was about to leave town. It was an idea that would come as no surprise, all things considered. Silas Levin was a convincing man and he had convinced them both to do as he said, or else. He wondered if "or else" had come to pass.

"Damn. Nothing." Nothing he had seen in those messages stated anything other than what had actually gone down. Even last night, there was no indication Alex was going to flee. He replayed the events in his head. Had it been the men who came out to speak to them in the parking lot? They'd only offered condolences for suffering losses during the game. Regardless of how menacing they appeared, neither discharged threats.

Jacob stood from his desk and sighed. He knew what he had to do and started toward his boss's office to tell him about the car. The first few steps into the corridor took much longer than they should have, but he pushed forward and cracked his neck from side to side as if that alone would grant him the strength to continue.

"Hey, man." Billy approached from around the corner. "What's going on? I hear you and Alex had quite the night last night."

"Wait. Have you talked to Alex today?" Jacob stopped dead, almost stumbling over his own feet.

"I touched base with him late last night and he replied that he was heading home."

Jacob outstretched his palm. "Can I see the message?"

Billy's brow creased as he reached into his pants pocket and retrieved his phone. "Sure. I guess." He unlocked the phone and opened the messages. "It's right here. What's going on?"

"Nothing. I just need to see what he said." Jacob snatched the phone and examined the message.

"Okay, dude. Chill out."

Jacob's face wore uncertainty. "This is it? That's all he said? 'Talk to you tomorrow, bro?'"

"What were you expecting? You read it with your own eyes. He said you guys had a good time and I missed out and see ya. So, yeah, that was all he wrote." Billy grabbed his phone. "What the hell's going on with you?"

Resigned, Jacob replied, "I need to see the boss. That's all. I have to tell him... I need to tell him that the submittal isn't coming back for another few weeks." He couldn't do it. He couldn't say what swirled in his mind, that it seemed Alex had jumped bail, and for reasons he would need to learn.

"I don't envy you, bro. Good luck with that. Hey, you see Alex, tell him maybe I'll take him up on the next game. Who knows? I just didn't get a warm fuzzy from the owner over there. You know."

"Oh yeah, I know." Jacob started into the hall once again.

ETHAN PEERED AGAIN THROUGH THE SIDE-VIEW MIRROR OF the cruiser. "I see it. The tow truck's here." He opened the passenger door and stepped out, turning to face the oncoming truck.

Riley glanced into the rear view and then stepped out to join him. "I'm not sure which direction to go with this. The wife says she hasn't seen him and he's not at work. I'll tell you, Ethan, I'm not getting a good feeling about this."

"But you don't see anything?" he asked.

"No, which might be more troubling."

"Maybe not, Riley. It could be a very good thing. All we can do now is get his SUV towed and hope he turns up. I mean, look, we didn't see anything suspicious inside. That's a good sign. He didn't run out of gas or have the hood up, meaning it wasn't likely he had car trouble, and even if he had, I'm sure his wife would've been the first to know."

"Okay, so then what you're saying is he just walked away." She placed her hands on her hips. "A guy just walks away from his family, his job, and his car, for what reason?"

Ethan shook his head. "I wish I knew. I really do." He started toward the truck that had just pulled up behind them. "We have to wait for something to break free." He waited for the driver to exit. "I'm Officer Pruitt. That's my supervisor, Officer Thompson."

"You all made the call?" The slim man in baggy Dickies and a shirt with his name embroidered on it spit onto the road.

"Yes, sir."

"I figure you'll want me to take it to the impound lot then?"

"If you wouldn't mind," Ethan replied.

"Consider it done, Officer. I will need to get the truck closer, if you'd be so kind as to move your police car."

"Sure thing." Ethan started back to the cruiser. "We have to get out of his way so he can hook it up."

"Oh, right." Riley returned to the driver's seat and pulled the car around Alex's Toyota 4Runner and then off onto the shoulder in front of the abandoned vehicle. When she stepped out of the car, the faint sound of a ringing phone caught her attention. She cocked her head, straining to listen and hoping to identify a location. A few steps forward and she listened again.

A small ravine lay about fifty feet ahead and was covered in tall weeds that had dried out in the summer sun.

"That's where it's coming from." Riley turned back and waved to her partner. "Ethan? Over here."

"I'll let you do your thing. I need to see what my partner wants." He turned away from the tow truck driver and started his approach. "What's up?"

"I heard a cell phone. I'm pretty sure it's a cell phone."

"Where?"

"The ravine up there. We need to check it out." She started toward the overgrown gully between the shoulder of the road and a strip of desolate farmland. It appeared that the ravine was used as part of a watering system for the field that was now abandoned. "I stepped out of the car and I heard the noise."

"We didn't hear Jack Squat when we were checking out the vehicle." Ethan followed only steps behind.

"I know. Someone must've just called him. We might've just gotten very lucky." She continued until reaching the edge of the ditch and retrieved the flashlight from her belt. "Let's hope we can see in this mess of weeds."

Ethan also retrieved his flashlight, regardless that it was midday, and aimed it into the tangled dried brush. "Wait. Don't we have his phone number? Laughlin's number?"

Riley stopped in her tracks. "Yes, we do." She dialed the number from her phone. A low ring tone, some sort of classical music, resonated. "Do you hear that? It's coming from in here."

Ethan stepped to the edge of the gully and pushed around the weeds with his legs. "It stopped. Call it again."

She dialed the number. "Down there. I think it's coming from down there." Riley pointed a few more yards ahead and trudged through the edge of the brush. She trained the light in the center and deepest part of the channel. "I see it! I need gloves. Do you have any gloves?"

"In the car. I'll be right back." Ethan jogged back to the patrol car but stopped as he approached the tow truck operator. "Hang on. Don't take it just yet. We found something."

"You got it, Boss," the driver replied.

Ethan retrieved a forensics kit from the trunk of the car and hustled back to Riley. "Here." He handed her the gloves.

"Thanks." She dropped her phone into her pocket and squatted down into the grass. Pushing away the brush, she formed a clearing in the center and reached in. "It's lying on top of some brush, above the water. Thank God it hasn't rained in days or we'd be looking at a phone that didn't work."

"Just be careful, Riley. There are snakes in there." Ethan hunched over with his hands resting against his knees. "You got it?"

A small grunt, and Riley pulled up again. "Yeah. I got it."

Ethan pointed into the clearing. "Over there. Less than a foot. Is that? Does that look like keys to you?"

Riley peered down again. "Sure does." She reached in again and pulled out the keys. Upon returning upright, she held out the evidence. "This just went from bad to a whole lot worse."

JACOB CLEARED HIS THROAT AND KNOCKED ON HIS BOSS'S door.

"Come in," the voice from the other side of the door answered.

He turned the handle as if he was moving in slow motion and opened the door. "Hey, Ty, I'm not interrupting you, am I?"

"Jacob. No, not at all. Have a seat." He motioned to the seat across from him. "What can I do for you?"

"Um, you asked me to come see you if I heard anything about um..." He felt his phone vibrate in his pocket. "I—I'm sorry." He pulled out the phone to check the caller ID, praying it was Alex. He peered at the screen and shot a look to his boss. "Excuse me, Ty, but I think this call could be critical to what I'm about to say. Do you mind?"

"No. Go ahead and take it, if you have to."

"Hey, tell me you have news?" Jacob lowered his tone as he spoke. "I'm here with my boss right now."

"Sorry," Riley replied. "But I thought I should let you know. We found Alex's cell phone and his car keys."

"But not him?"

"No. Not him. But now we know he's gone without a phone and he didn't take his keys."

Jacob was silent as his mind spun to think of something to say.

"Jacob, a man just doesn't walk away like that, you understand this, right?" Riley asked.

"Of course, yeah. Um, okay. I really have to go. I'll call you back." He ended the call. "Sorry about that. That was my girl-friend. I told you she was a cop, right?"

"I'm aware." Ty leaned back in his chair and regarded Jacob with growing concern. "What is it? Is this about Alex?"

"Yes. She said they found his 4Runner on the side of Hillcrest Road and that they also found his cell phone and keys—in a nearby ditch."

"What?" Ty pulled up in his chair and leaned over his desk. "What are you saying, here, Jacob? That Alex has gone missing?"

"It's looking that way, Ty. I'm sure the next call the police will make will be to Alex's wife." He fiddled with his fingers for a moment. "Since our phones are company-owned, is there a chance, and we'd probably have to get the okay from the police, but do you think we, or you could ask that they check his GPS for where he might've gone last night?"

"You said they found his phone. So he clearly doesn't have it. Jacob, is he...?"

"I don't know. The cops don't know. But I guess you're right. I wasn't thinking that since they now have the phone." He shook his head. "I'm sorry, I'm just a little taken aback by all this."

"You and me both. Look, tracking the GPS might not be worthwhile, but that doesn't mean we can't see who he called or texted and give that information to the cops. Since it's a company phone, Corporate should be able to request the records, I think."

"Okay. Good. Yeah, I think that would help the cops find him." He stood.

"Jacob? You don't look good. Is there something else you want to say?"

"No. I guess I'm just—scared. Scared for Alex and his family. He's got kids, for Pete's sake."

"I know he does. I'll reach out to the police department and see what I can do to help, okay?"

Jacob nodded. "Thank you."

CAPTAIN WARD SPOTTED THE PATROL CAR ENTER THE PARKING lot from his office. He made his way to the bullpen in anticipation of his officers' return. When the door opened and Riley walked inside, he began, "I got a call from someone who might be able to help."

"Who?" Riley eyed him as she walked to her desk.

"Alex Laughlin's boss reached out to me. He knew you'd found Alex's phone and said it belonged to the company."

"That's great." Ethan returned to his desk. "We'll be able to see who he was last in contact with."

"Exactly," Ward replied. "He also said Jacob had taken a call from you, Riley. And that was how he was told about Alex."

"I called Jacob because he'd been out with Alex last night and I knew he was worried."

"It's okay. I'm actually glad because getting into that phone is going to be critical. Where is it, by the way?"

"I have it." Ethan opened the kit and placed the phone that was inside a baggie along with the keys on top of his desk. "We followed protocol down to the T. Didn't want to leave anything to chance."

"Good call." Ward examined the evidence. "Let's get it logged into Evidence and we'll go from there." Ward started back toward his office. "Thompson, while Pruitt's handling that, you mind if we have a word?"

Riley eyed Ethan then returned her attention to the captain. "Sure thing." She followed him into his office. "I know I should've gotten your buyoff before calling Jacob..."

"This isn't about that." Ward dropped into his chair. "This is about what Jacob was doing with Alex last night. Now, I don't know much, which is why I asked you in here, but from what Ty Henry, Alex's boss, said, he and Jacob went out together. Any idea what that was about?"

"According to Jacob, it sounded like Alex wanted to vent about work or family. Nothing unusual about that."

"You mind telling me why Pruitt was there last night too, then?"

"How do you...?"

"Doesn't matter how I know. I know. He was off-duty. What was he doing there and were you in contact with him?"

Riley cast down her sights. "I asked him to spend some time with Jacob."

"Why would you ask him to do that? They aren't the best of friends, even I can see that."

"I've been having—visions. Unpleasant ones about Jacob, and I can't identify a reason, so I asked Ethan to pry a little. But it didn't result in anything new. It was a waste of Ethan's time."

"Okay. So when that little meeting was over, Pruitt went straight home?" Ward pressed on.

"By your tone, you already know the answer to that," Riley replied.

"As a matter of fact, I do. It's my understanding Pruitt decided to stick around there for some time. Meaning he probably saw Jacob's buddy too."

"He did."

"What are we going to do with that information now, Riley? I would say, with the wife's consent, the time's come to call this deal what it is."

"A missing persons'?"

"You got it," Ward replied. "So first and foremost, let's get Pruitt in here and find out what he knows."

"And Laughlin's cell phone?" she added.

"We'll get the company's assistance and see what we can find." Ward inhaled a deep breath. "In the meantime, help Pruitt with that evidence. Then I want you both to come back in here and let's open us up a Missing Persons' file."

JACOB'S WHITE MUSTANG PULLED ONTO THE DRIVEWAY AND caught Riley's attention from the living room. "Scooch now, CJ." She closed the lid of her laptop and hopped off the couch to open the door. Her eyes couldn't hide her emotions this time and as he approached, tears welled. "I'm so sorry, babe."

"It's okay." Jacob returned her embrace. "It's okay, Riley. Come on. Let's get inside."

She pulled away and wiped the tears that had pooled. "How's everyone at the office doing with the news?"

"Not great." He continued toward the kitchen. "I could use a beer. You want one?"

"No. Thanks."

"Sorry, I forgot." He opened the refrigerator and popped off the lid to a bottle of Sam Adams and tossed back half of it. "Anything yet from his phone?"

"No. It's going to be a little while. We've only just opened the investigation." Riley watched as he chugged down the rest of the brew. "I know how upset you must be, but we need to talk about last night. I have to know everything that happened. Jacob, we're going to have to talk to everyone Alex was last seen with."

"I have to give a statement?"

"Yes, you do." She paced the kitchen floor and the cool tile felt good on her bare feet. "This must've been what the visions were about."

"What do you mean? They were of me, not Alex."

"I know, but you know how they can be deceiving sometimes. They don't always make sense, but they're always foreboding. I just can't see if he's..."

"See what? If he's dead?" Jacob replied.

"Yeah. If he's dead."

"Well, if you can't see it, then that must mean he's not, right? He probably just took off somewhere."

She walked toward him. "But why? Why would he do that?

He has a family, children—a good job. It doesn't make sense. Please, Jacob, is there anything else I should know? This is your friend we're talking about. That should mean something to you."

"He was never a friend, just a guy I worked with. Christ, I was doing him a favor."

"What do you mean?"

Jacob appeared to realize his admission. "I mean, by hanging out with him. Letting him vent, you know? He only asked me because no one else wanted to go."

"Then who were those men who talked to you both last night? And then the one who talked to you alone?"

"What?" His brow creased. "What are you talking about? What men?"

Riley's shoulders sank. "Please don't be mad, but Ethan decided to—stick around—after you two wrapped up. He said two men came out and talked to you and Alex. Who were they, Jacob? It could be important."

Jacob stepped back with his face masked in confusion. "Wait. What? You had Ethan stay there? Was he like staking me out or something? What the hell, Riley?"

"I didn't ask him to. It doesn't matter because it was a good thing he did. What with the visions and everything. I was scared you were hiding something, and I couldn't see it."

He nodded with an air of superiority. "Let me get this straight. You couldn't read my mind, so you sent someone, your partner, a guy who doesn't like the fact that we're together, to keep tabs on me?"

"Well no, not exactly."

"Sounds exactly like what happened. You realize no one can

read minds, except you, right? So what do you think everyone else does? Send spies to track their significant others?"

Riley raised her head in defense of her actions. "I don't know what other people do."

"That's right, because you always had things under control. You were the one with all the knowledge in the world about everyone. If you think I'm hiding something from you, why the hell didn't you just ask?"

"I did—sort of."

"Sort of. Okay, look, um, I'm going for a drive." He raised his hands. "I'd appreciate it if you didn't follow me or send someone to follow me, okay?" He grabbed his keys from the table and started toward the door again, but then stopped and turned. "I should be able to keep some things to myself, Riley. Everyone should. But I guess I shouldn't expect that if I'm in a relationship with you." He slammed the door behind him.

14

The few streetlights that illuminated the single-lane roads through town made driving even more challenging this late at night. Jacob didn't need any more traffic issues after mowing down a stop sign last year before he decided to stay in Owensville and pray that Riley would give him a second chance. And now that she had, he'd blown it once again.

It was coming up on 10pm. Jacob was tired and had been circling the streets for almost an hour and still had no idea what to do. Riley always had his best interests at heart and had risked her life for him. She'd gotten him out from under the thumb of the Indianapolis mafia, no easy feat. And this was how he would repay her, accusations and storming out of the house—her house.

Maybe the root cause was really based in fear. Alex Laughlin had disappeared, leaving behind his wife and children. He wasn't the type of man to do that, not that Jacob believed, in any case. And to hear that Riley had Ethan, of all people, tailing him; it just didn't sit right. But now he was beginning to feel a growing dread that Alex was gone for good, maybe even dead. What had transpired after they parted ways last night? Had the men tracked down Alex? And for what reason? They did exactly as Silas Levin had asked. Unless those men weren't on the side of Levin and only victims of Levin's scheme to swindle hefty sums of money. Maybe those same men caught wind of it. If that was the case, then Jacob could be next.

He found himself driving along the street where Captain Dan Ward called home. The man who had helped Riley cope with her abilities, watched her family split in two, and now cultivated her career with the police department. Ward had almost as much influence over Riley as Carl had, but in a different manner. Carl seldom doled out advice; he only listened to her and spoke his piece, if asked. Jacob hadn't been around for a chunk of Riley's relationship with Dan Ward. It had developed prior to Jacob and Riley dating and then when he left for college, all she had was Ward and Carl—and then Ethan.

He pulled to a stop in front of the captain's house. Jacob needed his advice. He had to know what to do to smooth things over and, of course, find Alex. He'd begun to wonder if trouble was following him or if it followed Riley.

The front porch light burned, a good indication the captain was still awake. Jacob approached the steps and climbed them until reaching the door. With his fist curled, he rapped softly on the door. A light flickered on in the entryway and shone through the door's side window. Jacob pulled straight and thrust his shoulders back in some strange attempt to not appear as weak and feeble as he felt.

"Jacob? What are you doing here? Is Riley okay?" Ward stood

in a white t-shirt and grey athletic shorts; his socked feet curled over the threshold.

"She's fine. We had a fight." His bogus swagger melted away in an instant, as though he was about to confess to some childhood prank gone awry.

"Come in." Ward stepped aside and closed the door after Jacob entered. "You want something to drink? Probably water or soda, since you're driving."

"No, sir. I'm fine. I was just hoping you could tell me what I should do."

The captain shuffled into the kitchen and filled a glass of water from the tap, setting it in front of Jacob on the counter. "About Riley? Son, if you think I'm some expert on how to contain Riley Thompson, then you don't know her as well as I thought you did." He folded his arms and examined Jacob. "This must be about your buddy, Laughlin. I'm sorry he's gone missing. I truly am."

"Yeah, me too." Jacob sipped on the water. "She's been having visions, you know."

"About you?"

"Yep. It freaked her out, and me too. Now with this? What are we going to do, Dan? What can we do to find him?"

"*We* can't do anything. The Owensville Police Department, headed up by yours truly, can. We've already opened an investigation. The wife is coming in first thing tomorrow. We're going to try to track down his friends or any other family. In fact, it's best if you come in and make a statement too, seeing how you were the last person to see him."

Jacob hadn't considered that small but significant point. "I didn't have anything to do with his disappearance."

"Of course you didn't, son. But we're going to need to know what you two did last night. Riley must've told you that."

"She didn't have to. She had Ethan tail me. Anything you need to know, you'll be able to learn from him." Jacob's eyes flashed with irritation.

"I see now why you're so bent out of shape." Ward nodded. "That is something." He was silent for a few seconds longer, appearing deep in thought, before he began again. "Go home, son. Smooth things over with Riley because what choice you got? You and me both know she needs you just as much as you need her. I'll address this with her tomorrow. In the meantime, we'll do everything we can to find your buddy. I promise you that."

"Thanks, Dan." Jacob started toward the door again, but stopped and turned back. "There is something maybe I should've said to Riley."

"Is that right?"

"As we were leaving the Crooked Horse last night, a couple of men came out and started talking to us. I didn't think much of it because it didn't seem important. And I thought Alex had left, but maybe one of them followed him."

"Can you give a description?"

"I can."

"Good. Come down to the station in the morning and let's talk more about this." Ward pulled open the door. "You should've led with that, son."

WHEN THE FRONT DOOR CREAKED ON ITS HINGES, RILEY'S eyes snapped open as she lay in her bed. The time hit 11pm and the expectation that Jacob had returned was predicated on the detail that Ward had texted her. He was always looking after her, regardless of whether she was in the right and in this case, she was not.

His steps sounded in the hall as he tiptoed along the wood-planked floors, apparently trying hard not to wake her. Sleep wasn't in the cards for Riley tonight, at least not until Jacob returned and apologies could be professed.

Light spilled in from the hall as Jacob pushed open their bedroom door and slipped inside. He made his way to the bed, shedding all but his boxer shorts, and crawled under the light-weight covers.

"Hey," she whispered with her back to him.

"I woke you, I'm sorry," he replied with a rueful quality.

"I wasn't asleep." Riley turned over and regarded him in the darkened room. His eyes held regret and she was sure hers did too. "I shouldn't have done what I did. I went behind your back and I'm sorry."

"I shouldn't have flown off the handle like that. I know you were worried about me." He held her gaze as though he would never let it go. "I'm scared, Riley. There are things I've done, kept from you, in an effort to help someone else. I think it could backfire on me now. And I think my friend might've paid a price for some-thing he didn't owe."

Riley took in a breath before sitting up and switching on the side table lamp. The soft amber glow revealed the depth of Jacob's fear, and now she could see everything he'd tried so hard to keep from her. "We're going to have to keep up appearances."

"I'm sorry, what?"

"This poker game you and Alex were in last night. I have to

assume this is the reason he's now missing. I'm sorry, but your face says it all."

"Of course it does," he replied.

"I won't let that happen to you. So we're going to have to come up with a plan to make sure no one knows you're working with us."

"Working with who?" Jacob finally sat up. "The cops? I don't know, Riley. Alex asked for my help and I helped. Silas Levin wanted us to throw the games, make the players believe we were novices, and then he swoops in and cleans house. Not obviously, though. He's smart about how he plays it."

"The men who approached you and Alex in the parking lot, were they in the game too?"

"Yes, and they lost a lot of money, but they thought we did too, so there weren't any hard feelings. Well, I didn't think there were."

"Okay. So, tomorrow, you'll give us a description. Ethan's got pictures of your conversations, but they're just too grainy. Then we'll see what we can dig up and keep trying to locate your friend."

"You said we should have a plan," he added.

"It's finally clicked. I know why Carl showed me those cards that day, six months ago. It all comes down to this. He knew it was coming, somehow, and it was a warning. I only wish I'd realized it sooner. I might've been able to prevent whatever happened with your friend. But I just couldn't see it then."

"You were in so much pain after losing Carl. How could you have put two and two together then? But you can now. And that's what we'll have to focus on. Maybe this is why you had the visions of me."

"But I've had others like that—about Dan not too long ago. So maybe this is the same thing, a warning." She considered the idea forming in her mind. "You're going to have to keep playing this game with Levin. You'll have to pretend you have no idea what happened to Alex. That should be easy because you two weren't close and we really don't know what happened."

"And then what?"

"Then we'll find a way to take him down. And the rest of them because I suspect none of the people participating in those games are upstanding citizens. We'll find out if they're involved in Alex's disappearance and we'll take down each one of them."

SILAS LEVIN PUSHED BACK HIS THICK SALTY HAIR AND STOOD with his legs shoulder-length apart in front of the door. This condominium building was owned by the person behind that door and was the one who Silas Levin had come to see. He cleared his throat and rapped on the door.

A heavy-set man greeted him with an impish grin. "Silas. I was concerned you wouldn't show, considering the late hour. Please, come in."

With some hesitation, Silas entered the lavish penthouse condo. "It took me longer than I anticipated. I apologize for the time."

"These things happen. I do hope you have what you promised." In stark contrast to Silas, Eli Foster was robust with olive skin and deeply receded black hair. His origins were too difficult to pin down, though he spoke with a clear midwestern accent. "Can I offer you a drink?"

"Thank you, no. I won't be taking up much of your time and I still have a long drive ahead of me."

Foster walked to a wet bar opposite his enormous big screen television and poured a shot of gin for himself. "Surely you don't intend on driving back to that Podunk town of yours tonight?"

"I'm afraid so." Levin forced a smile. "I have to get the bar ready to open by midday." He retrieved a manila envelope from his back pocket, its thick, rectangular shape leaving no room for doubt as to its contents. "I have the money for you."

Foster waddled toward him. "All of it?"

"Just what we agreed upon—for now."

"Of course. That's all that is required of you, Silas—for now." He slid his sausage-like index finger under the lip and ripped open the envelope. A broad smile stretched across his lips as he nodded. "Excellent. I'm sure it's all here. No need to count it."

"Thank you, Eli. I appreciate your trust." Silas shifted his weight. "If there's nothing else?"

"Right, of course, your long drive back." Foster stepped closer to Levin and locked eyes with him. "You know, Silas, you would've been better off staying here in Chicago. We had a good thing going. You would've been running the region by now."

Levin nodded. "It's my loss, Eli. I readily admit that. However, I'm hoping that once we're done here, we can still part ways in a congenial manner."

"I wouldn't want it any other way, my friend." Foster laid his ham-hand on Silas' shoulder. "Your debt will be repaid, and you'll be free to live as you please. But should you not fulfill your end of the deal, you remember the price you'll be forced to pay."

"I remember and that won't happen. I should be going now

and let you get some sleep." He stepped back less than a foot, waiting for permission.

"Goodnight, Silas. Same time next week?" Foster walked to his door and held it open. "Maybe a little earlier, if you can swing it."

"Yes, goodnight, Eli." Silas stood in the hall again, his back to the door as it closed. A sigh of relief escaped him and he started down the long corridor. He pondered if there was a way to finish this thing with Eli sooner rather than later. The longer he dragged it out, the more things could go wrong. And pissing off Eli Foster was not in his best interest.

As he reached his car and turned the engine, Silas headed back onto the highway and prepared himself for the three-hour drive back to Owensville. It would be 3am before his return. And then he would have to do it all again next week, assuming things went to plan and the game continued to prove beneficial. It remained to be seen if he could pull off what he had the other night. Recruiting others was key and they would have to be gullible enough to take the bait.

His primary concern, however, was the local cops. More specifically, the one everyone said had an unusual gift. He didn't buy into mumbo jumbo, but folks around Owensville seemed pretty adamant about it. There was only one way to be sure and that was to cozy up to the cop's boyfriend, a man he had already understood would play the game if needed. Perhaps he would be needed again.

THE BLACKNESS WAS DISORIENTING. ALEX LAUGHLIN wouldn't be able to see his hands in front of his face were they not bound behind his back. Sweat poured down his cheeks and neck and soaked his long-sleeved dress shirt. His bladder was so full, it brought pain every time he took a breath. But the idea of pissing his pants would be a sign of weakness and they might take advantage of that. Nevertheless, nature was calling—screaming—at him and he didn't know how much longer he could take it.

The men hadn't shown their faces in what he thought was at least a few hours. His lids were heavy, though his heart pumped adrenaline to the point of trembling. No reason for his capture had yet been revealed, but he assumed this had to do with the game. He'd done everything he was supposed to do, so why was he taken? What could possibly come from this? He had no money. There would be no ransom paid.

Someone had messed with his 4Runner. The damn thing sputtered and just died and yet, he found himself less than two miles from his house with a disabled car. He had pulled over to the shoulder when he noticed the headlights behind him. A feeling of relief surged, until two men approached from either side. One thumped his knuckle on his window.

It all had happened so fast. He was yanked from the driver's seat, his phone dropped to the ground and then—black. He awoke briefly and found himself in some warehouse and based on the light outside, it appeared to be mid-morning. Then he was given something. Something in his arm. That was the end of that.

When he awoke this time, he had a splitting headache, a cotton-mouth, and he quickly figured out that he was bound to a chair that was chained to the floor of this building. Was it the same place? There was no way to tell. But one thing was certain, he was alone.

15

One of the lesser known talents of Lowell Abrams was that he also served as the department's sketch artist. So when he sat down with Jacob this morning, he appeared to put aside his wise-ass exterior and coaxed a detailed description of the men who had approached Alex and Jacob two nights earlier.

"This look like them?" Abrams turned the sketch pad to Jacob.

"Yep. That's them, all right."

Abrams looked at Riley. "Let's pair this up with what Pruitt has on his phone and run this through the system, see if we can find a match." He handed her the sketches.

"This is good work, Abrams, thanks." She turned to Jacob. "Looks like you can head in to work now."

"You don't need me for anything else?"

"No. This is a great start. I'll see you tonight." Riley returned to her desk.

"Okay. What am I supposed to tell everyone at the office?" Jacob asked.

"Nothing. Right now, we don't know anything," she began. "Your boss, your co-workers, you can't discuss this with anyone."

"Laughlin hasn't been missing long enough yet," Ethan began. "Technically, we're jumping the gun a little, so we'll need to keep that in-house for now."

"Got it." Jacob reached for his keys. "I hope that helps. I want Alex to come home safely."

"We all do." Riley opened the door for him. "I'll talk to you later." She waited for him to leave before returning to the bullpen where Abrams and Ethan remained at their desks. "Well? What do you guys think?"

"I think we have a couple of different situations brewing here," Ethan began. "Most importantly, Alex Laughlin is missing under suspicious circumstances. On that, we can all agree. Secondly, we've got a couple of men who were involved in an illegal poker game who were the last to see Laughlin."

"What's your point, dude, besides stating the obvious?" Abrams asked.

"My point is, I think it's time we get Silas Levin in here. We all know he was the one to set up this game or games. It's his bar, for Pete's sake. He could be the one responsible for Laughlin. At the very least, he's a conspirator."

Captain Ward appeared from the corridor with a coffee in hand. "I'm not so sure that's the best course of action, Pruitt. I admire your fervor, however, if we haul in Silas Levin, he won't hang around long after that. That said, I think there could be another approach to this scenario."

"What you got up your sleeve, Cap?" Abrams asked.

He peered at Riley, and based on her expression, she seemed to grasp the concept of his plan before he said one word. "We're going to need Jacob for this, you understand that, right?"

"I do," Riley said.

"What are you talking about?" Ethan asked.

"Jacob's going to have to go back and keep playing this game. It's the only way to find out what Levin is running and if he was involved in Laughlin's disappearance. Him or his buddies."

"You want Riley's boyfriend to go undercover? Is that what I'm hearing, Captain?" Abrams asked. "Because last I checked, he wasn't a cop."

"You're hearing correctly, son. I think it's the best way to get information without running off the only one who can help us find Alex Laughlin."

"I agree," Riley added. "Silas appears to already have a level of trust in Jacob. He'll need to exploit that to get the information."

Ethan stood from his desk. "Hang on here. Far be it from me to agree with Abrams, but he's right about Jacob not being a cop. And you're going to have him take part in an undercover operation to take down an illegal gambling ring or whatever this is. You're putting his life in danger, Riley. How can you, of all people, be okay with that?"

"Because we aren't going to leave him hanging in the wind. You managed to keep out of sight when you were there the last time. I have every confidence you can do that again. And..." she peered at Ward again. "I assume we'll want him to wear a wire?"

"I would say that's a correct assumption. It's the only way to figure out what and who we're dealing with."

Abrams shook his head. "Being on the same page as Slim over there is bad enough," he nodded to Ethan. "But getting your boyfriend to wear a wire when we have no idea who these people are is putting him in one hell of a tight spot. Even the most trained officer is walking a thin line trying to pull off something like that."

"Look, Silas Levin knows every one of us," Riley said. "We've all been in contact with him. Jacob has too, but on a different level. He's the only one who can pull this off. How much time do you think we have before Laughlin turns up dead, if he isn't already? We can't wait."

"She's right, fellas," Ward added. "Let's see if we can get some background on these guys Abrams sketched out as well as any and all information on Silas Levin. The more information we have, the better we can prepare Jacob." Ward returned to his office.

Ethan eyed Riley. "I can't believe you're okay with this. I would've thought you of all people would want Jacob to stay clear of any more trouble. After what we all went through..."

"I know what we went through. I was there." She glanced at Abrams. "We all were. But this is different. We're talking about a rigged poker game here. Not a cartel drug bust."

"Uh, and a kidnapping or murder," Abrams interjected. "Don't forget that. I'm just saying, Pruitt's got a point. Captain's got a point and so do you. None of this is good news, Thompson. But now we're stuck with it. So what are you gonna do?"

"I think you and Decker should go to County and have another chat with Sims. Now that he's been behind bars for a while, he might be more willing to talk, especially if it might lead to a plea deal. I'm starting to believe he was in on this game too. We know the murder of his wife was about money, money he lost somehow." She peered at her colleagues. "Come on, guys. I can't be the only one to see the connection here."

"No. I suppose you could be right about that," Ethan said. "Putting Decker and you, Abrams, on this is a good call."

"Fine by me. I'll bet he hasn't gone to sleep yet, so I'll get his ass down here." He picked up his phone and made the call.

Riley perched on the edge of Ethan's desk. "I think Laughlin is alive."

"Okay. Any particular reason why you think that is?"

"Because I can't see anything else. When we were checking out his SUV, his phone and keys. I didn't get anything."

"I hope to God he's alive, but if he is, how the hell are we going to find him?" Ethan leaned in and lowered his tone. "It's all well and good for Jacob to keep up appearances with Levin, but how much time do you think this is going to take? And what if it comes down to Levin threatening Jacob to do his bidding in exchange for keeping Laughlin alive?"

"You're assuming Levin is behind the kidnapping," she said.

"Or murder. But yeah, I guess that's what I'm saying. I think we'll find out these men were working for him too."

"No. That doesn't make sense. That would mean half the table was being forced to lose money. I don't buy it. This is a side deal with Levin. And I can't be sure who has Laughlin, but if Levin doesn't, I'm betting he knows who does."

ELI FOSTER SHOVELED AN ENORMOUS BITE OF SCRAMBLED egg and toast into his mouth before reaching for a nearby mug of coffee and guzzling a healthy amount. A piece of egg dangled from his lower lip while he finished swallowing down the food. A moment later, he gently dabbed away the stray morsel with a white linen napkin that had rested neatly in his lap.

"I want you to go see what Silas is running in that backwater town. Whatever it is, he's making a killing and paying off his debt too quickly. I need to keep him under my thumb a while longer so that he learns his lesson. We're going to need to put some obstacles in his way."

"How should I do that, sir?" A wiry man with dark thinning hair and smooth skin sat across from him with only a cup of coffee in his hand.

Foster held the napkin to his face and blew his nose into it. "Get in on whatever he's doing. Buddy up to anyone else you think can get you closer to him. If he gets out of this deal unscathed, others are going to see that. We can't afford for that to happen."

"Okay, Boss. I'll go down there today." He pushed up from the breakfast table.

"Oh, and one more thing, Gage, don't fuck up whatever he's working on. Your only job is to keep me abreast of his operation. Nothing more."

"Sure thing, Boss."

A LOUD CREAK SOUNDED WHEN THE METAL DOOR WAS PUSHED open to the room where Alex was being held captive. He knew it was morning because the sun was now shining through the small window near the ceiling. As daylight flooded the area, he realized he was in a commercial space of some kind. Perhaps an office that wasn't finished on the interior yet? It was difficult to say. There weren't many places in Owensville that were currently under construction and he supposed he wasn't in Owensville anymore.

"Good morning." An athletic man in dark jeans and a grey t-shirt entered.

He looked to be in his forties, early forties, most likely, but Alex didn't recognize him. "Is it morning? Hard for me to say."

The man peered down between the chair legs where Alex sat. "Oh, man. I'm sorry about that. Someone should've let you take a piss."

Alex looked away, angry and embarrassed. "What do you want from me? What the hell did I do to you anyway?"

"To me? Nothing. To my bosses, well, they think you were in on a scheme to swindle them out of some cash, brother."

Now it was being pieced together. Alex figured it must've been the men who approached Jacob and him. They had to have been the ones to tamper with his vehicle and force him to break down. Then they knocked him out cold and now he was here. "Look, I don't have any money. You have to understand that."

"I don't have to understand anything, brother." He held a glass of water to Alex's lips. "Drink up."

Alex didn't want to give him the satisfaction of obeying, but he was parched. His stomach growled and his head still ached. The water would help.

"Dude. Don't be stupid. Drink the water."

The man pushed the glass against Alex's lips and his instincts kicked into gear. He lapped up as much water as he could, feeling almost sick as a result.

"Okay, okay. That's enough." He pulled away the glass.

A few droplets trickled down Alex's chin, and for a moment,

his thirst abated, but it wasn't quenched. "Is this Silas's doing because I did everything he asked of me."

"Silas? Silas Levin?" The man reared back in laughter. "That little piss-ant? No, man. Levin's who you're going to get for us. See, we know you have an in with the cops in that jerkwater town. Your buddy, Biggs."

"Why the hell did you come after me, then? If you wanted Biggs, he was right there." Alex regretted his comment. He'd just thrown Jacob under the bus for no other reason than to try to save his own ass. "I mean..."

"Oh, I know what you meant, dude. Glad you aren't my friend. We couldn't take Biggs because Levin has you under this thumb, not him. The deal was with you."

"How do you know any of this?" Alex asked.

The man shook his head in disbelief. "Man, you really have no idea who you're dealing with, do you? You think this is about some fixed game? It's not. The people you played against, the ones who've been in on Levin's game for weeks now, those guys don't fuck around. They're high-stakes players who don't like being played."

"Lieutenant Moody, it's good to hear your voice." Riley grinned as she held the phone to her ear. "Thank you. Listen, I was following up on the sketches we sent over earlier and the photos. I know they weren't good quality." She nodded and peered at Ethan while the lieutenant spoke. "Yes, sir. That would be great. We appreciate your help. Captain Ward sends his regards. Yes, we'll speak to you soon, then. Goodbye." She

returned the phone to its cradle and looked at the rest of the officers, all three of them. "He turned them over to his people to run
through facial recognition and see what comes up."

"It'd be nice if we had those kinds of resources." Chris Decker,
who had been called in after serving on the night shift, had joined
the others in their search to find Alex Laughlin.

"It would, but at least we have friends in the Indianapolis PD,"
she replied. "He says it might take the afternoon, but he was
having them rush it through."

"What do we do in the meantime?" Abrams held a toothpick
and began to pry out of his teeth whatever it was he had eaten for
lunch. "Get your boy ready?"

Ethan regarded Riley. "You haven't told him yet, have you?"

"There isn't supposed to be another game until tomorrow
night," she began. "We discussed it in general terms, but I was
hoping this might be resolved before then. And he wouldn't need
to get involved any further."

"Our priority is to find Laughlin," Decker added. "Abrams and
I are going to head up to see Sims in just a little bit here, so if we
get something, I'll let you know. You're right, we could finish this
today if we find out who these men are and what they want with
Laughlin. But if we don't, Riley, you're going to have to prepare
Jacob for tomorrow."

"I know, and I will. Ethan and I will stay on top of the IDs on
the men while you two head out."

Abrams pulled his feet off his desk and slowly stood from his
chair. "All right. Let's go talk to the murdering asshole and find out
why he killed his wife."

While the night shift officers prepared to leave, Ethan
approached Riley and perched on the edge of her desk. "I really

hope we don't need Jacob to get involved in this. I don't agree it's the right thing to do."

"I know you don't. Like I said before, it's a last resort." She studied him for a moment. "Gracie's leaving tomorrow, and honestly, I'm kind of glad she is with everything that's going on right now. I don't want her to worry. She's going to have enough on her plate with her new internship."

"She will."

"How are you doing with all this? Her leaving, I mean," Riley pressed on.

"Good. Fine, yeah. It's her life and I want her to be happy and it seems like this will make her happy."

"And you? What about your happiness?"

"Riley, why do you ask me these things when you already know my answer?"

"I don't always."

Ethan smiled. "Sure you do. You don't need me to confirm it." He pushed off her desk and returned to his own. "I'll keep looking into Laughlin's phone records to see if anything pops up."

Riley returned to her task, but Ethan's words haunted her. It was the second time someone had called her out for her gift. It wasn't like she could turn it off, but it was clear it had negatively impacted those closest to her. She felt like Ethan was pulling away, distancing himself from her so he wasn't confronted with his feelings for her. Could she blame him? She'd wanted him to be happy with Gracie, but what she saw behind his eyes just now, happiness wasn't in the cards for him at the moment. She wondered if Gracie had felt the same.

With too much time on her hands, perhaps now was the opportunity to address the issue with Gracie since she was leaving in a day. And there was no way of knowing what would happen in the next 24 hours. Even she couldn't foresee what lay ahead and that was terrifying in and of itself.

She reached for her keys and stood. "I'm going to run out for a bit. All we're doing right now is waiting for IPD and our people to visit Sims. I need some air."

Ethan regarded her for a moment. "Sure. If that's what you need to do. What do I tell Ward when he gets back?"

"Just that I ran out. He can call if he needs me. I won't be long." She pushed out the door and walked to her patrol car. She gazed back at the stationhouse and for a split second, considered an idea that seemed completely foreign to her. As much as she loved this town and loved her job, the consequences of her abilities had become too great on those very people she loved. Maybe the time had come to make a change.

16

The home where Riley's mother, Ellen, lived was shaded by a large sugar maple tree in the front yard. The tree had been planted after Carl's son, CJ, died, a sort of memorial to the young man who was killed after trying to protect her and Dillon. In the sixteen years since then, the tree had grown substantially, its canopy offering shade under which to sit and read, something Riley did often in her younger years. Now it looked greener and lusher than ever as it protected the home.

Riley approached the front steps and knocked on the door before inserting her key to open it. "Hello? It's only me." She stepped inside and surveyed the living room and kitchen. "Anyone home?"

Gracie trotted down the steps. "Riley, what are you doing here? Sorry, I was just upstairs packing my things."

"Where's Mom?"

"She had an early shift at the restaurant." Gracie moved in for an embrace. "Shouldn't you be at work?"

"I'm working. Just taking a break to come see my little sister before she leaves." Riley placed her keys on the side table and walked into the kitchen. "Have you eaten? I could go and grab us some lunch."

"I ate already. Mom made a huge breakfast this morning before she left. I'm still full." Gracie followed her. "How's Ethan? I haven't talked to him yet today."

"We're working on something right now. I can't really say much about it just yet. But don't worry, he's safe."

"I wasn't worried." Gracie cocked her head. "But should I be?"

"No, of course not. It's Owensville. Nothing happens here."

"Except when it does." Gracie held her gaze. "What's going on, Riley? I can tell when you're hiding something from me. You think you're protecting me, but you're not. I'm an adult now."

"I know you are, Gracie. I'm sorry if I've made you feel differently." Riley moved closer. "I'm so proud of you for finishing school and doing this internship. It's everything Dillon and I ever wanted for you."

"Yes, well, I got off easy compared to you two." Gracie walked toward the cabinet and retrieved a glass before filling it with tap water. "I'm sorry you both were forced to stay here and pay for my school."

"We weren't forced to do anything. We wanted to," Riley replied. "We wanted you to get out of Owensville and do what you wanted to do with your life."

"Then why do I feel like crap about it? You and Dillon are here taking care of Mom, working your jobs, and I'm off living a good life in the big city."

"That's right and that's exactly how we wanted it; don't you see that? Gracie, I'm happy here." She considered for a moment her earlier misgivings. "Dillon loves being a teacher. It's everything we wanted for ourselves too."

"But all you've gone through, Riley, both of you. The tornado, which I don't even remember, then last year with the whole mob thing. I mean, that was scary."

"It was, but that's my job. And besides, the best thing to come out of that was that I have Jacob back in my life."

"That's true. You two have always belonged together."

"I suppose that brings me to another reason for my visit," Riley began. "Ethan. Have you thought about your future?"

"Not much. I like him, don't get me wrong. And I know he has feelings for me, but I can't make any promises. He knows that. We'll try the long-distance thing."

Riley regarded her carefully. "That's the only reason you're having doubts. Distance?"

"Yeah, of course. It's a big deal."

"It is."

Gracie turned away her gaze. "Stop. I know what you're trying to do. Don't. I hate it when you try to look inside."

"I'm sorry. Sometimes, I can't help it."

"Yes, you can. You just don't want to. You like it—knowing everything about everyone. It makes you feel safe and secure, like no one can ever get the better of you, or take advantage of you. It's how you protect yourself."

And there it was—the truth—from her little sister who Riley didn't believe had the maturity to understand. She had underestimated Gracie.

"I think Nate has it too," Riley said.

"He does. I've spent enough time with Jack and all of them to have seen it. He's young and can't control it the way you can. There's going to come a time when you'll have to help him, Riley. You had Carl. He's going to need someone too."

"My God, you really are grown up, aren't you?"

"That's what happens." Gracie tipped out the rest of the water from her glass and returned her attention to Riley. "And to answer your question about Ethan, I don't know how all that will play out because he's still in love with you. I knew that when he walked away from me the other night. We were about to... anyway, he said he had to leave. I knew for sure then. So, I don't think it's the distance that's going to kill this relationship. It's you."

RILEY SAT IN HER PATROL CAR IN FRONT OF THE HOUSE, staring at it as if she could exorcise its demons and remove the sins of the past. Her grandfather's suicide, her father's drunken bouts that were taken out on her mother. Now it seemed Gracie, the little girl who had followed her around like a puppy for years, had realized what Riley had become. She directed her anger on this house, but all it succeeded in doing was reflecting back on her own insecurities. And there were plenty of them. No matter how hard Riley tried to be a tough, stoic cop, Gracie had just reduced her to her ten-year-old self, who lacked self-esteem and feared her power, just as her half-brother did now.

"Stop." Riley closed her eyes and finally turned the engine. Her family had always tiptoed around Riley's abilities. Perhaps they were afraid of her after all. But not Gracie. That was the reason she was here. It was her job to keep Riley in check now that Carl was gone. But she was going to be leaving too. Who would keep her in check then?

Static sounded through the radio receiver before a voice began. "Riley, we got it."

She picked up the receiver. "Got what?"

"IPD has names on the sketches. You need to get back here now."

"On my way." She placed the radio in its cradle and pulled away from the curb. This was too important for the distractions in which she allowed herself to indulge. It had been a mistake to see Gracie. She hadn't been prepared for the gut check.

A man was missing, a friend of Jacob's, and that was what she needed to focus on now. She needed to put in the back of her mind Ethan's feelings and Gracie's harsh but spot on words.

Riley pressed harder on the accelerator and sped through the quiet streets, through the downtown area, and arrived at the station a good five minutes sooner than she should have.

She pushed inside. "Who are they?"

Captain Ward hovered over Ethan's desk as the two viewed the images and reports from the Indianapolis Police Department. "Where have you been?"

"I went to see Gracie. She's leaving tomorrow. I thought I had time."

"You thought wrong. Come take a look at this." Ward gestured for her to view the monitor. "Lieutenant Moody sent this over not twenty minutes ago. This one here is Anton Meisner. Thirty-four, a mile-long rap sheet, and currently on parole. Hails from Chicago, same place our Mr. Levin is from."

"And the other?" Riley asked.

"That's Eugene Vaughan." Ethan pointed to the report. "Same as the other guy, from Chicago, only he's not on parole. But he has served time in Ohio for armed robbery. So still a scary dude. Forty-two years old and last known address was Chicago's Southside."

"What are we dealing with here, then?" Riley pressed on. "These aren't more mob thugs, right?"

"Not from what we can tell," Ward replied. "But they're definitely into some shady stuff. Lieutenant says both these guys are known associates of a man by the name of Dennis Ackerman."

"Yeah, and he seems like a real piece of work." Ethan flipped through the report. "Says here Ackerman was nixed from a World Series of Poker tournament in Las Vegas back six years ago. Got caught cheating. Had a group of men working with him who were throwing games."

"Sounds a little like Silas Levin," Riley said.

"You got it, Missy." Ward returned his attention to Ethan. "We keep digging into these guys and I bet we'll find a connection to Levin somewhere along the line. These big-time gamblers run in the same circles."

"Okay, now we know who they are. We still don't know where Laughlin is. What's our next move?" Riley continued.

"If this was a ransom situation, they would've called his wife already," Ethan began. "I think this is a way to get at Levin somehow. I don't think the end result is to get rid of Laughlin but to keep the two separated from one another. Maybe until the next game? Keep Laughlin out of commission so Levin is forced to find another solution?"

"You might've hit the nail on the head," Riley replied. "But there has to be a way to find out where they're hiding him, if that's the case. How can we get a hold of these men?"

"I'm not sure that will be possible." Ward pushed up from Ethan's desk. "If we reach out to Levin and tell him what we believe is happening, Levin will stop the games. If what we suspect is true, that'll spook the hell of these men. They'll disappear. If that happens, there's no telling what they'll do to Laughlin, assuming we're correct and they do have him."

ALEX HAD BEEN ALLOWED A FEW MINUTES TO USE THE bathroom and walk around the shell of a building. He still had no idea where he was being held and hadn't yet been told why or by whom, though it clearly had something to do with the two men who had pretended to console Jacob and himself prior to his abduction.

The man from earlier who had offered him water returned. "Here, put these on. Then you go back in the chair." He tossed him a change of clothes. "You should be grateful for the gear. I had to go to Walmart for you, asshole."

The man turned his back to Alex to allow him a modicum of privacy. His clothes were soiled and reeked of body odor. But then he considered the man's words, who had yet to offer up his name. *Walmart*, he thought. Not that it narrowed down many possibilities. After all, there was a Walmart in just about every town now. But there was also one in Owensville. It had opened last year on the north side of town and had already put out of business the local grocery store owned by a couple who had lived in Owensville their entire lives. They left for greener pastures, or retirement, he didn't know which. But the fact remained, there was a slim chance he was still in Owensville.

Alex pulled on the fresh clothes and felt slightly more human. "I'm dressed."

The man turned to him. "Eh, better than what you had on before. And you don't smell like piss, so that makes my life easier. Back in the chair you go." He grabbed the back of the chair, hitting the ground with the legs to reinforce his demand.

Alex obliged because there was no other choice. He sat down and wrapped his arms around the back of the chair. His muscles still ached. "Do what you gotta do, bro." He waited while the man secured the ropes and tape to his hands and feet. At least they hadn't gagged him—yet. "Can I ask you something?"

"What?"

"Does my wife know?"

"I assume she knows you're missing."

"That's not what I mean. Has anyone called her, you know, asking for money or anything? Cause I told you people I don't have any money."

"That's not what this is about. I told you that you didn't know who the hell you were dealing with. The man running the show doesn't need your money."

"Then what? What the hell am I doing here?"

The man peered around to ensure their solitude. "Look, they don't pay me enough to know the whole plan. But I can tell you that you're here at least until the day after tomorrow. I don't know what's going to happen after that." A final tug on the ropes and he started to leave.

"Wait. Why the day after tomorrow?" Alex shouted as the man left. "Shit." He searched his mind and tried to recall what day it was now. Time had passed almost in slow motion since he'd been here. He thought it had been a day, maybe two. And if that was the case, then tomorrow was Thursday. "What the hell's going on Thursday?"

Then it dawned on him. "The game. They want me to stay away from Silas's game." He considered the reason for this, but he just didn't have enough details to put all the pieces together. "Jacob." Was he going to be there? Surely he'd alerted the cops. Well, his wife would've for certain. But not showing up at work? Yeah, they all had to know. How could they not?

Another man Alex had not seen before navigated through the steel beams in the open area and approached him.

"Mr. Laughlin." Standing at least six feet tall with a medium build and brown hair, he continued to meander toward Alex. "I thought it was time we should meet." When he offered his hand, he smiled. "How insensitive of me. Your hands are literally tied. I'm Dennis Ackerman."

Alex appeared defiant. "Is that name supposed to mean something to me?"

Ackerman smiled again. "Oh good. You still have your sense of humor." The well-dressed man with tanned skin and a heavily lined face squatted to meet Alex eye to eye. "Mr. Laughlin, you're here because you were helping an old friend of mine play a game he and I used to play a long time ago. When I heard he resurfaced in that little town of yours, I thought I should see what he was up to. Turns out, he's up to his same old tricks. Tricks I had to pay for."

"I have no idea what you're talking about."

Ackerman laughed through his nose, keeping his lips pressed tightly together. "Oh, you think you're protecting him?"

"I promise you, I'm not trying to protect anyone."

"Your family, maybe? Friends?"

At this, Alex turned deadpan.

"That got your attention. Good." Ackerman stood upright again. "Here's the deal, Mr. Laughlin. I need to send a message to my old friend, Silas Levin, and your being here is going to accomplish just that. See, the thing is, I already paid the price for his misdeeds. He owes me. It took me sending in a couple of my guys to figure it out, but we got there in the end. I know what he's playing and why. He has some very serious people breathing down his neck. I don't know what he did to make that happen, but I assume that was the reason he's reverted to his old tricks."

"If I'm here, what am I supposed to do to help you?"

"You're being incredibly helpful just by staying put. Now I get that there are probably people out there looking for you, but I had to play the odds. And the odds those four cops in your tiny town are good enough to track me down are slim and none."

Alex considered the one cop whom he had heard about and revealed a sly grin.

"Is there something I should know, Mr. Laughlin?"

"No. Nothing."

"So here's what's going to happen. We derail Silas's plans, which will in turn send his not-so-friendly associates his way and they'll be the ones to solve my problem. Silas won't have the means to get out of his predicament."

"And you'll be the one to bail him out?" Alex asked.

"Oh, no. Not a chance in hell. I'll be there to watch him burn. That's why you're here. And you'll stay here until his world starts to crumble around him." Ackerman started to leave but stopped and turned on his heel. "I hear you're one hell of a good poker player."

"That's what they tell me."

"Well, maybe we'll see what happens when all of this is said and done. Enjoy your stay, Mr. Laughlin. Please trust that it will be temporary, providing you continue to cooperate."

17

HVM Builders was a solemn place in the wake of Alex's disappearance. Jacob tried to work, as did the rest, but his thoughts strayed to the whereabouts of a man he considered only a colleague, but now perhaps considered more as a friend. A friend who was in danger and who Jacob was the last one to see.

A woman whose eyes were reddened appeared in the corridor and was being escorted by Jacob's boss, Ty Henry. It was Alex's wife, Zoe. Jacob wanted to say something to her, offer words of comfort, but there were no words. And of course, it was likely she was aware that Jacob had been with her husband on the night of his disappearance. He feared blame would be launched in his direction. So he peered into the hall, feeling like a coward. His boss caught his eye, but he didn't move away from Zoe's side. Instead, he continued to escort her, his arm around her shoulders, and guided her through the doors.

Jacob's heart sank in regret. He should've said something to her and now he felt small, lower than a coward. "I'll find him," he whispered. "I'll bring him home."

He swiped his keys and marched through the building, ignoring the stares of his colleagues because he knew they blamed him too. He could feel it. Jacob had to make this right. Somehow. Alex had dragged him into this, but now he was compelled to clear his name of any wrong-doing and find his friend.

Since he'd returned to Owensville, misfortune seemed to shadow him. This time, he was going to stop it dead in its tracks.

THE SIGHT OF JACOB'S CAR PULLING INTO THE PARKING LOT of the station caught Riley's attention as she peered through the window. "What are you doing here?" she said to no one in particular.

"What's that?" Ethan piped up as he pulled his attention from his work.

"Jacob's here," she replied. "He shouldn't be. I need him to keep playing his part."

"The part of the dutiful worker bee?" Ethan pressed on.

"Yes. If Levin or anyone associated with him is watching Jacob, we need him to keep up his routine. We can't afford for him to veer from the norm."

"And did you convey that to him?" Ethan asked.

"No." Riley turned her sights to him. "I didn't think I had to."

"He's not a cop, Riley. He's doing what anyone would do under these circumstances."

"You're defending him," she replied.

"I guess I am. Look, Jacob didn't deserve to get pulled into this and I'll be the first one to admit that. He's not my favorite person in the world, but I won't hold what happened to Laughlin against him."

"Good. Because he looks determined about something." She watched as Jacob pushed through the doors.

"Hey." Jacob headed straight into the bullpen. "We need to talk. All of us."

"About?" Riley asked.

"I just shied away from Alex's wife, who came into the office this morning to see my boss. I couldn't even look her in the eye, Riley. I was the last one to see Alex. She knows it. Everyone knows it. I have to do something to help find him. Please, tell me there's something I can do. Now."

Riley peered knowingly at Ethan before turning back to Jacob. "We're still working on a plan. The men who approached you two, we have their names and are working on getting background information on each of them."

"That's great. Why didn't you tell me?"

"Because all we have are names right now. We still don't know for sure if those men are responsible for taking Alex."

"Who else could it be, Riley?"

"I don't know. That's what we're trying to find out."

"Tell him," Ethan said.

"Tell me what?" Jacob regarded Riley. "What else don't I know?"

Riley shot a perturbed glance to Ethan. "If we don't make enough progress today, we're going to need you to show up at Levin's poker game tomorrow night, like you and I initially discussed. I'm still hopeful it won't come to that. We believe the people who have Alex, and yes, we believe Alex is still alive, are keeping him as a means to back Levin into a corner. Again, we don't have enough to go by yet, but we're working on it."

"Fine. I'm in. I have to do something to help bring him home. You didn't see the look on his wife's face. And he has kids. No, if this is what I have to do, then so be it. I'm tired of running scared, Riley. I feel like that's all I've done since I came home."

"That's not true. You had no idea about the people running the plant," she replied. "You can't blame yourself for that. I don't." She glanced to Ethan again.

"Right. Neither do I, man. It wasn't your fault, and this isn't either."

"Yeah, well, there's a whole lot of bad things going down in Owensville and I don't know if you two have noticed, but I seem to be the common thread."

"Well, you do have a point," Ethan muttered.

"Ethan!" Riley said.

"He said it."

"Ethan's right." Jacob sat down in the chair opposite Riley's desk. "Tell me what I need to do for the game tomorrow. I'm not nearly as good a player as Alex. What if I screw it up?"

She returned to her chair. "Okay, here's the deal. Right now, we don't know that you're going to have to participate. Our goal is to find out who these men are connected to and look for ties to Silas Levin. If we can establish that, we might find our motive and Alex."

"That said." Ethan walked toward them and leaned against the lateral filing cabinet behind Riley's desk. "We don't have much time. The guys at IPD are helping us out with background checks, thanks to the captain, but we don't have anything back yet."

"Nothing more on Levin himself?" Jacob asked.

"He's clean," Riley said. "We did, however, discover that the men who last saw Alex and you are associated with a man who served time for swindling some heavy hitters out of cash. And, he was expelled by the World Series of Poker operators for cheating in a final round game six years ago."

"These guys have to be connected," Jacob added.

"That's what we think too," Ethan replied. "Which brings us to Levin's game tomorrow night. Jacob, he can't know that Alex is missing."

"You don't think he already knows it?"

"If he does, he's playing dumb. I think he would've called off the game and he hasn't, right? You'd probably be in the know on that one," Riley said. "If tomorrow night comes and still no Alex, Silas is going to get real nervous. It's going to be up to you, who he clearly believes is on his team, to smooth things over. Tell him Alex had a family thing or whatever. I don't care what you make up, but he has to believe you'll be there to fill in for him and do whatever Silas wants you to do."

"Okay. I can handle that," Jacob replied. "But this isn't going down until tomorrow night. What can I do now to help?"

Riley considered an idea. "The other people in the game. Obviously, we know Sims was there at an earlier game last week, before you got pulled in."

"And that Abrams and Decker are meeting with him now," Ethan added.

"Right. And the men who approached you both, Meisner and Vaughan. But who else was there with you and Alex? Were you introduced to any of them?"

Jacob cast his gaze toward the ceiling as if thinking hard on the question. "No one in there was interested in giving names. I can tell you that much. But I do recall conversations afterward. A couple of the guys were talking. Not Meisner or Vaughan, but two others." He paused again and furrowed his brow. "I'm trying to recall their names. I'm sure they greeted each other."

"Anything you can remember, Jacob. It would be extremely helpful." Ethan appeared to try to prompt him. "What did they look like?"

"Like the rest. They all sort of had that—I don't know—that criminal element to them. Whatever that is. Shady, you know?"

"Stands to reason," Riley said. "They're in with shady people. Look, it's okay if you can't remember..."

"No, wait." He raised his hands. "Jeff, maybe. I think that was one of the guy's names. Kind of skinny, well-dressed. Super tan. Older, though. Maybe in his forties." He continued to ponder. "The one he was speaking to, I want to say...no it escapes me. I'm sorry."

"That's okay. Jeff is a good start and we have a description," Riley said. "Don't suppose you saw their vehicles?"

"As a matter of fact, I saw Jeff's. It was a newer model, maybe only a couple years old, Mercedes coupe. I couldn't say the model. It was dark. But it stood out to me because well, this is Owensville. Don't see a lot of luxury cars here and it was sleek, black. I saw him step into it."

"Okay." Riley wrote down the details. "This is good. This will help." She laid down her pen. "Look, you need to go back to the office. Go back to work, just like it was a normal day. If you're being watched, you shouldn't be here."

"Well, it's easy to play off, though," Ethan began. "Everyone knows you're his girlfriend. I'd say, to make things look normal,

Riley, you should walk him out, kiss him goodbye. Make nice for the cameras, if there are any."

She nodded. "Okay. Let's get you out of here."

Ethan pushed off the chair and returned to his desk as he watched the two of them leave. But he didn't sit down. Instead, he gazed through the window as Riley embraced Jacob. Their kiss appeared loving and passionate. He looked away, his face masked in grim defeat.

Riley returned inside. "If anyone's watching, I think we put on a good show." She returned to her desk. "I hate that this involves him. It scares me. The idea anyone is watching him; I'm starting to feel like we'll never catch a break."

"We will," Ethan began. "I don't think the two of you are destined to be entangled in criminal agendas. We'll get through this, Riley. We always do."

FOR GAGE PARKER, THE DRIVE FROM CHICAGO TO Owensville was anything but boring. Despite his line of work, he fancied himself an enthusiast of literature. In his spare time, he was known to devour a book inside of a day. And while his free time was scarce, he utilized it most effectively. Hence, the drive found Gage engrossed in an audiobook from one of his favorites in the spy thriller genre. Not exactly the great American novel but entertaining as hell.

He passed a sign for the small town in Indiana with a population of around 4,000. Chicago, it was not. But Gage was here to check in on his boss's client, a man who had owed Eli Foster a substantial sum of money. And whom Eli had been disenchanted with because he'd been paying back that sum at an increasingly alarming rate. Something was up and Gage had been tasked to find out exactly what that something was.

A row of boutique shops and a diner appeared ahead. It seemed Gage had reached the downtown area of Owensville. He pulled into a spot in front of the diner and stepped out of his black Camaro wearing pointed dress shoes, slim-fitted trousers, and a blue dress shirt. He'd underestimated both the heat and the casual attire of those around him.

From the moment he entered the joint, the folks inside eyed him with a hint of derision. "Afternoon, ladies and gentlemen." Gage tipped his head in response to the overwhelming attention.

"You can take a seat anywhere." Ellen was on staff this afternoon and brushed past him on her way to pick up an order.

"Thank you." Gage slipped into a booth that overlooked the parking lot. Perhaps he should've considered checking into his hotel room prior to venturing out into the town. He might've opted for a change of attire.

"What can I get for you?" Ellen stood at the end of the booth, pen and pad at the ready.

"Iced coffee and I'll take your BLT."

"You want fries with that?"

"Are they fat or skinny fries?" he asked.

"Fat."

"Then no. Just the sandwich and coffee. Thanks." He returned the menu to the holder on the table and retrieved his cell phone. *"I'm here. Will keep you posted."* The text message was sent to Eli Foster.

Within a few minutes, Ellen returned with his meal. "Here you go. Is there anything else I can get for you, sir?"

"No, thank you. This will do just fine." He unveiled a toothy smile while Ellen walked away. He lowered his tone. "She's a friendly one." With both hands, he picked up the healthy-sized sandwich and took off a large corner. "Oh, oh, this is delicious," he said aloud with a full mouth. "Wow." He turned his head toward the counter where Ellen stood. "Give my regards to the chef. Delicious sandwich. Perfectly cooked bacon."

"Thank you, sir. I'll let him know." She appeared slightly taken aback by his forward nature and it seemed she wasn't alone.

Heads turned and a few whispers sounded as Gage continued to eat his lunch, the occasional moan of delight sounding from his lips.

Ellen walked back into the kitchen and stood next to the cook. "You ever seen that man before?"

"No, ma'am, I have not. Don't mind saying he's a little odd, that one."

"I don't mind you saying because I completely agree." Ellen stepped into the hall that led to the restaurant manager's office. She picked up the old rotary-style phone mounted on the wall and dialed. The line rang twice before it was picked up.

"Officer Riley Thompson."

"Sweetheart, it's your mother."

"Is everything all right? Is Gracie okay?"

"She's fine. Everything's fine. Honey, the reason I called is because there's a man here."

"A man. Okay," she replied.

"He's acting strange. Definitely not from around here."

"Mom, I can't talk to someone just because they're acting funny. I mean, is he upsetting anyone else?"

"Well, no. It's just, he's making a bit of a scene. Going on about the food and such. Honey, something's not right with this fella and I thought you should know."

"Okay. I'll come by, and if he's still there, I'll see what's up with him."

"Thank you, baby." Ellen hung up the phone and wiped her hands on her apron before returning to the kitchen.

"You call Riley?" the cook asked.

"Sure did."

"Good thinking."

RILEY STOOD FROM HER CHAIR AND REACHED FOR HER KEYS.

"Where are you off to?" Ethan asked.

"The diner. Mom says some strange man waltzed in there acting funny, as she put it."

Ethan stood up and gathered his things. "I'm coming with you. With all that's going on, we can't afford to overlook anything. And you going alone isn't an option. You got a problem with that, I suggest you talk to the captain."

"I don't have a problem." Riley approached Ward's office. "Hey, Captain, Pruitt and I are going to stop by the diner. Mom says some strange man came in. We're just going to go check it out."

"Sure thing. I'm going back and forth with the lieutenant, hoping to get some answers on the history of our two men. You let me know if something smells funny."

"I will." She returned to the bullpen. "Let's head out." Riley pushed through the doors and unlocked her cruiser.

Once they were both inside, she fired up the engine. "Mom's

pretty relaxed when it comes to people in the diner. Maybe this guy is looking to cause a problem."

"At this point, Riley, it would not surprise me," Ethan replied. "Oh, by the way, I'm going to take Gracie to the bus depot later this afternoon, if that's okay with you. I mentioned it would be best if she left a day early. Lord knows what's going to happen tomorrow. I know we have a lot of balls in the air right now."

"Funny, she didn't mention that to me." Riley considered their earlier conversation. "Go, it's fine. Decker and Abrams should be back by then and I'm sure they'll have plenty to say about Sims."

"Thanks. I'll come straight back. There's too much at stake for either of us to have any personal issues going on."

She peered through the windshield. "I'm starting to wonder if we shouldn't confront Levin. Maybe us waiting is putting Alex Laughlin's life in too much danger."

"I'd say just the opposite. We don't have anything on him, except what Jacob has to say about the poker game. And if he's smart, Levin's got a good lawyer who will tear Jacob apart because he's your boyfriend." Ethan took in a deep breath. "We're on the right track. I know you want to find Alex. So do I. So does the rest of the team. But we're doing everything we can to make that happen as quickly as possible." He turned to her. "Unless you can pull a rabbit out of a hat."

"Right now, I'd do anything to be able to do that." Riley turned right and the diner appeared in the distance. "I'll bet that's his car."

"The shiny black Camaro? Yeah, that'd be my guess too. Kind of sticks out like a sore thumb around here."

Riley pulled in front of the store next door to avoid the patrons in the diner spotting her car. She didn't want to alarm anyone, especially with a strange man inside. "Let's try to keep a low profile."

"We're in uniform, Riley. That might be a challenge," Ethan replied.

"You have a point." She approached the diner's glass door and pulled it open. What she had wished to avoid was, of course, exactly what happened. With a smile, she politely nodded to those who'd craned their necks to see the officers walk inside.

Ellen spotted her and waved her over out of view of the man in question.

As she and Ethan approached, it was too late.

"Oh, looky here. Local law enforcement." Gage wiped his lips with his napkin. "Afternoon, officers. Here for some lunch? You have got to try the BLT. Best thing I've ever eaten in my life." He raised two fingers. "Scout's honor."

Riley raised her lips into a half-smile. "I've had the BLT and you are absolutely correct. Best thing ever. Hands down." She turned away and looked back to Ellen with raised eyebrows.

"I told you so," Ellen replied in a low voice.

"I wouldn't mind a coffee," Ethan said to Ellen.

"I'll take one too." Riley pulled out a stool at the breakfast counter and sat down. She eyed for Ethan to do the same, and in a hushed tone, began, "What do you think?"

"Could be something. Don't suppose you took note of the plate when we came in?"

"You bet your ass I did. Illinois."

Ethan nodded then turned sharply when he felt a tap on his shoulder.

"Sorry to bother you, Officer, I was just wondering. See, I'm new around here and wanted to know where a good place might be to put my head down for the night."

"Just one night?" he replied.

"For now. I'm playing things by ear. You know, waiting to see what hand I'll be dealt."

Riley turned deadpan as she peered into the kitchen, avoiding contact with the man.

"Well, you know, there isn't a lot of choice here in town. You could try the Ramada Inn off the highway. It's not far," Ethan replied.

"What about you, Officer, ma'am? Any suggestions for a city boy like myself?"

Riley pasted on a smile and turned to him. Her head grew fuzzy. She peered into his brown eyes, his smile so wide and bright, she felt the need for sunglasses. Her heart pumped a little harder, her hands grew a little clammy. It was happening here right now and she had to control it. People would stare. The man before her would think she was crazy. *Hold on. Just look. Just look,* she thought.

"Officer? Are you okay?" Gage pressed on.

"Um, yeah. Of course. Sorry, I was just thinking. My partner's right. The Ramada's probably your best bet."

"Well, I thank you both for your suggestion and I will take it under advisement." He patted Ethan on the shoulder. "You have a wonderful day and enjoy your lunch."

Ethan waited for the man to return to his booth. "You saw something."

She nodded almost imperceptibly. "He wants Levin. He's here for Levin."

18

With the ongoing investigation into the disappearance of Alex Laughlin, Captain Dan Ward had ordered all hands on deck, meaning the night-shift officers. Lowell Abrams and Chris Decker had been on duty going on eighteen hours straight. Their return from the county jail where Sims awaited arraignment for the brutal murder of his wife was much anticipated. Though upon their arrival, both appeared on the verge of exhaustion.

Captain Ward stood in the bullpen, hands on his hips, eyeing the men as they entered. "Well, I have to say, boys, you two have looked better. I'm starting to think you ought to go home and try to catch a few hours' rest before we kick this thing into high gear."

"I might have to take you up on that offer, Captain," Abrams began. "I'm starting to feel like I've hit a brick wall. That said, we do have some news for you on the Sims front." He turned to Decker. "You want to fill him in?"

The more laidback and judicious Officer Decker began, "Sims

was more than a little reluctant to speak to us, but when we told him Laughlin went missing, he seemed keen on answering our questions."

"Did you promise him anything in return? A deal?" Ward asked.

"No, sir. Wasn't our promise to make," Decker replied. "He was, nevertheless, willing to talk because it seemed he wanted payback for how things went down." He returned to his desk and dropped into his chair. "Where are Thompson and Pruitt?"

"Heading back. Should be here any minute. They tell me we got us another visitor in town. Things are starting to heat up. So tell me, what did Sims have to say?"

Decker shot a glance to Abrams, who sat across from him. "There's no doubt in my mind that Sims killed his wife because he lost a shit ton of cash at a poker game in the backroom of the Crooked Horse."

"We suspected that." Ward's attention was diverted. "Oh, and here they are now. Good. You two are back just in time to hear what happened at County."

Riley made her way inside. "Maybe we'll be able to figure out why another stranger's arrived in town looking to keep tabs on Silas Levin."

"Is that so?" Abrams replied. "Interesting."

"How's that?" Ethan asked as he trailed behind Riley.

"Turns out, Sims had been involved in the last several games Silas Levin was running," Decker continued. "He started pulling in some big cash, then it all went south on him."

"I'll bet Levin planned it that way," Riley replied.

Decker looked at her. "That'd be my guess. So he keeps going to the games, keeps trying to win his money back, but then the last one, last week, apparently was the final straw. He made a bad bet and lost it all."

"Did he tell you who was at the game?" Riley asked.

"I have a list of names. Couldn't tell you if the names are aliases or not, but we'll run them. Point being, Sims says Levin's running a con. Sims lost his shirt, took it out on his wife, and you know the rest of the story."

"It's starting to make sense now." Riley moved in toward the others who had gathered around Decker's desk. "The man we saw, I didn't get his name, but something told me he's after Levin." Riley didn't need to clarify what that something was. Her colleagues were well aware of her special talent of insight. "If Levin's running a con, why? He only purchased the Crooked Horse, what, a year ago, maybe? Why go through all the renovations and opening up a new business just to risk it all getting shut down?"

"That's what we'll need to find out," Ward replied. "Could be he needs the money. Maybe business isn't as good as we think it is."

"That's very possible." Riley turned to Decker. "Let's run those names Sims gave you and see if any of them have a history with Levin. That'll give us a start. Anyone care to guess how long Levin's been running this operation?"

"From what Sims said, about three months or so," Abrams replied.

"Okay. So something happened to him three months ago that made him decide it was time to run the con. We need to know what that was. We already have a dead woman and a missing man we can tie back to Levin in some form," she continued. "I'm not waiting for the next body to turn up. It's time we get to the bottom of Levin's story."

"You heard the lady," Ward said. "Let's divvy up these names and see if we can get a hit. Thompson, you and Pruitt need to find the man from the restaurant. If you got a plate, run it. I want a tail on him. I want to know if he's going to see Levin like you believe he will."

"Shouldn't be too hard," Ethan said. "The guy's driving a new black Camaro with Illinois plates."

"Chicago?" Ward asked.

"If he's in with the rest of these guys, then most likely," Riley said. "Why?"

"I'll just need to let the lieutenant know because he's helping us track down the whereabouts of Meisner and Vaughan, the fellas we think might've had a hand in Laughlin's disappearance. Maybe there's a Chicago connection, I don't know, but I'll work on that. The rest of you have your orders." He started toward his office for a moment. "Actually, scratch that. I told Decker and Abrams to go catch a couple hours' rest. You two should really do that and then come back. After I get off the horn with the IPD, I'll start on the list of names. You two come back later tonight and we'll see what we're dealing with. We have ourselves a plan?"

"Yes, sir, Captain," Abrams replied.

"You got it, Cap. See you in a few," Decker said.

RILEY FOUND HERSELF BEHIND THE WHEEL OF HER PATROL car once again, with Ethan in the passenger seat. This time, they were on the lookout for the shiny black Camaro and the mystery man who drove it. "I wish we'd turned up more than a corporate owner on those plates."

"That would make our jobs too easy, Riley. At least we can confirm it's based in Chicago," Ethan replied.

"Well, we can hope this guy took us up on the recommendation to check in at the Ramada."

"You really think he's going to go there?" Ethan said.

"Hey, it's all we have right now. Better to rule it out. I'd like to go straight to Levin and talk to him, but..."

"Captain would have your head on a spike if you did that. You said it yourself. Nothing can change. Everyone has to keep to their routine so Levin doesn't realize what's happened. I would say this." He turned to her. "Jacob's going to have to say something. If tomorrow night happens, and he's there, Silas is going to wonder where Alex is. Don't you think it might look strange that Jacob didn't tell him the guy went missing?"

"Maybe, but the explanation could be that he'd decided to take a vacation."

"Riley, you can't be serious. No way Levin will buy that lame excuse. No. The sooner Jacob talks to Levin about this, the better, in my humble opinion."

She peered at him for a brief moment. "Fine. I'll tell him to stop by the Crooked Horse after work tonight and talk to him. Let him know what the deal is and if he still wants Jacob in the game tomorrow night."

"Good. Thank you. See? Sometimes I come up with good ideas."

She smiled at him. "I never said you didn't. You're a good cop, Ethan. No one's ever questioned that."

Ethan peered through the windshield. "Here we are. You want to take a drive through the lot to see if his car is here?"

"Yep. Doesn't look like there are a lot of cars here to begin with." She entered the parking lot and drove slowly through the near-empty space. "I'm not seeing it. You?"

"No. Nothing yet. Why don't you let me jump out and I'll run inside and have a word with the manager?"

"Sure. If he can let us know if he sees the car, that'll help." She rolled to a stop and Ethan hopped out.

"Be right back." Ethan disappeared inside the sliding glass double doors.

Riley pondered the fallout of Jacob becoming further involved in this underground gambling operation Silas Levin appeared to be running. With Alex Laughlin missing, she feared for Jacob's safety, but in order to find him, someone needed to be on the inside. Unfortunately, that someone was Jacob.

She spotted Ethan returning to the car, and as he pulled open the door and slipped inside, she blurted out the words. "He's going to have to wear a wire."

"Sorry. What's that?" Ethan closed the passenger door. "Who's wearing a wire?"

"Jacob. It's the only way we'll get anything hard against Levin and anyone else in that room who might know where Laughlin is."

"Okay. Do you want me to tell you what the manager said?"

Riley shook her head as if clearing it of all thoughts. "Yeah, sorry. What'd you find out?"

"Our man in the black Camaro has not shown up. But the manager said he would let us know if he did."

"Not what I was hoping to hear." She turned over the engine

and pulled away from the hotel. "We're going to have to drive around and hope that we spot him."

"You're thinking the Crooked Horse, aren't you?"

"So you *are* a mind reader." Riley headed onto the highway and toward the center of town.

"I know Ward mentioned this, but are you sure you want Jacob to wear a wire?" Ethan asked.

"I just don't see any other way. We have to know who's behind the kidnapping and I don't think it's Levin. The men who took him, I'm sure they don't work for Levin."

"I follow you, but there's a connection between the three of them and that's what we need," Ethan pressed on. "Riley, I know you understand how dangerous this could be for Jacob."

She shot him a brief glance. "I understand that I've had terrifying visions about him recently. I don't know if this is the reason or not, but I imagine it is. So yes, I understand a great deal what this could mean for Jacob. But if we do nothing, if we allow this game to continue, we'll lose Laughlin and Silas Levin will flee town quicker than you can say 'fold.'"

They reached the center of town once again and both peered into the distance in search of the elusive car.

"The bar's just ahead," Riley began. "I'm going to go down the side street here, just in case. I don't want anyone watching us driving slowly by."

Ethan gripped the hanging bar above his door and continued to gaze into the distance. "Slow up. Let me have a good look-see here." He squinted and studied the front of the bar as best he could from where Riley drove through. "I'm not seeing the car." He continued to survey the area. "Damn it."

"I don't see it either. Okay, here's the deal. I'll drop you back off at the station so you can take Gracie to the bus depot. I'll take another loop around town and see if I can spot him."

"You want to meet me back at the station then? I won't be but an hour, at the most."

"Sounds like a plan." Riley pulled out of the side street and headed back to the station.

WARD HELD HIS PHONE TO HIS EAR. "LIEUTENANT MOODY, you have saved the day. Thank you so very much for your assistance. I'll wait for the email and will be in touch." He ended the call wearing a wide smile and typed in commands on his computer. "Let's see what we have here." Ward placed his glasses on his face and studied the emails that had just arrived from IPD.

He opened the first one with the name Eugene Vaughan as the subject header. He already knew a little about Vaughan, but the lieutenant was working on finding a connection to Silas Levin. And it seemed he'd found success.

"Well, I'll be damned. I knew it." Ward leaned back and folded his arms across his chest. "You're working for Dennis Ackerman, a known associate and co-conspirator of Silas Levin from back in the day."

Ward quickly opened the other email that had just arrived. This one was about the other man by the name of Anton Meisner. He began to read the report and shook his head. "Damn. So he's got both of you here keeping tabs on Levin. Why? And why the hell would you take the kid? More importantly, what did you do with him?" He picked up the phone again. "Lieutenant, sorry to bother you again. Hey, I just perused the information you sent over. Now that we know there's a connection to this Dennis Ackerman, what can you tell me about him, aside from his stint cheating at the World Series of Poker tourney back in 2013?" He paused to listen. "Uh-huh. And you feel pretty confident Levin was in on the deal but managed to make a clean getaway?" He shook his head. "I see. Any employment history on Ackerman? I sure would like to talk to someone who's seen him recently." Ward peered through his window and spotted Jacob pull into the lot. "Okay, well, thank you. We'll keep working things on our end. Sure do appreciate the help. Speak soon." He ended the call and made his way to the bullpen.

"Jacob. What can I do for you? Didn't expect to see you this afternoon. Riley's not here, I'm afraid."

"I know she's not. I just got off the phone with her."

"Okay, then. What's going on?" He turned on his heel. "Why don't we sit down in my office."

Jacob followed him and took a seat opposite Ward. "Riley thinks I need to speak to Silas this afternoon and tell him about Alex."

"She mentioned that to me. I can see the concern on your face. You're worried. Frankly, I don't blame you one bit."

"Look, Dan, I have no idea what I've stepped into. It certainly wasn't intentional and now I'm trying to find my co-worker who wasn't really a friend and I seem to be digging myself deeper into a hole."

"Forgive me, son, but you did say you wanted to help and that you were the only one who could."

"I did."

"Then what's the problem besides getting cold feet, which by the way, son, doesn't make you a coward or anything. Don't want you to think that at all. You're not one of us. And by that, I mean you're not an officer of the law. You're not trained for this regardless of what your past efforts have shown."

"I guess I felt that if I waited until the game tomorrow night and told Silas then, I'd be protected, you know? I don't think he'd do anything in a room full of people during a so-called friendly card game."

"I take your point. Go on," Ward said.

"If I go in alone—today—what protections do I have?"

"Are you asking me to send you in there armed?"

"Maybe, yeah."

Ward pursed his lips until they turned white. "I hear what you're saying, but I'd be hard-pressed to agree with you, with one exception."

"And that is?"

"This boils down to Riley's visions, doesn't it? That's why you want to go in armed."

"You and I both know she's right more often than not about these things."

Ward nodded. "Yes, yes she is, but you also know they can manifest themselves out of her own fear of what's to come. Not necessarily what will be." He pushed back in his chair. "But I'll tell you what. I'll go with you on this front, so I'm going to make sure you're protected. I have something I personally own. Can't be police-issue, you understand that, right?"

"Of course. Thank you, Dan. I'll feel a whole lot better."

"I imagine that's true. When are you planning on going in for a visit?"

"As soon as we're finished here."

"Then let's get you saddled up."

~

THE CROOKED HORSE HAD ONLY JUST OPENED ITS DOORS IN preparation for the Happy Hour crowd, which was due in at any moment. Jacob pushed inside and waited for his eyes to adjust to the dim lighting that was its trademark setting of the mood. He instinctively placed his hand atop the 9-millimeter tucked in the back of his jeans, beneath his white undershirt and the opened button-down shirt over top. The gun felt foreign to him as though he carried some sort of crutch. He supposed that was what this was, a crutch. Nevertheless, it was there as a means to provide protection in the event Silas Levin didn't like what he had to say.

Jacob spotted Silas behind the bar, setting up the glasses and top-shelf liquor, and made his approach. "Afternoon, Mr. Levin."

He spun around. "Jacob Biggs. What are you doing here? Wasn't expecting to see you until tomorrow night, as per our arrangement."

"I needed to talk to you about something. Something I think could—will—impact your plans for tomorrow."

Silas, with his perfectly styled hair and slender physique, leaned over the bar top. His arms braced against it, revealing their well-toned shape. "Is that so?"

"My friend, Alex, no one's seen him in more than a day. Every-one's starting to worry. His family, other co-workers, friends. And me. Which is why I'm here."

Silas pulled upright again and folded his arms, widening his stance. "You're telling me he's missing?"

"It's looking that way, Mr. Levin. I'm really concerned about him. Have you heard from him, by any chance?"

"Why would he have reached out to me?"

"I—I don't know. I've been asking around, you know. But it seems he hasn't been in contact with anyone. His wife's getting pretty upset. They have two young kids."

"So what you're telling me is that I shouldn't expect to see him at the game tomorrow night. Is that what I'm hearing?"

"Honestly, I'm really hoping he'll turn up before then. Maybe he's just gone out on some bender, I don't know."

Silas nodded. "Well, you understand that just because he might not show his face doesn't mean you aren't still obligated to. We did have a deal."

"Yes, sir, I know that. I have every intention of holding up my end of the bargain. I'm just saying, without Alex, I don't know how things will go down, that's all."

"What about your girlfriend? She's a cop, if I've heard correctly. Is she out looking for him?"

Jacob felt his heart jump into his throat. He hadn't known Silas was aware of his relationship and now telling him there was an active investigation just didn't seem like a wise decision. But lying, well that could open up another can of worms. "I don't know, actually. I didn't want to make a whole thing of it."

"You didn't? Then why on earth are you here?" Silas's eyes bored into him, searching for the cracks in his story.

"I thought you should know. That's all. I didn't want you to be caught off-guard tomorrow in the event he doesn't show."

"I see. You were protecting me. That's very kind of you, Jacob, but I don't see this as a problem as such. I just see it as you'll have to pick up the slack. I assume you can handle it?"

"Of course. Yes. That won't be a problem."

"Good. Then there's nothing more to discuss. Tomorrow night,

10pm. I'll see you then." Silas wore a pleasant smile, but his eyes remained hardened and trained on Jacob.

"See you tomorrow." Jacob made his way to the exit.

Silas watched as the door opened and light spilled into the bar. Upon the door closing again, he retrieved his cell phone and dialed a number. "Mr. Foster, sorry to bother you."

"No bother at all, Silas. To what do I owe the pleasure?"

"I wanted to be sure we were all on the same page. I seem to have a small situation brewing and I wanted you to know that our arrangement still stands."

"A situation? Something I should know about?"

"You sure you don't already know, Eli?"

"I haven't a God damn clue what you're talking about, Silas. But you better check your tone."

"Sorry. No offense. I just wanted to touch base with you. Nothing changes. This minor hiccup will sort itself out on its own, I'm quite sure. You have a good day and I'll see you soon." He ended the call. "If it wasn't you, then what the hell happened to the kid?"

19

The whereabouts of the stranger in the Camaro remained unsolved, though Ethan was hopeful the hotel manager would contact him should the man turn up at his establishment. It was the best shot they had to put a tail on him. Though it seemed clear he was there for Silas Levin, at least, according to Riley and her sixth sense, as it were.

For now, however, as late afternoon arrived and the air grew oppressive, he stood on the front porch of Ellen Thompson's home. The brief interlude to take Gracie to the bus depot only complicated Ethan's emotional state. Riley and the rest of the team were back at the station, ready to pull an all-nighter, if necessary, to solve the case of the missing Alex Laughlin.

The door opened and Gracie, with her dark hair pulled back in a ponytail, wearing a form-fitting tank top and shorts, appeared. "Hi. Come in. I'm just about ready."

Ethan stepped inside and noticed her bags sitting by the front door. He wished she wasn't leaving. Maybe if she were to stay, his feelings for her would evolve with time. Of course, that was wildly unfair to her, but it wasn't going to happen in any event. Gracie was a determined young woman with an amazing future ahead of her. He began to feel that future would not include him. "Afternoon, Ellen. How are you?"

Ellen appeared from the kitchen, looking as though she was ready for bed. "Ethan, I appreciate you driving Gracie. I know how busy you are."

"It's my pleasure."

"Riley said you all were going to be working late tonight. Does it have anything to do with that man who came into the diner for lunch today?"

He shied away, peering down at his feet. "Well..."

"You can't say, can you?"

"It's best if I don't. But please know that you're safe and there's nothing for you to worry about."

"I stopped worrying about myself a long time ago. But a mother never stops worrying about her children."

Gracie descended the stairs with a backpack slung over her shoulder. "Sorry about that. We should head out. Don't want to miss the bus."

"Have a good evening, Ellen." Ethan grabbed Gracie's bags and stepped through the door.

"Goodbye, baby." Ellen reached around Gracie's shoulders for a full embrace. "You call me when you arrive, okay?"

"I will, Mom. I promise."

"I'm so proud of you. You've accomplished so much."

"With the help of my siblings. I'll pay them back one day." Gracie kissed her mother's cheek. "Bye, Mom, I love you." She caught up to Ethan outside.

"All good?" he asked.

"Yep."

He opened the passenger door for her and closed it as she stepped in. The lid of the trunk was raised and he placed her bags inside, slamming it shut again.

Gracie waited while he slipped into the driver's seat and turned the engine. "Thanks for taking me, Ethan."

"You already thanked me, but you're welcome." He pulled away from the curb. "Did you say goodbye to your brother?"

"I did, and the kids. I'll miss all of them. Riley too."

He felt her eyes on him, studying him, trying to read his current state of emotions.

"I wish things had been different between us, Ethan. I want you to know that."

"Different?" he asked without taking his eyes off the road.

"Yes. I wish we'd connected on a deeper level. But it's okay. It would've only complicated things. Long-distance relationships are hard enough without having a third-party involved."

This time, he turned his sights to her. "I told you, Gracie, there's nothing between me and your sister."

"I know that. It doesn't mean you don't want there to be. And honestly, Riley would never admit it, but I think she likes having you to fall back on."

"What? Why would you say that?"

"Because it's true."

"She's with Jacob. She loves him."

"Yes. She loves him. They have history, but he broke her heart and I don't think she has it in her to truly forgive him. The way we grew up, Ethan." She shook her head. "Riley, all of us, had been put through the wringer. Mostly her because of—her gift. Which, by the way, I hate calling it that because it implies she wanted it or that it makes her special. She never wanted it. No one would ever want something like that. And now, with my half-brother..."

"What?"

"Nothing. My point is, forgiveness is a wonderful concept but difficult in practice. Riley needs you, Ethan. And for that reason alone, we could never have worked out."

Maybe she was right. Riley was going to keep him on a short leash not out of some egotistical need, but out of fear of losing Jacob. It wasn't right and it wasn't fair, and in all likelihood, she didn't know she was doing it. Clearly, Gracie could see it. Perhaps Jacob could too. It wasn't going to be a question Ethan would ever pose to him or Riley, for that matter. So what was the solution? Could he find another and force Riley's hand? It was too much to think about right now. He was exhausted. They had a critical investigation to work on and his personal life had to be put on hold for the foreseeable future.

"Here we are." Ethan pulled into the parking lot of the bus depot and cut the engine. "I'll get your bags from the trunk."

Gracie stepped out of the car and hoisted her backpack over her shoulder.

With both bags in his hand, he started toward the entrance. "You ready?"

"Right behind you." She trailed a few steps and upon reaching the entrance, she jogged ahead. "Here, I'll get the door. Your hands are full."

"Thanks." Ethan walked inside and set down the bags in the waiting area. "I guess this is it."

"I guess it is." She stood inches from him.

"I do care for you, Gracie."

"I know you do." She raised on her tiptoes and pressed her lips gently against his. When she pulled away, she continued. "Maybe in another life."

"Maybe," he replied.

Gracie rolled her bags toward the back of the depot and disappeared beyond the doors.

GAGE PARKER PULLED HIS CAR IN FRONT OF THE CROOKED Horse and stepped outside. He surveyed the lot and nodded. "Business looks good." He'd stopped by earlier in the day but didn't spot Silas Levin, and after a quick drink, he made his way to the Ramada. Now in a fresh change of more casual attire, he'd returned in hopes of making his presence known to Mr. Levin. He tugged on his t-shirt and hiked up his Levi's before sauntering into the bar. He pushed open the doors. "Well, well, well. Looks a little livelier in here now." He made his way to the bar and perched on the edge of a stool.

"What can I get for you, sir?" the bartender asked.

"An old-fashioned with your finest bourbon, please." Gage peered around. "I don't suppose your boss is in now?"

"Mr. Levin? He's in the back. Let me get you your drink and I'll go track him down."

"I'd appreciate that, thank you very much." His toothy smile was bright enough to light a ten-foot radius around him.

And just as the bartender had returned with the old-fashioned, Silas appeared.

"Your ears must've been burning," Gage said.

"I'm sorry? Do we know each other?" Silas asked.

"We run in similar circles." He sipped on the drink. "Oh, now that is superb, my good man."

"Thank you." The bartender turned to Silas with a concerned look on his face.

"Similar circles, you say?" Silas approached him from behind the bar. "Who, might I ask?"

"I'm pretty sure you know a man by the name of Foster. Eli Foster?"

Silas's face drained of color. "Sure. I know him. We're business acquaintances."

"Business acquaintances. That's one way to put it." Gage captured his eyes and refused to let go.

"He sent you, did he?"

"Mr. Foster merely wants to be sure your arrangement is still good. You know, that you're keeping everything running smoothly."

"I am indeed. And I've kept him abreast of my progress," Silas replied. "I'll tell you what, you be sure and let Eli know that on your way home, would you?"

"Oh, I'm not going home just yet. This is a quaint little town you've got here. I think I'll hang around for a day or two and see the sights." Gage threw back the rest of his drink and firmly set the glass on the bar. With a pronounced licking of his lips, he boisterously declared, "Delicious."

ETHAN'S THOUGHTS WERE OCCUPIED WITH GRACIE, THAT was, until he passed by the Crooked Horse on his way back to the station. He slowed his car and spotted the sleek black Camaro parked in front of the bar. "Holy shit. There you are."

He snatched his cell phone and dialed. "Hey. He's here. Our Camaro guy is here at the Crooked Horse."

Riley pulled away the phone from her ear. "Captain, it's Pruitt. He's got a visual on the Camaro."

"Where?" Ward quickstepped to her desk.

"The Crooked Horse."

"Okay," Ward placed his hand on his chin. "Tell him to keep out of sight, but if the guy leaves, I want him to follow. We can't afford to get sidetracked again."

Riley nodded and returned to the phone call. "Captain says to stay put and follow him when he leaves."

Ethan furrowed his brow. "Shouldn't I go inside or something?"

"No. That guy is going to wonder why the same cop who trailed him into the diner is now showing up at the bar. No. Captain's right. This is our best chance to keep tabs on him this time and see where he goes next. Are you good with that?"

"I'm good. I'll keep in touch." Ethan ended the call. "Shit. I can't just sit here and wait." Maybe this was his opportunity to show the captain that he didn't need Riley holding his hand. He was a damn good cop, and right now, a man was missing. And whoever that guy inside was had something to do with it, he was sure. One thing Riley was right about, the man would recognize Ethan from the diner. So what was the plan? How could he get what he needed without jeopardizing the case?

A knowing grin surfaced as he recalled the bag he kept in the trunk of his patrol car. Civilian clothes. He rarely needed them and they'd probably been in that bag for weeks, but he could change out of uniform, go inside, and the man would probably not even look twice at him.

Ethan pulled his car around to the alleyway behind the row of stores and retrieved the clothes. A quick change and he looked like any other guy on the street. A ball cap would've been nice, but he didn't have one in his bag. "This will have to do." He locked up his car and started on foot to the bar.

He made it to the door and stood poised to enter but stopped short before opening it. "Go inside, sit at the bar, and listen. That's all you have to do." Ethan had slightly less experience than Riley had under her belt. While he'd been faced with troubling situations, he mostly had Riley to fall back on. Not this time. And maybe it was about time.

Ethan opened the door and casually walked inside, keeping his head down just a little to avoid direct eye contact with anyone. He didn't know where the man would be or if he would be engaged in conversation. The idea was to blend. At six feet one inch, that was a little hard, but if he didn't, it could mean putting himself in danger. The captain would definitely be pissed then and so would Riley.

The bar was just ahead, and as he briefly peered up, he spotted the man in question. It was the peculiar stranger Riley was sure was after Silas Levin. Only there was no Levin, not at the bar, at least. Meaning any significant conversation might've already occurred. Regardless, Ethan pressed on and sat down at the bar.

The bartender approached. "What can I get you?"

The look on his face suggested he was about to ID Ethan. He needed to think fast. "Bud Light, please." He widened his eyes and faintly shook his head.

The bartender creased his brow with confusion. "Sure, man. I'll get that for you right away."

It was a small town and this place was one of only two bars. The other one was generally frequented by the older crowd. Ethan was here just the other night with Jacob. He feared the bartender would recognize him. But he narrowly avoided the situation.

The bartender returned. "Here you go—sir. Start a tab?"

Ethan retrieved his wallet and handed him a credit card. "Thanks." The look on his face conveyed his heart-felt gratitude and the bartender nodded and smiled in reply. It seemed he'd figured it out.

As Ethan tossed back a swig of beer, a booming laugh sounded. He turned to his right and realized it was the stranger and his raucous laughter.

"Did you see that?" Gage Parker raised his bottle of beer toward the TV mounted above the bar. "He missed the shot! How much are they paying that guy anyway, am I right?" He nudged the man next to him.

"Sure buddy."

"Boy, what a shitty team you people got here. Now the Bulls, they were something back in the day. They aren't shit now, but you can't beat what old Phil Jackson did for them."

"What the hell are you talking about?" the man next to him piped up. "The Pacers are a respectable fifth in the conference. What are your Bulls at? Like 15th?"

"13th." Gage regarded the man with empty eyes.

"Whatever."

Ethan could tell the Camaro man had had a few already. What he didn't know was what kind of drunk he was. However, that question might be resolved soon. Silas Levin was making his way behind the bar. This was why he was here, and he needed something. Things were about to get interesting.

"Hey, man, maybe it's time for you to head out. We can catch up tomorrow." Levin's silky, placid tone would've convinced anyone to concede.

"I bet you'd like that, wouldn't you, Silas? I have my orders. I'm supposed to keep my eye on you." Gage pulled down the bottom lid of his right eye and leaned over the bar.

They know each other, Ethan thought.

"Eli thinks you got something going and maybe he wants in on it," Gage pressed on.

"Okay, I think you've had enough." Silas reached for the beer bottle.

Gage's hand clamped down on it. "I'll tell you when I've had enough. You think you're the one giving orders here?"

"I think this is my bar and my responsibility to cut off anyone who's had too much to drink. Why don't you go sleep it off, Gage, and come back tomorrow, when you've had time to recover."

Now Ethan had two names. Eli and Gage. What were the odds he'd get a last name out of either of these guys?

Gage stood from his stool, swaying a little. "Fine. Your beer is too warm anyway. But I'll catch you on the flip side, Silas." He started to leave and fired off a look at Ethan.

"What the hell you looking at?"

Ethan's stomach dropped and his heart raced. "Nothing, man. Have a good night." He kept his head low but could feel Gage's stare. He sipped on his beer and waited, not looking back.

"Buncha assholes around here." Gage pushed through the doors.

Ethan released the breath he'd held on to and peered up again.

"What are you doing here, Officer Pruitt?" Silas walked toward him. "Took me a minute to recognize you since you're not in uniform."

"Just enjoying a beer, man. Is that all right?"

"Hey, it's fine by me. You're the ones who've been harassing me for weeks. You know who that guy was?" He nodded toward the exit.

"Nope." Ethan tossed back another swig, doing his best to appear aloof.

"Me neither." Silas held his gaze for another moment before returning to the bartender.

Ethan had managed to avoid detection by the Camaro man, but Silas had figured it out. Right now, though, maybe that didn't matter, because he had two names.

20

The bullpen of the stationhouse was littered with files, reports; any leads they could track down to find Alex Laughlin. And still—nothing.

"We're running out of time." Riley pushed off the chair and paced the room. "We ran the names and found the relationship between Ackerman and Levin, but we're no closer to finding Alex than we were this morning. What if they kill him?"

"You're the one with the power," Abrams began. "Why the hell can't you find him?"

She whipped around. "Because it doesn't work that way, okay? I wish it did, but it doesn't."

"Back off, man," Decker said. "We're all tired, but there's no need to lash out. If Riley could do something, don't you think she would?"

"Okay, we're not getting anywhere here," Ward interjected. "Riley, sit down. Abrams, cool your jets. Getting pissed off isn't going to help us find Laughlin."

Ethan pushed through the doors. "I have names."

Riley spun around. "What? Why aren't you in uniform? You're supposed to be tailing the Camaro guy. Don't tell me you lost him."

"He's staying at the Ramada. The manager confirmed it with me. And his name is Gage."

Ward approached him. "How do you know that?"

"Because Silas Levin called him that."

Ward raised his hands. "Okay, you're going to have to back up and start again. What the hell is going on and why are you in plain clothes? You were in uniform when you left to take Gracie to the bus."

"I was. I changed. Look, that's not the important part. What's important is that Gage is the Camaro guy and he's working for someone named Eli. I don't have any last names."

Ward moved toward him, standing inches from Ethan's face, and placed his hands on his hips. "Did you engage this man? You had orders to follow him. That's all. Boy, you'd better have a good explanation for this."

"I'm sorry, Captain. I—I didn't want to sit there and follow the guy. I knew he'd be going to the hotel, so what was the point?"

"The point was to see if he was meeting anyone," Riley said. "Jesus, Ethan, do you know what could've happened?"

"Last I checked, Riley, I was a cop. I had a hunch and I followed through. Kinda thought that was my job."

"What went down, Pruitt?" Ward demanded.

"I called Riley to tell her the guy was at the Crooked Horse."

"Which was when I told you Captain said to stay put," Riley replied.

"Based on what you said at the diner, Riley, I knew he was

there to see Silas Levin. I had to know what their conversation would entail. So I changed into the plain clothes I keep in a bag in my cruiser and went inside. I wasn't going in there in uniform, that was certain. Levin already thinks we're harassing him."

Ward folded his arms and spread his stance. "Continue."

"I sat at the bar, saw the man, and ordered a beer. He didn't recognize me. I was fine. He's something else, though, I'll tell you. Loud, obnoxious, and a little drunk. Anyway, he drew the attention of Silas, who I guess had been in the back or something. So Silas came out and told the guy he'd had enough and asked him to leave, basically. And he said his name—Gage. So Gage starts putting up a fuss. He then mentions a man by the name of Eli and how Eli told him to keep tabs on Silas."

"And then what?" Abrams asked.

"Nothing. Gage spouted off a few more things and even approached me for a hot minute, but he didn't recognize me. Unfortunately, Silas did, after Gage took off. I smoothed things over. It's fine."

"I doubt that." Ward started toward Abrams' desk. "Do we have anything with those names on them? Eli or Gage?" Ward shot a glance to Ethan. "You took an unnecessary risk tonight, Pruitt."

"I know I did, Captain, and..."

"And it's a good thing you did. This could be the break we needed."

Riley shook her head. "If this Gage hadn't been drinking, he would've realized who you were. We'd seen him only hours earlier."

"I'm okay, Riley. Everything turned out the way it was supposed to."

"This time." Riley approached Abrams' desk. "If Gage is working for a man named Eli, we should cross-reference the name with any of Silas' known associates. Same as we did for Ackerman."

"Ackerman had a record," Decker began. "And we don't have a last name."

Ethan advanced and placed his hand on Riley's shoulders. She inhaled a quick breath in response.

"What?" He took his hand away. "What is it? Are you okay?"

The team stared at her like she was a circus freak. "I'm fine. I just—saw something. A piece of something." She turned to him. "You said Silas knew who you were."

"That's right. He said we've been harassing him."

"I saw him looking at you just now. His eyes. Ethan, he owes money and he's scared."

"Scared of who?" Decker asked.

"Eli, maybe? I don't know. But he must be pretty afraid for me to pick it up from Ethan. He fears for his life."

Ward nodded. "Okay, here's what we're going to do. I know it's late. I know you're all tired and want to go home."

"Not me, Cap. I got plenty of shut-eye earlier." Abrams smoothed back his hair and wore arrogance on his face.

"Besides Abrams. We're all exhausted. But I think the way we find out what Levin is afraid of is to search records on his bar. Riley, if he owes someone money, it's likely to be this Eli character. Why else send someone to keep an eye on him?"

"But this doesn't seem to have anything to do with finding Alex," Riley pressed on.

"It might, in a round-about way. I don't know yet. What I do know is that we have to determine how Silas paid for the bar, the renovations, the whole shebang. He's a gambler, at least, he was. He must know a lot of shady people. People who lend money and break legs if they don't get it back."

"Or worse," Abrams replied.

"Exactly." Ward eyed the team. "We find out how he got the money for his bar and I'll bet we'll find out who Eli is."

"Then what? How do we get to Alex?" Riley asked. "He has to remain our focus or else..."

"I know. But this will all tie together. I'm sure of it, based on what you're seeing. So let's dig into his finances and see what we can turn up."

Alex remained bound in the chair, bobbing his head as he tried to stop himself from drifting off to sleep. He had no idea of the time, only that it was pitch black outside. They'd fed him and had given him water. He wasn't suffering, though his family must've been. If only he could get word to his wife. She must have been beside herself, not knowing what to tell the kids. The notion that they were scared and worried made his eyes sting with tears. The whole thing had gone sour so quickly and he didn't know if there was a way out. Right now, it seemed no one was looking for him.

But they'd told him after tomorrow that things would change. The game was tomorrow night. They wanted to keep him far away from Silas Levin, but to what end? None of this was making sense.

A light flickered on and Alex squinted until his vision adjusted. The man who had been tasked with looking after Alex had returned. "What time is it?"

"It's late," the man replied.

"Why are you here?" Alex asked.

He continued his approach and walked around the back of Alex's chair.

"What are you doing?"

"I'm untying you." With a pocket knife, he cut the ropes and freed Alex's hands. He continued around the front and cut the zip ties from his ankles.

"I don't understand. I thought I was going home in a day or two."

"Going home?" The man shook his head. "That's the last place you're going."

Adrenaline exploded inside him. "What are you talking about?" This was it. They weren't going to let him leave.

"Stand up," the man said.

He hesitated.

"Stand up. Now."

Alex took in a deep breath and rose from the chair. "I had to do what he said. I didn't have a choice."

"We know. Look, here's the deal. Things have changed. We've been made aware of developments that will impact our plans."

His heart began to slow again. Thinking he might be shot at any moment apparently wasn't going to be the case.

"You're going to be taken back to town. And you and your buddy will be in that game tomorrow. But here's the deal: you're going to go against Silas's demands. You won't lose and, in fact, you have to win. You have to take all of it."

"I don't know what kind of poker player you think I am. I'm average at best."

"Really? Is that how you want to play this? You think we don't know that you've played online poker for the past six years and have raked in a couple hundred thousand dollars? You only stopped because the Feds made it too hard to get access to the sites. You used that money to help buy your perfect little house in that backwater town. And you moved there to stay under the radar because the Feds wanted you to help them find other players. Rat them out."

"I wasn't going to rat anyone out."

"Wise decision. Point being, you're better than you've let on. And you're going to take everything from Silas Levin. There are people who want more from him than even we do. We hadn't anticipated their arrival. You'll be the catalyst; they'll finish the task."

"How do I explain my absence?"

"You can contact your wife, but if you go home, you'll be putting your entire family at risk. The people who are there already will be watching, make no mistake about that. My suggestion is to tell her you're safe, and in a day or two, you'll be able to explain everything. Tell her to keep her mouth shut. That's the best thing for her to do right now. As far as the cops are concerned, because we know they're looking for you, you'll tell them you had to leave town for a short while."

"What about my car? Don't you think they're going to wonder why I left my car and my cell phone?"

"Hey, people disappear for all sorts of reasons. Family life, financial troubles. Dude, I don't care what you say, but you sure as hell better make it believable."

"If I can't go home, where am I supposed to go?"

"You have friends, don't you?"

Alex thought of the friends who would let him crash on their sofas and he couldn't think of more than one or two. "I don't see how this is going to work. I've been gone for how many days?"

"You've been gone for less than 48 hours. The cops won't do shit so long as you give them a reasonable explanation. If they start sticking their nose into this, you can kiss your family goodbye, do you understand what I'm telling you?"

Alex nodded. "So I go back to town, make up some bullshit story I took off for personal reasons. Marital trouble or some shit. Then I take Silas Levin for everything at the game tomorrow night. What about my friend? The one who was with me when you people decided to turn my life upside down."

"You're going to convince him to do the same thing."

"Christ. Are you shitting me?" Alex replied.

"Look, he's got a cop for a girlfriend. Dumbass should've gone to her at the first sign of the shady deal with Levin, but he didn't."

"Because I asked him not to. I knew Levin wasn't screwing around."

"Well, at least you got that right. The people who've come to town wanting something from Levin aren't going to get it. And they'll handle it from there. My boss's hands will be clean. And after that, you can go about your merry way." He started to leave. "Find yourself a place to hole up for the night. I'll dump you back into that shithole town." He stopped and turned squarely to Alex. "You fuck this up, there won't be any second chances."

ETHAN RUSHED TO HIS FEET. "I FOUND SOMETHING." HE walked to the printer and yanked off two pages. "Here, I found this in public records."

"What is it?" Ward ripped the papers from his grip.

"Bankruptcy," Ethan added. "Silas Levin filed for bankruptcy three years ago."

"Before he purchased the bar." Riley made her way to Ethan's desk. "I wish we could get hold of his banking records."

"Not without a warrant," Abrams replied as he sat at his desk. "And we don't have nearly enough to request one of those."

"Not yet." Decker stood and walked toward Ethan and the others. "Let me see." Ward handed him the report. "So he bought the bar last year, sank a ton of money into renovations."

"Where did he get that money?" Riley asked. "There's only one answer. Eli."

"Okay, how do we prove that?" Ward asked. "We need something with Eli's name on it. A company name, anything."

"Uh, Cap, I think I may have something here." Abrams slowly rose from his chair. "I checked out the permits issued for the renovations and several of them were issued to a company by the name of Chi-Town Builders."

"Are you kidding me?" Riley looked at Ethan. "Wasn't that the name of the company that the Camaro is registered to?"

"Yep."

"Please tell me the owner of that company is Eli something or other," Ward asked.

"Foster." Abrams eyed his colleagues. "Eli Foster."

"Bingo." Ward appeared triumphant. "Foster's company gets the contract for the renovations, bails out Silas Levin, and now Levin is in debt to him. What's Foster's background?"

"I'm checking the database now." Abrams feverishly tapped on his keyboard. "Okay, according to Chicago PD records, Eli Foster served time for money laundering. Had a couple of shell companies. Don't know how they were financed. Got released after a year and that's all she wrote. Nothing pops up on him until the articles of incorporation on his company back in 2014."

"A couple of years before Levin purchased the bar," Ward added. "We know Silas has connections in Chicago. This was clearly one of them. But that doesn't explain how Dennis Ackerman and his cronies resurfaced or why."

"There may not be a connection between Foster and Ackerman. Levin was involved in the poker arena years before he purchased the bar. He had to have had something going with Ackerman and Ackerman served time for it. That much we know," Riley said.

"So all of this is just a coincidence?" Abrams asked. "All these people converging on our little town at once?"

"I don't think so." Riley sat on the edge of her desk. "Levin started this backroom game, what, a couple of months ago?"

"Something like that," Decker replied. "Then we had Sims go nuts and take out his wife a week ago."

"Yeah. So things in the game must've been getting pretty high-stakes by that point," Riley added. "Could be the bar isn't bringing in enough to pay off the loans we suspect he must've received from Eli Foster. I mean, he dumped a ton of money into that place. Just look at it."

"Right," Ward began. "Folks around here won't pay top dollar, so he had to lower his prices to keep customers coming in. Losing money hand over fist, I'll bet."

"He starts this game because he knows poker. He knows how to cheat at it and get away with it," Ethan said. "It's starting to make sense now."

"He's using it to make money to pay off his debt," Decker

added. "Only things were getting out of hand with the death of Sims' wife. So he started looking for help and he got it from Alex."

"Unwillingly, I'm sure," Riley continued. "And then he managed to rope Jacob into his scheme as well."

"Okay, but how did Ackerman find out this was going on?" Decker asked. "Where's the connection there? What brought him and his people to town?"

Riley shook her head. "I don't know. If we find that out, we'll probably find Alex."

21

In the dreamy hours of the night, en route to a grey dawn, Alex Laughlin knocked on the door. His heavy and blood-shot eyes squinted at the burning porch light. Stubble dotted his face and worry lines had deepened on his forehead. He appeared to have aged five years over the past two days.

His wife, Zoe, cracked open the door only a sliver. "Oh my God. Alex." She slammed it shut again to release the chain and pulled it open. She thrust her arms around him.

In his weakened state, Alex stumbled back but regained his stance. "It's okay. It's okay. I'm home." He held on to her like he hadn't done in years, maybe ever. Her hair smelled of rosewater and her nightgown was silky smooth. "I'm so sorry."

She pulled back angrily. "Where have you been? What the hell happened? Why didn't you call me?" Tears streamed down her cheeks as she clenched her fists and lightly pounded on his chest. "I thought you were dead."

"I know. Let's go inside. Please."

She stepped aside to let him in and closed the door.

"I can't even imagine what you've been through these past two days. I—I wanted to reach out."

"Why? Why didn't you?" Her emotions climbed to the surface again as her voice quivered and tears continued to leave salty trails along her face and down her neck.

"I got tangled up in something and I can't say what right now, but I need you to trust me." Alex hadn't slept more than a few hours during his capture. He hadn't showered, his black hair required a comb, and while he wore fresher clothes, they too had begun to reek of body odor. "I need some water." He shuffled into the dimly lit kitchen and grabbed a bottle from the fridge, gulping it down until not a single drop remained.

"Alex, you have to tell me what's going on. Are you in danger?" She followed him into the kitchen. "Are we in danger?"

He recalled the words of his captor. *Don't go home unless you want to risk your family's safety.* "Not if I can help it."

"What's that supposed to mean? Jesus, Alex. We need to call the cops." She reached for her cell phone on the kitchen desk.

"No!" He rushed toward her and swiped the phone from her hands. "You can't. I have to handle this on my own. But I promise you, I will handle it. I just need for you to not say anything. Not to the cops, not to anyone."

"I don't understand. Are you just going to stay here and, what, hide out or something?"

"No. I'm going to go to work, like always. I'm going to tell everyone that I left of my own volition; family problems, financial, whatever, and that now I've returned."

"The cops have been looking for you. You understand that,

right? Your boss—everyone. You're going to tell them you took off on your own? Without your car or your phone?"

"I know how this must sound."

"I don't think you do." Zoe wandered through the kitchen with apparent confusion. "What the hell is going on, Alex? It's me, your wife. You have to tell me everything."

He approached her and took her hands. "I want to, I swear I do, but I can't. Not yet. If you don't trust me on this, I don't know what will happen."

JACOB ROUSED AT THE SOUND OF THE FRONT DOOR OPENING. HE stood from the sofa and walked toward the foyer when Riley entered.

"You're still awake?" She closed the door behind her. "You didn't have to wait up."

"Yes, I did." He pulled her into an embrace and kissed her lips. "It's four in the morning. I was beginning to think you weren't coming home at all."

"I should've called. I'm sorry. I thought you'd be asleep."

Jacob started back into the living room. "How can I sleep? I assume I'll still be in on that game tomorrow night. By the look on your face, it doesn't appear much progress has been made."

"It has, but maybe not the right kind of progress." She sat down next to him on the sofa. "Jacob, we found out that Silas Levin owes money and that appears to be the reason he started up the high-stakes poker games. It was how he made his living back in the day. He was a con man."

"What about Alex?" He asked.

"I wish I had news. Decker and Abrams analyzed the shoe prints from around Alex's 4Runner, but it didn't tell us much. We got us a size ten and eleven, but when we compared it to the photos Ethan took that night, well, it was too difficult to know for certain. Regardless, we have names of who we suspect are his abductors, but no idea of a location of where they might be holding him."

"Did you consider the idea he might already be dead?" Jacob's gaze hardened.

"We did. The good news is that scenario seems unlikely given the type of people we think we're dealing with. These guys don't appear to be murderers, just cheats and thieves."

"So, I take it we're going to let this thing play out and hope we aren't too late to find Alex."

"Yes. That appears to be our only move right now. I wish it wasn't. I wish there was more I could do."

"I take it as a good sign you can't do more, that you can't see more. If you could, it might mean Alex is dead. We both know how it works for you. Sometimes it's easier if the person can show you things from, you know, beyond or whatever."

Riley appeared deflated. When it mattered most, when a life was at stake, it seemed her so-called gift was virtually useless. "Maybe we should just try to get a couple of hours of sleep. I don't know what's going to happen tomorrow—today, actually. But we need to be sharp and ready for anything. Alex's life could depend on it. And so could yours."

Jacob followed her to their bedroom. The small room was decorated in floral and with soft and pretty things around, and it made him feel loved. It was everything Riley tried hard to hide about herself. She wanted those around her to see her as strong, resilient, and in need of no one.

"Sit down." Jacob squatted and untied her shoes.

Riley lowered herself onto the edge of the bed. "You don't have to..."

"I want to." He pulled off her shoes, placing them neatly next to her nightstand.

"I have to secure my gun." She unhooked her holster and stood in bare feet before padding to her closet to lock up her weapon. Upon her return, Jacob smoothed out a t-shirt on the bed. "Here you go."

"Why are you doing this? I'm okay."

"I know you are. I just need to show you that I'm here for you. That I understand who you are, who you *really* are. And that no matter what happens, I will always be right beside you."

She placed her hands gently on his cheeks, and in a playful manner, replied, "You're not dying, are you?"

"You tell me." He immediately regretted the comment. "I didn't mean..."

"Of course you didn't. Thank you for reminding me that I'm not alone. But I miss him, more than ever."

"He was an important part of your life for as long as I can remember. We'll get through this, Riley. You can only do what you can do and no one should expect more than that."

"They know what I can do and they expect me to fix everything, to solve everything. I just can't. Something's preventing me from getting the answers I need."

"I disagree. This time, it isn't up to some mystical force you inherited. You aren't trying to get justice for a heinous act that left a devastating power in its wake. This time, it's bad people looking to take advantage of each other for reasons we don't know yet. I can see how hard this is for you. You feel responsible. Everyone looking to you for answers. But Riley, what your gift does is search for the humanity in a situation. That's not what this is about this time. Look, I'm sitting here telling you what your gift can do, but you already know. Carl's guided you. Dan's guided you. I'm only here for support."

THE DAY HAD ARRIVED. JACOB SAT AT HIS DESK, STARING AT A computer screen but having no idea what he was viewing. A man entered the corridor and Jacob cast an unconcerned glance. But when his eyes focused, his mouth fell agape. He jumped from his chair and rushed into the hall. "Alex? Alex, what the hell? Are you okay?" He grabbed Alex's arms and checked him over as though he was a wounded man. "Jesus, where have you been? We've all been looking for you."

"I'm sorry, man. I messed up. I messed up, big time," Alex replied.

"What?" Jacob pulled back, the comment striking him like a punch to the gut. "What are you talking about? Man, we thought you were dead or something. Kidnapped or some shit."

"I know. I had to leave."

Others heard the sound of Alex's voice and appeared in the corridor. Some rushed to him, slinging their arms over his shoulders, welcoming him.

"Holy hell, dude. You have any idea how many people have been looking for you?" Craig asked. "Man, I gotta get the boss." He jogged deeper into the office until he disappeared.

"I'm okay. I promise. Please don't make a thing of this. It's my fault." Alex shrugged off his co-workers.

"Don't make a thing of it?" Jacob was in shock. He thought of what Riley had gone through and the rest of the cops. They'd all feared for his life and had worked through the night in an effort to find him. "You have no idea the lengths people around here have gone to figure out what happened to you. To try and find you. And your only response is for us not to make a thing of it?"

"You're pissed. You all are. I can see it and you should be. Like I said, this was all my doing. No one else's. And I'll suffer the consequences of my actions."

Ty Henry, the Director of Design and Architecture, appeared in the hall and marched toward the growing crowd that surrounded Alex and Jacob. "Oh my God, Alex." He pushed inside the circle and wrapped his arms around the slightly shorter man. "You're okay. You have no idea the thoughts that have been running through my mind. What happened? Have you contacted the police yet? They've been searching high and low for you."

"I will. I wanted to see you all first."

"And your family? Your wife? She must be so relieved," Ty said.

"She is, yes. We're all fine now. Can we talk for a moment, in private?"

"Of course." Ty led Alex back to his office.

The rest of the colleagues dispersed, but Jacob could only stare at Alex as they walked to his boss's office. In a moment of almost panic, he realized he had to call Riley. Jacob returned to his office and closed the door, reaching for his phone. "It's me. He's back, Riley. Alex is here, right now, talking to Ty."

"What?" Her tone was a hybrid of joy and concern.

"He says he's sorry and that it was all his fault." Jacob pushed his hand through his hair, still masked in disbelief. "I—I don't know what or how or why, but he's back. And he appears to be unharmed."

"I have to see him, Jacob. I have to look in his eyes so I can see the truth. Can you bring him to the station now?"

Jacob peered into the hall again, though no one remained. "He's in with Ty. Should I interrupt him? I have no idea what he's saying."

"Yes, please. We need him down here like now. I can't believe he just waltzed in like that. And he's not hurt or anything?"

"He doesn't appear to be. I'm freaked out over here, Riley."

"Just get him down here as quickly as you can."

"Okay." He ended the call and marched down the hall toward Ty's office. With a light rap on the door with his knuckle, he began, "It's Jacob."

"Come in." Ty's voice sounded on the other side.

Jacob opened the door to find Alex sitting in the chair opposite Ty's desk. "Man, Riley wants you down at the station as soon as possible."

"I figured that would happen." Alex looked to Ty. "Is it okay?"

"Yes, of course. Go. They need to see that you're okay. I'm sorry this happened to you, Alex. We'll have to discuss later what we need to do to get past this."

Alex pushed up from the chair. "I understand. Thank you." He walked to Jacob. "I can go down there by myself."

"If it's all the same to you, I'd prefer to drive you there."

"Yes, I think that would be the wise choice," Ty said. "Thank you, Jacob. Please keep me posted."

"I will."

Riley stood in the center of the bullpen, staring at her phone as though it might ring again.

"Hey, what's going on?" Ethan approached her. "Who was that?"

She slowly turned to him. "Jacob. He said Alex just strolled in to work like it was nothing."

"What?" Ethan spun around. "Where's the captain?"

"In the kitchen. I think the others are in there too."

"Holy crap. What the hell happened to him? Is he hurt?" Ethan started moving in all directions, appearing unable to settle on one.

"No. Jacob says he's fine. I told him to bring him down. They should be here in a few minutes."

"Who should be here?" Ward emerged from the hall with a coffee in hand. "Riley, you look like you've seen a ghost."

"Alex is back." Her monotone delivery matched the shock she wore on her face.

"What do you mean, he's back?" Ward pushed toward her. "Is he okay?"

"According to Jacob, he walked into the front doors of HVM like it was nothing. I just got off the phone and Jacob's bringing him in now."

"I don't believe it." Ward spotted Abrams and Decker appear from the back. "Alex Laughlin is here."

"Where?" Abrams looked around.

"Not here, in this building, but here in town. He's back. Jacob's bringing him in now."

"You're serious?" Abrams asked.

"Damn right I am."

"Does his family know?" Decker added.

"Son, I am just as in the dark as you are at the moment. We'll have to sit tight until they arrive. Then we'll find out where the hell that kid's been. I better call the lieutenant. He's had guys working round the clock to help us out." Ward started toward his office. "Let me know when they arrive."

"Will do, Captain." Riley shook her head. "I still can't believe it."

"It's a good thing, though, right?" Decker asked. "I mean, he's alive and that's what we all wanted."

"Of course, yes. But Jacob said Alex was going on about how it was all his fault." Riley returned to her chair and slowly sat down. "I don't know what to think right now. I sure as hell didn't see this coming."

"None of us did, Riley,' Ethan said. "Maybe now this whole thing can be put to bed."

"I think this is only the beginning," she replied.

The room fell silent. It was as if a miracle had occurred, yet no one could really believe it. They were sure it had been the men who approached Jacob and Alex two nights ago. No phone, no keys. It seemed impossible he was alive, let alone walking into work as if nothing had happened.

Riley tried to refocus, to wrap her head around this new result. It would change the entire dynamics of the investigation. Was there even an investigation anymore? "We can't let Jacob go through with the game tonight. There's no point now," she said to no one in particular, though her three colleagues listened intently.

"Look, maybe the time's come now, now that Alex is safe. We just go and arrest Levin for illegal gambling. The rest isn't our problem." Chris Decker returned to his desk and sat down. "I agree with Riley. No way in hell should we allow Jacob anywhere near that game tonight. He doesn't need to be there. Not anymore."

"I hear what you're saying," Abrams began. "But we're still dealing with a situation whereby the man who owns the bar is fearful for his life, by all accounts. People are here and they are after him, make no mistake about that. Thompson hit the nail on the head. This ain't over. We haven't even scratched the surface."

The door opened and Jacob walked inside with Alex a few steps behind.

Riley jumped to her feet. "I can't believe what I'm seeing."

Alex slunk in as if he knew the trouble he'd caused and regretted every second of it. "I can't imagine what you all must think of me right now."

"Do you know what we've done to try to find you, man?" Abrams asked.

"Yes. Jacob told me and I just don't know what to say."

Ward pulled open his door and stepped out. "How about you start by explaining what the hell went down two nights ago. And you better not leave out a single damn word."

22

The revelation of Alex Laughlin's whereabouts for the previous two days had been far less remarkable than the officers had expected. He'd spilled his guts and yet Riley knew there was more to the story. In fact, she sensed the entirety of his story had been fabricated but sat there in silence nonetheless. Laughlin didn't know what she was capable of, and had he known, he might've worked harder to spin his tale. As it was, his transparency, or lack thereof, all but assured Riley this game was far from over.

"And so you just decided to come back and face the music, is that what we're to believe?" Ward sat perched at the edge of Riley's desk and he peered back at her, seemingly for confirmation she hadn't bought it either.

"I realized what I'd put everyone through, especially my family, and I knew it couldn't continue. I got myself into this mess and it was time I owned up to it. I can't tell you all how very sorry I am." Alex turned to Jacob. "And that goes double for you. I'm sorry, man."

Jacob nodded half-heartedly.

"Well, what's the plan now, Captain?" Abrams pulled his feet from his desk and sat at attention. "We have our supposed victim back, safe and sound."

"That we do. I think it's time we huddle up and sort through this mess and figure out a plan of action." Ward stood. "Jacob, would you see to it Alex gets some food in him. You too, for that matter. It's past lunchtime as it is."

"Sure. I'll run out and get everyone some food," Jacob replied.

"Take him with you. Don't want him pulling another disappearing act on us, now do we?"

Jacob nodded and led Alex outside.

Ward turned to Riley at their departure. "Now I know you have the gift of sight, but it doesn't take a genius to see that boy is lying through his sparkling white teeth."

"He is, and it's because he's afraid. They threatened him— threatened his family," Riley said. "What he left out was that they want him in the game tonight. He doesn't have a choice."

"To what end and who?" Decker stood from his desk and walked toward Riley, leaning against the filing cabinet behind her.

"To make sure Silas Levin loses everything. Alex knows he has to go in there tonight and do exactly the opposite of what Silas wants. The men who held him, they know Silas's back is against a wall and that he has debts that need to be repaid. They're going to ensure he can't repay them. It's Ackerman who's behind this, just like we suspected."

"How is that possible? What do they know that we don't?" Abrams asked.

"I can't say. These people, they hang around in similar circles. Someone obviously said something and word got back to Ackerman."

"What I still don't get is why they took him in the first place," Ward began. "Take him then let him go? Do they believe that won't raise a whole lot of red flags?"

"Again, Captain, I just don't have an answer for that." Riley regarded her colleagues. "Alex is terrified, that much I know. I think our priority has to be to ensure the safety of his family and then to keep him and Jacob safe tonight."

"You still want Jacob in on that game?" Abrams asked. "Why?"

"Because if anything changes, apart from the fact that Silas is going to be a little surprised to see Alex, he'll bail. And if he does, we won't find Ackerman or his men, who we know took Laughlin. Those men still have to account for their crime of kidnapping, even if Alex won't admit that's what happened. This can't have all been for nothing. Ackerman is after Silas for something. And Silas will do anything to keep the people he owes money to off his back."

Ward folded his arms. "Wires. Both those kids are going in there with wires. There's no other way to keep them safe."

"For Pete's sake, Captain, that could make them far less safe," Decker said. "What if they get a pat down?"

"They didn't for the last game. Why would that change?" Ward replied. "That's the deal or there is no deal. And we'll turn this over to the big boys and let them put Laughlin's family in Witsec or whatever the hell they want to do with them."

"I don't mind saying, I'd prefer to go that route," Abrams said.

"Well, this is still our town," Ward began. "Either we uphold the law or we fold like a bad hand."

Captain Ward negotiated with the county to have access to their surveillance tech. While he waited at their nearest station, Riley and Ethan were tasked with following through on safety precautions for Laughlin's family.

Riley pulled alongside the front of the home and stopped the engine. "Let's go have a talk with Mrs. Laughlin." She stepped out of the car with Ethan following closely behind. Upon approaching the door, she knocked lightly.

A young woman, not much older than Riley, slowly opened the door just a crack. "Yes?"

"Mrs. Zoe Laughlin? I'm Officer Thompson, this is Officer Pruitt. We're here because of your husband."

The woman opened the door a little wider. "Is he okay? He left here this morning."

Riley raised a pre-emptive hand. "He's fine, although I'm sure you're aware of the events of the past few days."

"Yes, I'm aware."

"Then you'll understand it when I say that we're here to escort you and your children to your nearest relative."

"We have to leave? Why? Alex said everything was okay now."

"It isn't yet, but it will be soon. I promise you. Are your children here?"

"Yes. It's summer vacation. They're home." She stepped aside. "Please, come in."

"Thank you." Riley walked inside. "You have a beautiful home."

She nodded. "My sister lives in Terra Haute. We can stay there for a few days. She won't mind."

"Perfect. It won't be more than a day or two, I guarantee. Our priority is to ensure you and your kids are safe."

"Please understand, Mrs. Laughlin," Ethan began. "You won't be able to tell her why you're there. Not the real reason. It'll only make an already difficult situation worse."

"I understand, but I'm still waiting to hear the real reason." She regarded them with uncertainty. "Is this supposed to happen now?"

"It would be best, yes, ma'am," Riley replied. "We can escort you to the edge of town. From there, the County Sheriff's office will take you the rest of the way."

"Of course. I'll go pack a bag and get the kids ready. It'll just be a few minutes. Can I get you some water or something?"

"No, thank you." Riley bared a tender smile. "This will be over soon."

Zoe nodded and disappeared into the hallway.

Riley's shoulders dropped and she exhaled a breath. "I feel terrible for her."

"It's for their safety. Just try to remember that," Ethan replied.

"I know. I just hate lying to people. She's scared out of her mind. I don't know what Alex told her, but I have a feeling he might've told her the truth, which is probably what he should do, but it's placed a terrible burden on her."

"You can't do anything more than you're doing, Riley." Ethan held her gaze. "You're a good person. I know I've said this before but dealing with the emotions of others—I don't know how you do it and don't completely fall apart."

"Oh, I fall apart sometimes. I just don't show anyone."

Zoe returned. "Okay, we're ready." She held the hands of her two young children. A boy and a girl, who appeared to have no understanding of why they were leaving but didn't seem concerned by it.

Riley nodded. "Then we should head out."

They returned to the cruiser while the mother of two loaded her children in her minivan and started the engine.

"Once we make sure she's safely in the Sheriff's hands, we'll head back to base and check to see how they're coming along." Riley pulled out behind her and trailed the woman. "You don't see any tails?"

"No. We're not being followed." Ethan eyed the side-view mirror and peered back over his shoulder. "I just want to make sure we keep it that way."

"Me too." She kept her eyes glued on the minivan as it worked its way through town. "After this, do you mind if we take a quick detour? It won't take long."

"Not at all." Ethan studied her for a moment. "I'm glad it was you I was assigned to."

She turned to him with mild confusion. "What do you mean? When you joined?"

"Yeah. I mean, I could've been paired with Decker, or worse, Abrams. But Captain put me with you."

"That was a long time ago, Ethan." She continued to keep her sights on the vehicle ahead.

"Four years. I knew I wanted to be a cop, so that's what I did. And I couldn't imagine a better partner."

"This is it. Town limits." Riley flashed her lights at the Sheriff's car ahead.

The deputy returned the gesture before pulling out onto the road just behind Zoe Laughlin and her children.

"You sure she'll be okay the rest of the way?" Ethan asked.

"I'm sure. The county guys know what they're doing." She turned to him. "And besides, I have a gut feeling." Riley smiled before turning around and heading back.

Ethan looked on until it seemed he figured out where she was heading. "This minor detour of yours—Carl?"

"I want to talk to him for a minute. Is that okay?"

"Of course it is."

Riley pulled to a stop near the entrance of the church's cemetery. She unbuckled her seat belt and opened the door. "I'll only be a minute."

"Do you want me to come with you?" Ethan asked.

"I need to do this on my own." She stepped outside and began walking. A brief turn back and she noticed Ethan keeping an eagle-eye watch over her.

Riley walked across the perfectly manicured grass until reaching the headstone. Carl, of course, didn't have any family, so it was up to her to organize the funeral. As a Vietnam veteran, he had been buried with military honors. She wasn't sure if he would've appreciated that or not. Riley had witnessed some of the hardships he'd faced during the war. Their bond was such that it had become inevitable she would live through it as he had. Part of it anyway. Any more and she might have been driven mad with pain and grief. It was no wonder he was hardened.

Riley stood before his headstone and smiled at her recollection of the first time she met Carl Boyd, Sr. He frightened the living daylights out of her. There she stood, in front of his trailer as he opened the aluminum door. She was only ten and hadn't yet known the reach of her gift. In fact, in those days, she'd barely known what it was. But Carl changed everything.

Her legs had frozen in place as he peered at her with irritation.

"What do you want?" he'd said. Typical, crotchety old man. He never changed either. Except they'd grown to love each other and depend on one another deeply over the next fifteen years. And now he'd gone and left her to her own devices.

"You showed me the cards. I didn't understand it then, but I see now what lies ahead." She crouched down and placed her hand on the mound of grass before her. "I can't see it all, though. Not this time. I don't know how it will end. Why can't I see it? What's happening to the command of it I once had?"

He'd been gone far too long to reach her; she knew that well enough. Their connection had severed, and she was on her own to figure this out. But just talking to him one more time; perhaps it would bring clarity.

"I'm afraid for Jacob, but I have to go through with this. You know it as well as I do." She shook her head. "I really need you, Carl. I need your guidance."

Nothing. She felt nothing, not that she expected to, but maybe... Riley pushed up again and started back to the cruiser where Ethan waited patiently. She had been instructed to put such a tight rein on her ability that she no longer realized its full potential. Carl advocated for such a day because, deep down, he was fearful, both of her and for her. She'd given in to him and to Dan Ward, and to Jacob. She'd given in to all of them because she always strived to please those around her, regardless of her own feelings, her own desires.

Now that Carl was gone, Jacob was once again in a perilous situation, and Ward, as always, levied restraint in her, maybe of her. Perhaps the time had come for Riley Thompson to let go of that restraint, unleash her potential. Something inside told her this was required in order to make it to the other side. *The other side of what?* she thought.

Riley returned to the car and stepped inside.

"Everything okay?" Ethan asked.

"Fine. Thanks for giving me the time."

"Sure." He peered at her for a moment. "Did you—see anything?"

"No. I'm on my own this time." Riley turned the engine and pulled away.

THE STATION WAS JUST AHEAD AND RILEY HADN'T SAID anything the entire drive back. She parked and stepped out, immediately walking toward the entrance without waiting for Ethan, who jogged to catch up.

A quick overview of the parking lot and Riley noticed Jacob's car was still there. That was a good sign. It appeared Ward had also returned, meaning it was time to get the ball rolling.

Riley pushed through the doors and spotted the team in the bullpen, with Ward fiddling with the surveillance equipment. "Do you know how to use any of this stuff?"

He gazed up at her from the table where the equipment sat. "I'll have you know I keep up to date on my training, thank you very much. Just remember I've been a cop since you were in diapers."

She smiled on approach and placed a hand on his shoulder. "I know that, Captain. I'm only giving you grief."

Jacob walked toward her. "How'd everything go? Alex is in the restroom. Anything I should know?"

"Zoe Laughlin and her kids made it safely out of town. I don't foresee any problems ahead for them. The rest of us, I'm not so sure about."

Alex emerged from the hall. "You're back."

"Everything's fine, Alex. Your family will be safe, and when this is over, they can come home."

His shoulders sank in relief. "Thank you, Officer Thompson. Thank you."

Riley nodded before turning back to Ward. "How much longer before we can strap up these two?" She thumbed at Alex and Jacob.

"Just as soon as I can figure out how the hell this receiver works." Lowell Abrams sat at the table and turned knobs and pressed buttons as though he knew what he was doing.

Chris Decker appeared from the back entrance of the building. "Okay, the van's here. We're all set to get the gear inside and get her hooked up."

Ethan checked the time. "We still have about four hours. Anything else we need to get handled before we move this thing along?"

Jacob took hold of Riley's arm. "Can I talk to you for a minute?"

She peered at the team, who witnessed the exchange. "Sure." She followed him back to the breakroom. "What is it? We're right in the middle of this and I can't have you pulling me aside for personal reasons. It doesn't look good, Jacob."

"I know. I'm sorry. I just need to talk to you about things that might go unsaid otherwise should tonight not go to plan."

"Nothing is going to happen to you, okay? I would've seen it.

We are all coming out of this on the other side." She paused a moment, considering her choice of words.

"You did see something before, though, didn't you?"

"Yes, but it was more concern than anything else. Jacob, it's going to be fine." She placed her hands around his waist and her face masked in concern. "What is this?" From the waistband of his jeans, she retrieved the firearm. "Jacob, what are you doing with this? How did you get it?"

He stepped back sheepishly. "Dan gave it to me. I was worried when I went in there last night to tell Silas that Alex might not come tonight. Of course, all of that could've been avoided had we known..."

"But you have no idea how to use this. I can't believe he just gave it to you. Why would he do that?"

"Because I asked him to." He moved closer again. "I was afraid. The visions you had about me. I thought... I thought maybe this was it, you know. If it was going to happen, it would've been then. But it didn't."

"You can't take this with you tonight. No way in hell."

"Why not? I'm wearing a wire. Shouldn't I have some protection?"

"You will have protection. We're all going to be in that van not a block away. Jacob, no. I won't let you do this. It's far too dangerous. I'm sure the captain would agree with me on this one." She let out a sigh. "I know you don't want to do this. That you're only trying to keep Alex from harm. I respect that. But I'm going to be near enough to help, if it comes down to it. I know what I'm supposed to do now, Jacob. People have tried to keep me from accepting what it is I can do, but I know. And I can prevent anything bad from happening in there."

"I don't understand. You mean..."

"I've been told to control it. To stop it before someone really gets hurt. But if I can prevent something happening to the ones I'm sworn to protect, then that's what I'm going to do."

"At what cost, Riley?" Ward walked inside. "This won't be a situation that will require you to do anything more than be a good cop. There's nothing else for you to do."

"And if there is? If this gets out of hand, what then, Captain? I should walk away?"

"If it means you keep a lid on the fire inside you, then yes. I've seen that fire burn before. I've seen you bend a tornado to your will. Toss folks around like rag dolls. Riley, I don't want to see any more of it. It changes you. It kills a little part of who you really are." He peered at Jacob and returned his sights to Riley. "Before we go down this road any farther, I think you need to put a call into your dad."

"Why would I do that?" she asked.

"Because he knows things. He's seen things he never told you before. Things about your grandpa that you need to know. You already know how things ended for him. God forbid you should suffer the same fate. I won't have it, Riley. I won't have it at all."

23

As the evening settled in, the Crooked Horse was about to open. The young bartender inserted his key into the lock of the front door and opened it to a darkened space. He switched on the lights and let the door close behind him. Isaac Bell had moved to Owensville a few months ago, having dropped out of college in pursuit of an easier road to prosperity. Turned out, that road involved cozying up to the likes of Dennis Ackerman, a man who had discovered where Silas Levin resurfaced. The plan had been for Bell to be the go-between. Keep Ackerman abreast of Silas's plans. And he'd done his duty to the best of his ability.

Ackerman was particularly pleased by Bell's unearthing of the true reason Silas started up again. It seemed Silas's back was against a wall and he owed a sizeable debt to a man who would collect at any cost. When word got back to Ackerman about the arrival of said man's henchman, well, he needed to adapt. This was the reason behind the release of the kid, Alex Laughlin. He needed Alex to play the game with Ackerman's lackeys, Vaughan and Meisner.

Bell removed the chairs from the tables and set them down as he made his way through the establishment. With the chairs in place, Bell worked his way behind the bar and wiped down the top, dusted off the top shelf liquor, and polished the glasses. It was almost time to open for the night. He hadn't seen Silas yet, but then he didn't usually arrive until around 8pm and it was only four o'clock, almost Happy Hour. Isaac Bell speculated as to tonight's outcome, and as he did, retrieved his 9-millimeter and tucked it into his waistband. The apex of the past few months was arriving tonight, and all bets were off.

THE SUN WAS DRENCHED IN A BANK OF CORAL-HUED CLOUDS and dipped below the tree line across from the police station. Riley gazed at nature's picture show as she stood outside the doors with her phone in her hand. She reflected on what the captain had said. This was a man she trusted with her life and he would never lead her astray, but why tell her this now? What had he known about her own father she did not?

Their past had been tumultuous. From the moment Dan Ward was compelled to save Jack Thompson's life, the two played a game of tug-of-war ever since where Riley had been concerned. Dan tried to be the father Jack never was, especially when Jack left to start a new and improved family. Dan did his best to fill in and Riley loved him for that. Just as she loved Carl. But it was clear now something had transpired between the two and Dan had chosen to keep it from her. A revelation with which she now struggled to come to terms.

With the phone to her ear, Riley waited for Jack to answer. Her throat dried and her mouth turned to cotton. The relationship they shared was still strained, though it had improved in recent years, primarily for Gracie's sake. She'd been too young to remember the damage Jack had caused their family, particularly their mother. And Riley didn't want to taint her opinion of Jack. She had succeeded, save for the fact that Gracie didn't understand the tensions between her older siblings and Jack. Neither Dillon nor Riley could bring themselves to explain.

"Riley. Hi. I didn't expect to hear from you," Jack began. "Is everything okay? Gracie get back okay?"

"Hi, Dad. Gracie's fine. She arrived in the city last night."

"Okay."

The silence between them was nothing new, but Riley needed answers and it would be up to her to break that silence. "Dad, listen, um, I know about Nate."

"Know what?" His voice raised an octave.

"I know, Dad. He told me."

"I see. What is it you want, Riley? You want to talk to him? He's fine, just so you know. He's handling it like a champ."

She rolled her eyes. Jack still had no concept of just how difficult it was to handle such a thing and for a twelve-year-old, it would be nearly impossible. Nate didn't have Carl Boyd like she had. "I'm glad to hear that, Dad. I would like to, in the future, sit down with him and answer whatever questions he might have."

"Well, I'm sure he'd appreciate that. I really should get back to work, Riley..."

"Dad, wait." She took in a deep breath and gazed at the sky. "I need to ask you something. There are some things happening here that I have to deal with. Work things. And, well, I feel as though this thing inside me might want to fix what's going on. But Dan says maybe that's not a good idea. He said I should talk to you—about Grandpa."

Jack was silent for a moment, then began. "What did Ward tell you, Riley?"

"That I should ask you. He didn't tell me anything. Dad, this is important. If there's something about Grandpa I don't know..."

"There's a lot about your grandfather you don't know." He sighed heavily. "After the accident, the one that killed Carl's family, he was changed. More so than I'd ever seen before."

"That accident wasn't Grandpa's fault. Carl knew that."

"Oh, he came to that conclusion because of you, but at the time, your grandpa suffered a great deal."

"He took his own life in the house," Riley began. "Was it because of the accident?"

"No. It was part of it, but he suffered from controlling his emotions. And it resulted in some other folks getting hurt."

"What did he do, Dad?" Riley peered over her shoulder inside the station to see Ward watching her. He quickly turned away.

"He um..." Jack cleared his throat. "He lost his temper a few times and some people got hurt."

"What do you mean?" she insisted.

"Riley, I mean his ability included not just seeing through folks, it involved being able to move them at his will."

She immediately thought back to the warehouse and how she'd thrown around those men just like the captain said, like rag dolls. She almost killed one of them.

"Sometimes, if he got real angry, if someone did something

bad, he made them pay for it. And one time, it almost cost some- one's life. That was the reason he did what he did. The guilt he felt was unbearable. He saw no other way out."

Riley closed her eyes. "Why didn't you tell me this? You obvi- ously told Dan."

"I did. But only because he called on me a while back. Said you had an incident. I guess it was a similar situation. He asked if it could be explained, if it had happened before. So I told him it had."

"I thought it was just me." A bolt of fear shot through her. "Does Nate..."

"I don't know. If he can do that, he hasn't," Jack replied. "Riley, I was a terrible father to you three kids; a rotten husband. I know that. I'm trying to make amends."

"I know you are, Dad."

"Is it too late?" he pleaded.

"I don't know. I just don't know. Listen, I have to go now."

"Wait. Riley, if there's something going on with your job and you think you might—hurt someone—just step back. Pull back so you don't. Believe me, you don't want to live with that kind of pain and guilt. Your grandpa couldn't, and I sure as hell don't want you to go through that."

"Goodbye, Dad." Riley ended the call and peered up at the dimming sky. A tear ran down her cheek. She wiped it away and turned around toward the door. "It won't end like that for me. I won't let it."

Captain Ward stepped away from the door and turned his back as if he hadn't been watching Riley the entire time. When she entered, he began, "Everything okay?"

The rest of the team appeared busy with their own tasks as the hour drew near to their sting operation.

"You should've told me." Riley brushed by him and returned to her desk.

Ward followed. "Probably, but I didn't think it was my place, if I'm being honest."

She just wanted this night to be over. It should never have gotten this far and involved Jacob. "I'm not so sure we should go through with this tonight, Captain."

"If we want to hold accountable those responsible for taking Laughlin and put an end to this underground operation, we have no choice, Riley."

"Of course we have a choice. There's always a choice. We have enough with Laughlin's statement to arrest those men."

"No, we don't. He never saw either of them. We're only surmising they're responsible because of their connection to Ackerman and his to Levin. We have nothing if we don't go through with this."

He was right. She'd allowed Jacob to become embroiled in this dangerous game just to get the bad guys, ignoring her own visions and feelings about what might come to pass. "Okay. We move forward. But if this takes a turn for the worse, I won't let you stop me. I'll do what I have to do to keep Jacob safe."

Chris Decker emerged from the corridor. "I think it's time we line things up. Get the boys ready and get our equipment set up. The clock's ticking."

"That's probably a good call," Ward said. "Where are our two players?"

"I'll round them up." Abrams pushed up from his chair and started toward the back.

Ward turned to Riley. "We do this right, and we won't need any *divine* intervention, you catch my drift?"

"Yes, sir."

ISAAC BELL SERVED THE GROWING HAPPY HOUR CROWD AT the Crooked Horse. It was a far more upscale establishment than its competitor. Nevertheless, Silas Levin kept the prices low to entice his customers away from the other, more recognized watering hole. As a result, the Crooked Horse was in a hole. In fact, it was the entire reason behind the twice-weekly high-stakes poker games late at night in the backroom. He'd gotten word to a few of his previous associates, who in turn brought in a few extra players to make things interesting. While few, if any, lived in Owensville, they traveled from Terra Haute and other towns just to join in. Silas Levin had a reputation and plenty of people wanted to see him live up to it. A few returned, others had given up hope when their stores dried up. This was why Levin had to recruit local, fresh blood. Alex Laughlin was primed and ready. The kid wasn't dissimilar to Levin himself, in his younger days. And the kid had come through, until he upped and disappeared. Now all he had was his friend, Jacob Biggs. He was moderately talented, but nothing like the phenom Laughlin was. Levin wondered if there weren't certain people behind the kid's disappearance. But now that he had Eli Foster's minion, Gage Parker, watching over him, there wasn't time to divert his attention. He had to get through tonight's game with plenty of cash in hand to turn straight over to Foster himself.

He only needed to get out from under Foster. If he could do

that, this would all be over. He truly had wanted to start anew but building a business in a small town where no one knew you and money was still in short supply had taken a toll. Nevertheless, Silas Levin wasn't a quitter. He was doing what he set out to do with the games and it would only be a matter of time before Eli Foster was in his rear-view.

"Hey, boss?" Bell approached him as he stood near the bar. "Is there anything I can do to help get ready for tonight?"

Levin turned around. "No. We'll be busy up front here for the next hour or so until Happy Hour finishes. We'll set up after that. No rush."

"Yes, sir." Bell started away but stopped again. "Oh, I heard that Alex Laughlin decided to come back from wherever it was he took off to."

Silas furrowed his brow. "Where did you hear that?"

"Lots of people around town are talking about it. A few of his co-workers who just left mentioned it too. I overheard them. That's a good thing, though, right?"

"Yeah. It's a good thing. Thanks for letting me know. I appreciate it." Silas started back toward his office with nagging concern. This was a good thing, but why hadn't the kid called to tell him? Turned out his buddy, Jacob, was right after all. He'd predicted Laughlin's return. Interesting.

There was no time to grasp Laughlin's reasons for disappearing and reappearing just in the nick of time. While the hair on the back of his neck stood, Silas ignored it; he had to. It could be addressed after the game, when the players had all gone home empty-handed.

Silas was at his desk, the nagging feeling eating away at him. "No. This can't be a coincidence. Biggs. He's got to be behind it."

He stood from his desk and swiped his keys before walking toward the front of the bar where Isaac still served the patrons. "I have to run out. I'll be back with enough time to spare. Just hold down the fort."

"Will do, Silas. No problem." Isaac observed as Silas marched out the door.

"Hey, man, can I get that beer, or what?" one of the patrons asked.

"Sure. Sorry about that." Isaac turned to retrieve the bottle of Bud and twisted off the cap. "Here you go. Four-fifty, please."

The man left a five on the bar top.

"I'll be right back with your change." He retreated to the back-room and made the call. "Mr. Ackerman, I thought you should know Silas left in a hurry. Something's up."

"Any idea where he's headed?"

"No, sir. He did say he'd be back in plenty of time for the game. I think it has to do with Laughlin. I did like you asked. I told him the guy reappeared and was coming tonight. He seemed a little surprised."

"Okay. I'll take it from here. Thanks." Dennis Ackerman, Silas's old business partner, ended the call. "Where are the boys?" he asked his subordinate.

"Grabbing a bite to eat before heading out for the game tonight. Why?"

"In the town, or what?" Ackerman continued.

"I don't know. I didn't ask. Did something come up? Anything I can help with?"

"Levin took off. Don't know where or why. I'm thinking he might be trying to track down our boy, Laughlin."

"Do you think the guy will hold up under Levin's pressure?"

"He'd better. If he doesn't and Silas figures out what we're doing, we're fucked. And if we're fucked, I'll make sure everyone's fucked."

THE BULLPEN LOOKED LIKE A COMMUNICATIONS COMMAND center. The surveillance equipment rested on the two folding tables in the middle of the room, ready to be loaded onto the van. It was the first operation of this kind Riley had seen since her tenure at the police department. In fact, she was pretty sure nothing like this had ever been necessary before, though she would need to ask Ward about that. He'd been a cop here when she was a kid, working under a different captain. She recalled meeting that captain. It seemed like a different place then. Her family had been called in because of Carl's son and all that he'd brought to town. Jack was still drinking in those days and Riley remembered he'd rubbed the captain the wrong way then. That was the beginning of the turbulent relationship between Daniel Ward and Jack Thompson.

Now, she was here, working as a cop, just as Ward had back in the day. Her life had changed substantially and that was mostly due to Carl and the events leading up to his son's death. The question was, could she stand up to the likes of Silas Levin when Jacob's life could depend on it? Just as Ward had confronted the men who killed Carl's son?

"I think it's time to get the van loaded up," Riley peered around. "Where are Jacob and Alex?"

"Last I checked, they were chugging back some coffee,

preparing for a long night," Abrams replied. "I'll go see what's keeping them." He started into the hall.

Ward eyed Riley as she examined the equipment. "It's going to be all right. It's part of our job and we'll get it done with no side effects."

"I know. I'm just a little nervous."

"Well, aren't we all?" He placed his hand on her shoulder. "Your boyfriend in there is courageous as hell. You know that, right?"

She nodded. "I wish you hadn't given him the gun."

"He told you about that?"

"He didn't have to. I found it. I told him he couldn't go in with it tonight. You're going to have to back me up on that one."

"Oh, I whole-heartedly agree with you. Not the time or the place. But he's risking more than he should. He's not one of us. I do wonder, though, if maybe he wants to be."

"I'll stop you right there. That isn't going to happen. He needs to stay as far away from this as humanly possible."

"After tonight, of course," Ward replied.

She smiled. "After tonight."

Jacob and Alex emerged from the back, with Jacob leading the way. "Abrams says it's time to saddle up?"

"It's time. Are you ready?" Riley asked.

"As I'll ever be."

24

The home where Alex Laughlin's family lived was on the outskirts of Owensville, a new development of about seventy-five houses that took less than two years to build out. Prior to that, the town was in a renaissance and housing was at a critical shortage. That shortage had been filled. And now the entry-level and move-up buyers had a place to call home.

Silas Levin crawled along the streets of the community in his newer model BMW 5 series. The silver sedan still stood out among the moderate family cars dotting the driveways as people returned home for the day.

The street lamps flickered on as daylight faded. They were the decorative kind meant to look like an old-fashioned gas lamp. It was intended to enhance to the home-spun, family-friendly ambiance. But what Silas was looking for as he steered up and down each street was a sign that Alex Laughlin was home. That would be the first place he would go, if in fact he'd returned as his bartender, Isaac Bell, had indicated.

He didn't know the precise address but knew the man's Toyota 4Runner and figured he'd gotten it out of the impound lot already. But there were no signs of it on the street or the driveways. There was another place he could try and that was Laughlin's work. HVM Builders, the company that built these cut-rate popsicle stick houses.

Silas pulled out of the community and started back toward town, though the drive wasn't far. The building was situated in a new commercial office area also built at the edge of town. There weren't a lot of places for these new developments to go except to the outskirts. Everything else had been built-out and the town hadn't yet done well enough to start the process of eminent domain, though Lord knew they needed to in some areas. He spotted the police station just ahead and continued on, sneering at the building. At least those assholes had cooled their heels for the past week or so. Harassing him the way they did and for what? They had nothing.

He slowed as he neared the station and peered over, wondering what the hell those cops did day in and day out. Nothing ever happened around here. That was when he saw it. Silas did a double-take and slowed down more. "What the—?" In the parking lot, he spotted the Toyota 4Runner, Alex Laughlin's 4Runner, no doubt. "That's interesting. What the hell you doing there, kid?"

An unsettled feeling crawled along his spine. He could be jumping the gun here, but what if he wasn't? Was it possible the kid was here to smooth things over, knowing full well his family would've gone to the cops the moment he didn't show up at home? It was possible, but somehow, Silas didn't think it was probable. He began to wonder. Had the kid spilled the beans? Had he told them about the games and the threats from none other than Silas himself? If that was the case, he might have to re-think tonight's game.

~

"I FEEL LIKE JAMES BOND OR SOMETHING." ALEX SMOOTHED down the wire that was taped to his chest. "You sure you'll be able to hear us?"

"Yes," Ward began. "We've run the tests, sound checks. We're all good to go. Just don't sweat too much."

Alex's mouth fell. "I—I don't..."

"He's joking," Riley said. "It's okay if you sweat. Nothing will happen. But you will need to relax. Stay calm. If Silas or either of Ackerman's people catches wind that you're wired, things will go south pretty quickly."

"Why don't you tell him he'll end up with a bullet in his back?" Abrams said.

"I'm being honest. What do you want me to do, lie to him?" Riley fired back.

"Okay, let's just settle down here." Ward raised a pre-emptive hand. "No one's going to end up shot or anything else. You two will play the game the way Levin wants you to play and when it's all said and done, when everyone's left the stage, that's when we'll go in. Not with guns blazing, but with handcuffs at the ready. We'll take Ackerman's people in first, then we'll go after Silas."

Jacob swallowed hard and nodded. "Okay. Okay. We can do this."

Riley gently grabbed his shoulder. "Yes, you can. I know

you've been in worse situations. This should be a cake-walk for you." She unveiled a sardonic smile.

"Sure. Cake-walk." Jacob sighed. "It'll be just like the other night."

"For you maybe," Alex said. "My orders are to go against anything Silas tells me to do. Look, it's my family's lives that are at stake here. I won't screw this up. I can't."

"Your family is safe," Riley continued. "Pruitt and I made sure your wife got out of town with the kids. Yes, you need to do what Ackerman's people told you to do. Otherwise, I'm not sure what his men will do or say. Silas won't say anything, not until after the game, I promise you. He would risk far too much if he let it be known the game was rigged. And by the time that happens, we'll be in there arresting him."

Abrams placed his hands on his hips. "I hate to break up this love fest, but we need to load up."

"You, Decker and Pruitt load up the van," Ward began. "I'll finish this up with Riley and we'll head out there in a few."

"Copy that, Captain." Abrams started back.

Ethan stood in place, peering at Riley.

"Everything okay there, son?" Ward asked.

"Fine." He let go of her gaze and followed the other officers.

"What's wrong with him?" Jacob asked.

"Just nervous. A little like the rest of us, I suspect," Ward replied. "Now come on. Button up your shirt and do a final check and then we are out of here."

SILAS RUSHED BACK INTO THE BAR AND HEADED STRAIGHT FOR

Isaac. "I'm going to need you to help out tonight. Get Renee to cover for you."

Renee was a lost millennial without a definable future ahead of her. She drank too much and didn't eat enough, but she showed up for work and that was all Silas cared about right now.

"Sure thing, boss. What's going on?" Isaac quickstepped to follow Silas to the backroom.

"We need to get the cameras up and running."

"What cameras?" He peered around.

"The ones in the back. I bought them when I purchased the place, but never got them installed. We're going to have to get that done tonight. At least the ones for back here. Now let's hustle."

"I don't understand. Did something happen?" Isaac's face masked in concern. "Is it the cops? Did someone squeal? It was that guy, wasn't it?"

"Shut up and do what I tell you, understand?" Silas stood squarely in front of him.

"Sorry, boss. I understand. I'll get it done." He opened the box where two cameras were packed away and began reading the instructions. "Do we have everything we need for this?"

"Yes. It'll be remotely operated through our wireless server and it'll record everything to the cloud." Silas walked around the room and peered up. "I just need to find a place to hide these. Can't afford for anyone to spot them."

"How about here?" Isaac pointed to a corner where a few boxes were stacked high on a shelf. "No one would look there." He continued around the room. "And here. That would be a good place too."

Silas examined the locations and nodded. "Good. Yeah, these will work." He patted Isaac on his back. "Now let's get started."

Gage Parker stood in front of the mirror in his hotel bathroom and smoothed down his dress shirt. He examined his refined features, his clean-shaven pointed chin, his thinning black hair, and brows that were brushed to precision. "Time to go."

He returned to the bed, where he grabbed his cell phone and started to reach for his jacket, but then thought better of it. The people around here weren't overly fashionable and he might stand out in the summer heat wearing a sport coat.

The phone buzzed in his hand and he examined the caller ID. "Mr. Foster, what can I do for you, sir?" Gage walked around the room, nodding as he listened. "I understand. Observe only. Got it." He returned the phone to his pants pocket and walked through the door.

Eli Foster was a man of few words and was surrounded by even fewer of those he trusted. Gage had been one who had gained his trust. He'd always done precisely as ordered, nothing more and nothing less. Tonight, all he was tasked with doing was observing Silas. He would do that and report back like the good little army ant that he was.

Upon stepping outside, moisture hung in the night air and he perspired the moment he started out. "God damn humidity." He pushed back his hair to keep it from falling out of place, as it was prone to do in this type of climate. Fortunately, the sleek black Camaro was just ahead and he started it with the remote in his hand.

As he drove away from the 3-star accommodation and toward town, there was only one thing on Gage Parker's mind; ensure Silas Levin understood who was in charge.

Officers Lowell Abrams and Chris Decker returned to the bullpen where Abrams began, "We're locked and loaded."

"Where's Pruitt?" Riley asked as she strapped on her sidearm.

"In the van, tweaking a few things," Decker said. "Are we ready to roll, or what? These guys need to get down there pretty soon."

"We're ready." Captain Ward emerged from his office and peered at the two kids in front of him, neither of which had ever served in any capacity such as this. No military training, nothing. He felt a little like he was leading lambs to the slaughter but wouldn't dare express that out loud. Of course, Riley probably already felt it in him. Though if she had, she hadn't said as much. Maybe because she was feeling the same way. He hoped the right call had been made. They were dealing with big city folks, dangerous ones, and these kids were his people.

"Then let's go." Riley started into the corridor and through the back door into the darkness. Two street lamps burned in the parking lot reserved for employees and deliveries. Only now there was a black van parked there that looked entirely suspicious. The small department had precious few resources and if it hadn't been for the county, they wouldn't even have this much.

They reached the van and Riley stepped inside. "Wow."

"I know, right?" Ethan wore an enthusiastic smile.

The other two officers and Captain Ward trailed inside, all seemingly impressed with the sophisticated setup.

"Well, we can't sit here and marvel about our handiwork." Ward stepped outside again where Jacob and Alex waited. "You'll take your car, Jacob. Remember, we'll only be a block away and with this." He tapped on Jacob's chest. "We'll know your every move."

"It's not my moves you should be worried about."

Ward nodded. "We'll know Silas's every move." He patted him on the shoulder. "Just remember to keep your cool and everything will go smoothly."

Riley stepped out. "We'll see you both soon."

Jacob stood there a moment longer while Ward and Alex disbursed. It was as though he was waiting for Riley to pull him aside for a few final words of encouragement. But she only nodded with a tender smile before retreating back into the van. He turned on his heel and followed Alex to his car.

"You ready to go, man, or what?" Alex stood next to the passenger door. "I want to get this over with so I can go see my family."

"I'm ready." Jacob unlocked his car and stepped into the driver's seat. When Alex entered, he continued. "I hope we're doing the right thing."

"It's a little late to second-guess it now, don't you think?" Alex replied.

"I'm not second-guessing anything. I just, hell, I don't know." He turned the ignition. "Let's just get the hell out of here." Jacob pulled away and entered the main road, and within a few seconds, the mysterious black van pulled out behind him, its headlights shining brightly. He peered through the rear-view mirror.

"Hey, man, it's going to be okay." Alex appeared to take note of Jacob's apprehension. "It'll be just like the other day."

"No, it won't." Jacob shot back. "We have to go against what Silas wants so those people don't hunt down your family. And when we do that, what do you think is going to happen? You think Silas will be understanding, because I sure as hell don't."

"Okay. Okay, I get it. But look, we go in there and you're agitated, how well do you think that'll play off, huh? Remember what Captain Ward said, we have to keep our cool or this thing blows up in our faces."

ISAAC APPEARED FROM THE BACKROOM AND MADE HIS WAY TO the bar to find Silas and his counterpart, Renee, behind it. "All taken care of, Mr. Levin."

"Good. Thank you." Silas checked the time on his phone. "I imagine my boys will show up in the next few minutes. We'll get them a couple of drinks and then I'll take them back to make sure we're all on the same page." Silas didn't mention that he'd seen Alex's 4Runner at the police station. He needed to examine the situation and understand its impact before the game.

The decision to proceed was made with caution in mind. The cameras, for one, they were for his protection, should anything fall into the hands of the cops. The conversation that would take place would give him assurances as to whether those idiot kids would follow through on their end of the bargain. If he got a whiff of wavering from either of them, he'd pull the deal. And finally, he knew Eli's man, Gage, would arrive at any moment. The idea still played in the back of his mind. If Eli wanted to know how he was managing to pay back his debts, then maybe he would invite Gage into the game. Of course, the man hardly seemed like a card sharp, and then there was the rather sizeable buy-in required to partake in the high-stakes setting. He doubted very much that Gage Parker had the money to participate in any event.

Silas Levin had taken all necessary precautions. If the cops were dumb enough to bust in and arrest everyone for illegal gambling, then so be it. It was far less difficult to rebound from that than answer as to why he was cheating his players out of thousands of dollars. The price to pay for that crime would be significantly larger than anything these backwater cops could dream up. In fact, Silas ventured to think it could well result in his demise. And that of his two protégés.

RILEY PULLED UPRIGHT TO PEER THROUGH THE WINDSHIELD. Ward was behind the wheel and Decker was in the passenger seat. Pruitt and Abrams continued to marvel in the technology they wished their department had. Meanwhile, it was Riley who remained concerned about the sting operation. "That's the location, up ahead."

"I know where we're going, Riley. Just relax." Ward peered back at her for a moment. "Once we park up, we'll test the audio and then it's full steam ahead."

She returned to her seat atop the bench that spanned the length of the cargo area in the van. Ethan perched on the edge of the bench and turned his sights to her. "Hey, you know better than any of us. This is going to go as planned. Otherwise, I think you would have said something by now."

"It's true. I haven't felt like anything is going to go sideways," she replied.

"Then why worry like this? I don't understand."

"It was something in Jacob's eyes," Riley said. "He believes something is going to happen. Something bad."

"I'm sure he's worried. He wouldn't be human if he wasn't."

"No, it's more than that." Riley sighed. "I can't see it, though. I can't read him. It's like he's learned how to block me out."

Ethan chuckled. "And how does one learn to do that? I'd like to know."

She shook her head.

"I'm sorry. I know this isn't the time for jokes. Look, I don't know what he's going through, or Alex, for that matter. He stands to lose a hell of a lot more if this doesn't go to plan than any of us. But I do know that we are all trained police officers. We can douse this flame should it start into a raging fire. You must know that."

"I guess I do. I don't know why I'm feeling so off. So hesitant."

"Because it's Jacob. And you love him."

Riley lowered her gaze. "Yeah. I do."

25

J acob pulled into the parking spot near the front of the Crooked Horse and killed the engine. He gazed at the building for several moments before turning to Alex. "We should go inside."

"I'm sorry." Alex turned away and stared through the passenger side window. "I'm sorry I got you involved in this. I never believed it would go down the way it has."

"I know you didn't. You were kidnapped, for God's sake. None of this was supposed to happen. But somehow, where I'm concerned, I never can seem to find peace." Jacob took in a deep breath. "We'll be okay. There are five highly-trained officers backing us up."

"Highly trained?" Alex asked.

"There are four trained officers and one who is probably highly-trained. Point being, they have our backs. Nothing's going to happen to your wife and kids. We'll walk out of here tonight, in just a few hours, unharmed, and the cops will get the bad guys.

And justice will be served to the men who took you." He opened the door and stepped out.

Alex stepped out of his side and the two met on the sidewalk near the entrance. "If you can hear me, flash your lights." He turned back toward the main street. A small glimmer of light sparked, then was out. "I hope that was them."

"You and me both." Jacob pulled open the door and walked inside. He plastered a smile on his face as he spotted the man who ran the show just ahead.

"Well, look who elected to show up." Silas made his approach. "Decided to come back and face the music, did you, Alex? Surprised you pulled that disappearing act."

"I just needed some time away. You know, family and marriage and all that. It can take its toll." Alex offered his hand.

"I hear you, brother." Silas returned the greeting. "Your buddy here, though, he was pulling for you to do the right thing. Glad you're both here." He turned on his heel. "Come sit at the bar. I'll pour you a couple of cold ones before we get started tonight."

Jacob and Alex eyed one another before following Silas back to the bar. Jacob hopped onto a bar stool. Alex sat next to him.

"How many are we expecting tonight, Chief?" Jacob asked.

Silas placed two bottles of beer in front of them. "Should be a good crowd tonight. Mostly regulars, though there may be a surprise guest or two." He eyed Jacob sternly.

"Sounds good." Alex chugged back his beer.

Isaac approached the men. "Evening, gentlemen. Mr. Laughlin, you know, we weren't sure you were coming tonight. Something about leaving your family?"

Silas raised a hand. "No need to get involved in the man's personal life. He's here now and that's all that matters."

"Sure. Sorry, man, no offense."

"None taken." Alex stared at him while he took another swig. "Just some personal business was all it was. Glad to be here now and looking forward to having some fun."

"Speaking of." Silas walked around the bar. "Why don't I show you our setup for tonight? Might be a good idea to know how things will be laid out."

Jacob pushed off the stool. "Sure thing." He looked at Alex. "Come on, man." Jacob briefly eyed his shirt, where the wire was strapped beneath. Without saying as much, he wanted to do his best to describe where they would be seated and what was around so when the team pulled the trigger, they'd have some idea what they would be coming up against.

Silas turned on the light in the backroom and illuminated the storage-like space. In the center was an octagon poker table, complete with green felt and storage cubbies for each player's chips. Soft padded folding chairs surrounded it, and by Jacob's count, there were eight seats. Six more would be in attendance tonight and he ventured to think that two of them would be the men who had approached them the other night and who they believed abducted Alex, though he himself was unsure.

At another end of the room, a rectangular folding table was set up and covered in a linen cloth. Empty bowls and glasses sat atop it along with a few bottles of the Crooked Horse's finest liquor.

Jacob continued to study the surroundings, cementing in his mind the exits and his and Alex's precise locations. If it was like the last game, they'd be positioned at the northwest side of the table. Meaning they would face the exit almost head on. That could be a very good thing.

"Everything look good to you two?" Silas asked.

"Perfect," Alex replied. "Just like before. So, can I ask, who will we be playing against tonight?" He looked at Jacob for a moment. "I want to be sure me and Jacob here are ready for whoever's coming."

Silas approached, walking to within a foot of him. He was only about an inch or so taller than Alex, but he loomed large in that moment. "You're interested in names now?"

"Uh, no, not really. I was just making conversation." Fear flashed through his eyes. "I'm just here to do like what we talked about, Silas. Nothing more."

"Good." He returned a slick smile and stepped back. "Then we should go back out there and have another drink. Tonight should be an interesting one."

"THANK YOU, ISAAC. BE ON THE LOOKOUT TONIGHT." DENNIS Ackerman, the former partner turned foe to Silas Levin ended the call. "Our man says Alex is doing his duty. Playing the part and hanging in there like a champ. We made the right call with that one."

"You're right," his partner said. "I think the other one would've been too difficult to sway. He didn't have anything to lose. Laughlin does."

"So the plan is," Ackerman continued. "Let Vaughan and Meisner get in there, play the game, and see how Alex plays. They'll know pretty damn quick if he's going to go along with the plan or keep to Levin's scheme."

"And if he chooses the latter?" he asked.

"Then Laughlin won't have a family to come home to,"

Ackerman replied. "But I don't believe it will come down to that. My main concern is what happens when Silas begins to comprehend what's happening. When he sees Laughlin and his buddy play like they're World Series of Poker winners."

"We'll go in after that, is that right?" he asked.

"That's the plan. We'll force him to lose his ass, then go in there and take the rest of whatever the hell he has. I spent six years in prison for that asshole. He's going to be held to account."

"What about the people he owes money to?"

Ackerman shook his head. "Not my problem. Isaac says it's Eli Foster."

"You know him?"

"You bet your ass I do. He's a player in Chicago and Silas must've been pretty fucking desperate to get into bed with him. Hell, he can have the bar for all I care. I just want Levin." Ackerman reached for his keys. "Better head down there. Don't want to miss all the action."

RILEY RETURNED A GLANCE TO WARD. "THAT WAS RISKY."

"It was. Much too risky for my tastes. Laughlin almost ended it before it began. Sounds like he recovered, so they're still on track."

Ethan stood behind Decker and Abrams, who were planted in front of two workstations. One was to monitor Jacob's wire and the other was set up for Alex's gear.

Decker pulled down his headset. "We don't know anything more than we did when they walked in. That could present us with a problem."

"Only if things go south, which I do not anticipate and neither should you," Ward replied. "Let those boys get settled in and see what they can do. We all need to have a little bit of faith, you understand? They need it from us right now."

Ethan peered at Riley. "It's going to plan so far."

It was clear he was making an effort to reassure her, but she still felt at odds with Jacob's behavior. Like maybe he might do something reckless. But it wasn't like him to be reckless. Well, not usually. The whole thing that went down when he returned to Owensville was reckless, but he was trying to rescue his girlfriend; ex-girlfriend. This time was different. He had no cause to do anything but stick to the plan. He needed to prove nothing, if that was what his intentions were.

"Riley?" Ethan asked. "You with us?"

"I'm with you. Sorry."

"Are you getting one of those feelings?" Ward asked.

"No. It's nothing like that," she said.

Both Decker and Abrams cast uncertain glances at one another as if they expected her to raise the dead and watch her head spin. It only made her feel more like an outcast.

"I just want this night to be over with. I know I was on board with this plan, but I'm concerned we've let it go too far."

"Riley, we have to know who took Laughlin and this is the only way to do that. Sure, we could've asked around, but what do you think that would've succeeded in doing? Silas would've walked away. Ackerman's men would've fled, and we still don't know for sure it was them. We need this to go down tonight or we have nothing. Less than nothing."

"The captain's right," Ethan began. "Jacob's smart. Smarter than I give him credit for. He'll do what he needs to do."

"*Hey, look who decided to make it.*"

Jacob's voice sounded through Decker's headphones. "He's on." Decker turned on the speaker.

The team hushed instantly. Riley leaned over Decker's chair as though it would help her to see what was going on, instead of just listening.

"I hope you're ready to lose tonight, Biggs."

"Who was that?" Riley whispered.

Ward only shook his head and waited.

"Guess we'll have to see about that." Jacob unleashed a laugh that wasn't his own.

"He's nervous." She shook her head. "Do you think it's one of Ackerman's guys?"

"I don't know. Just sit tight. We'll get more as he does," Ward said.

Riley dropped to the bench along the wall of the van. She lowered her head into her hands and continued to listen so intently, she hadn't realized Ethan was next to her rubbing her back.

"Let's head back, gentlemen." Silas's voice traveled through the speaker.

"Okay, folks. Now we're getting down to brass tacks." Abrams pressed a few keys on the keyboard and the volume grew from his speaker. "Our boy Alex is being awfully quiet. I'd worry more about him blowing it than Jacob."

SNACKS WERE ON THE TABLE NEXT TO THE BOOZE AND A bucket of beer bottles sat at the ready. The men entered, appearing jovial and unconcerned about the outcome of the game.

Eugene Vaughan, the forty-two-year-old with a paunch and receding hairline, sat down first. His colleague, Anton Meisner, the slightly more polished thirty-four-year-old, sat next to him.

Jacob nudged Alex almost imperceptible to anyone else, but Alex seemed to take note. With a subtle nod of his head, he was pointing out the obvious. Those were the men who abducted him, or so they believed through a process of elimination.

So far, the others were unknown. Jacob hadn't seen them before and it didn't appear that Alex had either, which meant Silas had fresh meat. Perhaps with the loss of Sims, he had to put out feelers for more unsuspecting subjects. But what he didn't know was that Jacob and Alex were about to run afoul with Silas.

Silas sat down. "Okay, gentlemen, buy-in is two grand."

He'd spotted Alex and Jacob the cash, as per the agreement, so each had tossed in their chips.

Silas began dealing the cards.

Jacob watched as each player viewed their respective hands. He was looking for a tell. And while he had nowhere near the skills of Alex, he'd picked up enough to grasp the situation. As he turned his sights to his friend, Alex's face became unreadable. No tell. Nothing that would give away his position. He was better than even Jacob believed. But the deal was, he had to win, and win it all. Denying Silas everything was the endgame here, and the night had only just begun.

Dennis Ackerman hopped out of his Cadillac Escalade and placed his hands at his waist. "So this is Levin's new place, huh?" He surveyed the grounds. "Why the hell would he come to this shithole town?"

"Because no one knows him here, I imagine." The man joined him and peered at the building. "Not a bad-looking place, though. Probably the nicest thing in this town."

Ackerman nodded. "You got that right." He patted his friend on the back. "Let's go and have ourselves a drink."

The two walked inside as the bar had begun to quiet down for the night. Folks still had to get up early and go to work tomorrow and it appeared as though only a few hard-core drinkers remained inside.

Ackerman revealed a broad smile at the sight of his informant behind the bar. "Mr. Bell. How the hell are you?" He extended his hand.

"Doing well, sir. And you?" Isaac replied.

"About as good as can be expected, all things considered. What do you have that's decent around here?"

"Got a pretty good pilsner, if you're interested. Otherwise, some top-shelf bourbon, if that's more your style."

"I'll take a shot of bourbon." Ackerman bellied up to the bar.

"And what can I get you?" he asked the man next to him.

"Same. Thanks." He too sat perched on a stool. "Pretty damn quiet in here."

"Yeah. It's getting late. Only got the folks back there to contend with mostly."

Ackerman leaned in and lowered his tone. "Anything going on with that front I should know about?"

"Nothing yet. They got started about forty-five minutes ago. Things usually start heating up after a few more drinks. Give it half an hour, tops. We should start seeing some action," Isaac replied.

"That's what I came for." Ackerman rubbed his hands together before taking hold of the shot glass. "Bottoms up, boys."

DECKER PULLED DOWN HIS HEADPHONES ONCE AGAIN. "Sounds like Alex is doing all right so far. Not sure about Jacob."

"He's not a poker player. At least, he wasn't until recently," Riley said. "As long as he can pretend and make sure he's winning, then he'll get through it."

"How long before Levin starts to feel the squeeze?" Abrams asked. "Gotta be coming soon."

"I'm sure it will." Ward turned to Riley. "I'm wondering if now is the time to have you check things out?"

"You want me to go inside?" She asked.

"You're most equipped to handle this when it comes to its ultimate conclusion," Ward said.

"She can't go in there alone. I'll go with her," Ethan said.

"No. We both show up and red flags will be sprouting up all over the place," Riley began. "The captain's right. I'll go. I'm in plain clothes. I doubt it's the same bartender, and even if it is, I can tell him I just clocked out for the night. Am I going to get kicked out for the sole reason that I'm a cop?"

"I don't know about this, Captain." Ethan stood as straight as he could in the van. "It's not like you're bullet-proof, Riley."

Ward snapped his fingers. "Ah. That's right. I brought a vest. Strap this on and head inside." He handed it to Riley.

"Are you kidding? Captain, look at what I'm wearing? You

don't think that'll show through my clothes? How would I explain that? No. I'm going in. I have my gun. I'll be ready."

"At least wear an earpiece." Ethan snatched one from the table where the equipment rested. "We need to have audio or you're going in there blind."

"I can agree to that." Riley placed the earpiece in her right ear and pulled her hair over it. "Okay. Catch up with you all soon." She slid open the van door and jumped out, walking the block to the Crooked Horse on foot.

Ethan peered through the door before finally shutting it again.

Riley was feeling better already. This was a good idea. At least if she was there, she could control the outcome by whatever means necessary.

26

The lighted sign for the Crooked Horse was mounted along the front of the small building. The term "crooked horse" was a horse slanted left or right, such as people who were left or right handed. It was said that a crooked horse had trouble holding its rider, however, the sign's imagery took another meaning. A horse holding a beer at a bar and appearing to be drunk. The inventive take on the saying drew Riley's interest as she approached the bar on foot.

"I'm about to enter." Riley's earpiece was hidden beneath her long blonde locks that were stick-straight. To any passersby, it would have appeared as though she was talking to herself. Luckily, it was late and a weeknight. In Owensville, that meant people had already retreated into their homes and were tucked up in bed.

Dressed in street clothes, a tank top with a light button-down shirt over top and a pair of cuffed denim pants, Riley easily blended with the rest of the patrons, of which there were few. And she caught the eye of the bartender, a woman whom she had not seen before. The few times she'd been inside the place was during the day and in uniform when a young man was serving drinks. This was an even better outcome than she had hoped.

The young bartender, slim and angry, eyed Riley as she approached the bar. "What can I get you?"

"Beer. Thanks." Riley sat on the barstool and surveyed her environment, keeping a particular eye toward the back where the game was taking place and Jacob was doing his best to play to both sides. A dangerous undertaking for the most highly-trained of law enforcement, let alone a young architect who'd already been faced with trouble in the recent past.

"That'll be six-fifty."

Riley handed over a ten-dollar bill and without a word, the woman retreated to the till and pulled out her change. Upon receiving the change, Riley left a two-dollar tip. "Thanks very much." She tossed back a swig of beer.

Riley didn't drink because it dulled her senses and all that came with it, and right now, she needed to stay sharp. But inside a bar, she needed to drink to keep from drawing unwanted attention. She knew the others were listening to her and felt more confident as a result.

"Evening, miss." An older gentleman who had been sitting at the other end of the bar moved next to her.

She'd seen this man in a mug shot. It was Ackerman. Riley glanced to where he moved from and noticed another, younger gentleman and figured he was his hired hand. Why the hell was Ackerman here? He'd already sent his men to participate in the game as they had before. This could be a problem when Silas realizes Jacob and Alex aren't playing by his rules.

"Evening." Riley nodded politely.

The man offered his hand. "Dennis."

"Riley." She returned the greeting. "Nice to meet you, Dennis."

"And you. I see you already have a drink in your hand. Care for another?"

"No thank you. Appreciate the offer, though."

"Sure thing. Can I ask you, Riley, what a beautiful young woman like yourself is doing in this place so late at night? And all alone?"

"Just got off shift and needed to relax a little."

"Oh sure. I've been there. What is that you do?"

She had to think fast. "I work at the hospital. I'm a nurse."

"Oh. I see. Then maybe you could use another one?" Ackerman laughed.

"Are you listening to this, Captain?" Ethan fired off a nervous glance. "She's talking to a guy named Dennis. That has to be Ackerman. What the hell is he doing there? I don't like this. We need to get her out of there."

"She's fine, okay? She can handle herself. Let her do what she needs to do to keep a lid on what's about to happen in there."

"We're just supposed to sit here and wait for it all to go down?" he continued.

"Cool your jets, bro." Abrams looked over his shoulder. "We still got ears on our boys in the game. We'll know before she does if it's taking a turn for the worse. And if it does, we can warn her. Jesus, man. Take a chill pill."

Ward placed his hand on Ethan's shoulder. "She's doing

exactly the right thing here. They've got a different bartender working, so no worries about the one you both met before. She's dressed down and hardly looks like a cop. Let her do her job, Pruitt."

Decker leaned over the table and viewed the monitor while he appeared to listen intently. "Hey. Hey," he shot back. "Something's going on."

"Put it on the speaker," Ward said.

"I guess I'm just having a good night, fellas. Beats the hell out of the last time I was here."

"Shit, that's Alex," Abrams said. "Sounds like he just won another hand. Silas is going to start suspecting something here real soon."

The sound that transmitted appeared to be that of moving chairs and a muffled voice in the background.

"What's happening? What's going on?" Ethan eyed the monitors as if he could see through them and inside the room.

"Maybe they're taking a break?" Decker said. "Sounds like they're getting up or something."

"I couldn't tell the muffled voice, though. Could've been Silas calling a break," Abrams replied. "Nothing from either of our boys at the moment..."

Then another voice sounded.

"Good thing. I need to take a piss."

"That's our boy. That's Jacob," Abrams said. "Good man. He's leaving the room."

Jacob emerged from the back and started toward the

restrooms on the other side of the bar. As he strolled through, appearing confident, he locked eyes with Riley. He noticed a man sitting next to her and it took a minute, but he realized who it was. His heart fell into his stomach. A brief look of panic crossed his face and he broke away from her stare. Why was she here and why the hell was Ackerman here?

He made his way to the men's room and walked inside, standing in front of one of the basins. "Shit. Shit. What the hell's going on? I hope to God you can hear me. Riley's out there talking to Ackerman." The audio was only one-way for fear an earpiece would be easy to spot. "We're winning our hands. I think that's why Silas called for the break. He knows something's up. I don't know how much longer we can hold on. If Ackerman's waiting for his men to come out, what then? What the hell is going to happen?"

No one was going to answer. Jacob had to continue on as though nothing had changed. As though he hadn't just seen Riley talking to a man who instructed his people to kidnap Alex. He inhaled a breath and turned on the faucet, placing his hands in the water. He splashed a small amount onto his face to clear his head, but it didn't work. "Okay. I have to go back out there. Christ, I hope you guys can still hear me. I need to check on Alex."

Jacob pushed through the door and on the other side was Silas with Alex next to him. "Oh. I guess I'm not the only one who needed to use the head. Go on in." He tried to walk around them, but Silas thrust out his hand, striking Jacob on the shoulder.

"You need to just hold tight for a minute. I've just had a very interesting conversation with your boy here." He turned to Alex. "Didn't I?"

In that moment, the door to the bar burst open. Jacob whipped around and spotted the three men, with guns brandished, rushing in.

"Owensville Police." Ward held out his badge. "I need everyone to stay where you are and put your hands where we can see them."

Silas's eyes narrowed as he peered at Jacob and Alex. "You fucking assholes. Do you have any idea what've you done? All you had to do was play the game. Goddamn it."

Ward continued through while Ethan veered to the right to secure the area and Decker and Abrams took the other side of the bar.

"Silas Levin?" Ward shouted. "The game's over. Time to come out."

Riley sat still, her eyes on Ward, but Ackerman in her periphery. She shot a brief glance to Jacob, who shook his head, fear and anger imbued in his eyes.

Levin emerged with his hands up and a broad smile on his face. "Decided to pay me another visit, huh? Couldn't leave well enough alone, could you folks? I don't know what the hell I ever did to you people, but you better believe a harassment charge is coming your way."

Jacob leaned in to Alex. "What the hell, man? What happened?"

"He knows. He knows Ackerman's men were back there too. Ward must've heard me on the wire. That's why they rushed in."

"I have to get to Riley. She's sitting next to Ackerman." Jacob took slow and deliberate steps out of the shadow of the corridor. He caught her gaze once again and her expression demanded he stop. He continued.

Riley's shoulders dropped as Ackerman slowly raised from the stool.

"Now what the hell is all this? I come in for a friendly drink and I'm sitting here with a beautiful lady and you people barge in and ruin the night for me?"

Silas turned to the man. "What the hell?"

"I was wondering when you'd realize I was here," Ackerman replied. "I heard you got yourself this place." He gazed around. "Not bad. Better than sitting in a prison cell for six years. You should've been there with me, Silas. Instead, here you were. And setting up games like back in the old days. You haven't changed one bit."

"How the hell?" Silas asked.

"I have people." He turned his sights to Isaac, who had appeared from the back.

Silas looked at his bartender. "You?" He shook his head.

"Okay, this isn't a reunion." Ward still had his gun trained on Levin. "You'd better get the rest of the people out of the back. I won't ask again."

RILEY'S HEAD GREW FUZZY. SHE KNEW INSTANTLY WHAT WAS about to happen. "No. Not now," she whispered. But there was no way to stop it. She gripped the bar top to steady herself. If she drew attention to it, panic would erupt and gunfire would follow. She couldn't let that happen. In the back of her head, a tingling sensation crawled and she peered at Jacob with a marked fear in her eyes. He had to see what was happening. She shook her head at him. Her breath grew labored and then it came.

"I know what you want to do, but you can't. Not this time."

The voice came from a deep place Riley didn't recognize. She stood inside an empty room, white walls and ceilings, devoid of anything. But a boy appeared. "Nate?" This wasn't possible. It was her half-brother. "What are you...how are you here?"

"You're my sister. I knew you were in trouble." He stepped toward her, his twelve-year-old lanky frame looking a little like a marionette. "If you do anything, he'll die."

"Who will die?" Riley was ripped from the moment amid the sound of a gunshot. Her senses returned and she remembered where she was. Beside her, Ackerman collapsed, clutching his chest. "Oh my God!" She leaned over him, pressing her hand against the blood that poured from him. She raised her head to find Decker. His hands shook as he held the gun. His face was ghost-white and his eyes were nothing less than saucers.

Jacob rushed to her. "Riley. Come on." He yanked her from Ackerman and pulled her behind a booth.

Another gunshot erupted. She searched frantically for its origins. "No." Her eyes landed on Silas who'd returned fire but had missed Decker.

"Hold your fire, Goddamnit!" Ward yelled. His arms flailed as he ducked behind a booth for cover. "Decker! Get down!"

It was Abrams who finally reached Decker and pulled him down. "Stay down, man!"

The gunfire stopped. No one was left standing; all had found cover.

"Where's Alex?" Riley asked Jacob as they crouched low. "What about the others in the room?"

"Jesus, Riley. I don't know. I don't know what the hell is happening right now. You were gone. You..."

"It was a vision. It doesn't matter. We have to..." She froze. "Do you smell that?"

"What?"

"Smoke. Oh God. I smell smoke." She raised up. "There's a fire! Everyone out!"

"Get down!" Jacob yanked her down again.

Ward turned his sights to her. "Shit. I smell it too. Get everyone out. Now!" He holstered his gun. "Abrams, Decker. Get outside. Call the fire department." He pushed through the bar. "Who's still in the back?"

Silas peered around the corner from the men's room where he remained in hiding. "Three others." He peered at Renee. "Go! Get out!" He rushed by Ward's side and led him to the backroom.

"I have to go with them." Riley stood again.

"No. Let them handle it. We need to leave." Jacob stood next to her. "Please, Riley, we have to get out of here."

"You go. I can't. I need to help them."

Ethan rushed toward them. "You heard the captain. Let's go." He grabbed Riley's arm.

"Stop!" She yanked it away. "Both of you. Stop pulling me! I'm a cop, for God's sake, and I'm going to help get everyone out. Jacob, you need to go." She started away.

"Shit if I'm letting you go back there without me." Ethan followed her. "Jacob. Help get the rest of the customers out of here. Please."

Jacob watched as Ethan and Riley followed Ward to the backroom. His eyes shifted around in search of Abrams and Decker, but they took whoever they could with them and were outside. His eyes landed on the young bartender. "It's time to go."

She threw down her towel and rushed around to him.

Smoke spilled into the main bar area, rising above their heads. "Stay low," Jacob said. He crouched down and led the way, his hand gripping hers and they started toward the door.

An older man, perhaps in his sixties, was tucked under a table. Jacob spotted him. "Sir, sir, come with us." He stretched out his hand. "It's okay. The door's just ahead. Please."

The man took Jacob's hand and crawled out from beneath the table. "Thank you."

Jacob nodded and led them to the door, which was still open as Abrams and Decker called for help and pushed away any remaining bystanders to safety. He led them through the door. "Step away from the building. Quickly!"

Renee and the older man did as they were told.

"Jacob?" Decker called out. "Is there anyone else inside? Fire department's on their way."

"Riley, Pruitt, and Ward. They went back to the poker room. We have to go back inside." Jacob approached him. "Come on."

"No. Jacob, you have to stay here. There's a back exit. They'll lead everyone out that way. It's too dangerous." Decker pointed to the side of the building. "Flames. We can't go back inside. The smoke is too thick and we have no idea how far that's spread."

"No fucking way am I staying out here, man. Are you crazy? Riley's inside."

Decker grabbed his arm. "Dude. Of all people, she'll be okay. I can't let you back inside. I'm sorry, man. Not going to happen."

27

The smoke thickened in an instant as Riley along with Ward and Silas reached the door to the backroom. Ethan caught up to them. "How many?"

"Three," Silas replied.

A bombardment of emotions slammed into Riley as though an enormous medicine ball had been hurled at her gut. "The fire's inside. It started in there." She reached for the door handle and gripped it before yanking it away and shrieking in pain.

"It's too hot in there." Ward peered at her with uncertainty masking his face.

He didn't know what to do. Riley sensed his fear, his apprehension. Instinctively, she kicked at the door.

"That's not going to help," Silas said.

"How could this happen?" Ethan demanded. "Did you do this?"

"No," Silas replied. "I wasn't in..." His expression hardened. "Oh God. Gage. Jesus, it had to be Gage."

"What?" Ward asked.

Ethan knew exactly who he was. In fact, he'd seen the man in action only yesterday. "He's crazy. I saw him. The man's insane. He can't be in there, though, can he?"

"No. He may be crazy, but he's not suicidal," Silas replied. "Where the hell is the fire department?"

"On their way." Ward examined all possible scenarios as he gazed around. "We have to do something. They're going to burn..."

Riley could do something. If she wanted to, she could put an end to this before anyone got hurt. "It has to be me."

"What can you do?" Silas asked.

Ethan and Ward glanced nervously at one another before Ward replied, "No way, Riley. Not a chance. No. We'll have to figure out another way."

"There's no time, Dan. You know that as well as I do. They have a few minutes, tops." She turned to Silas. "Is that where you store the liquor?"

He peered at his feet and nodded, appearing to understand the implication.

"Dan, when the fire reaches the alcohol, we both know what's going to happen. No one will stand a chance inside there."

Silas peered at them as if they were crazy. "I don't understand. What can you possibly do?"

Riley eyed Ethan and Ward. "Go. Let me take care of this."

"I'm not leaving you," Ward replied.

"Me neither," Ethan said.

"It's too dangerous. Please. We're wasting precious time. Take Levin and go." She eyed Ward. "You don't have a choice."

He relinquished. "Come on." Ward ushered Ethan and Silas away.

"What the hell? Are you serious, Captain?" Ethan tried to pull back.

"Let her do what she has to do," Ward replied.

"Riley, please don't! Just wait for the fire department," Ethan shouted as he was being pulled away.

She put him out of her mind. She had to focus on extinguishing the flames inside. There was still some time. She could feel their pleas for help. Their screams sounded above the flames. "Stand back!" Riley shouted through the door. "Get back now!"

Riley focused on the metal door. Her breath labored again and sweat dripped from her brow. The metal started to dimple, like it'd been hit with rubber bullets. It wasn't enough and she had to focus harder. The door screeched as it began to warp. Inside, their screams were growing louder. The flames were nearing them. She had only moments to open that door so they could escape.

"Help me," Riley whispered. "I need your help." She was calling on Carl, who could no more help her now than he could have helped his own family when they'd been killed in the accident. "Grandpa." She recalled what her father had said. Grandpa could do these very things and it changed him. But she was doing this to help, not hurt. This was not out of anger but out of a sense of duty to save those inside.

Riley knew she was alone. Carl couldn't help her; he couldn't offer words of wisdom or tell her outright what she should do. People would die if she did not act.

Her eyes bore into the door as it continued to twist and writhe until, finally, a hinge shot away like a bullet. "Come on. Open, you son of a bitch." The men inside yelled ever louder. She pushed harder. Another hinge flung away, striking the wall behind her like a knife. The door began to yield to her will. "Open!" she screamed with a voice she didn't know she possessed.

The door flew off completely and slid back, landing in front of the men. Their eyes were wide.

"Run! Come on, run!" she demanded of them.

They were in shock, but their feet began to move and they started toward her. She felt a rush of air get sucked inside and the blaze breathed it in deeply, exhaling a bright yellow flame so tall it reached the ceiling. A side window blew out. Riley couldn't see behind the flames. "Let's go. Let's go." She helped them through. "Back exit!"

Riley started toward the rear exit. The door was locked. With all the power she could muster, she pushed on the door and it swung open, slamming against the wall on the other side.

"Jesus, lady!" Anton Meisner, the younger of Ackerman's henchmen, yelled.

But they were out. They were all out, except Ackerman. Riley looked back into the corridor leading to the main bar. "He's already gone." The voice came from her head. It sounded like Nate's. Maybe she was going crazy, like her grandfather had.

The men appeared from around the building. Riley trailed only steps behind. When she emerged, Jacob was hunched over someone on the ground. She rushed to his side. "Jacob? What happened..." She stopped dead. "Oh my God. No. Is he okay? Captain!" She raised up. "We need help over here!"

Ward was in the middle of the parking lot flagging down the fire truck, though the flames would have drawn their attention. He started to jog back alongside the truck. "Hurry. Hurry!"

"Dan!" Riley screamed again. "Over here!"

He heard her this time and rushed toward her. "What is it? What happened."

Jacob slowly pulled up and the person below him was revealed. "He's gone." His head dropped into his hands.

"What? Alex?" Riley's eyes darted around in search of an answer, a reason for this. "What happened? I got everyone out. What happened?"

"The window blew out." Jacob tried to speak through his sobs. "I don't know how. It just blew and the flames and the glass. They got him. It was like an explosion."

Riley threw her hand over her mouth and shook her head in disbelief. "I did this. I did it. When I opened the door, I heard the explosion behind the flames."

"We need a medic over here!" Ward yelled at the firefighters.

"If you do something, he will die." The words of her half-brother reverberated in her mind. She thought he was talking about Jacob or Dan, or anyone else, but not Alex. "It's my fault. If I hadn't opened the door..."

"If you hadn't opened the door, everyone inside would be dead," Ward interrupted. "You couldn't have known this would happen."

Of course I could, she thought. Riley had freed the men inside the room. Bad men who were criminals and thieves. The one innocent man was now dead. And it was his blood on her hands.

DENNIS ACKERMAN WAS DEAD. HIS TWO MEN HAD JUST BEEN released from the hospital with minor injuries and were about to be arrested by the County police for kidnapping. Gage Parker, who everyone believed started the fire, was in the wind. That left Eli Foster, the man to whom Silas Levin owed a handsome sum of money.

Silas Levin was being charged with conducting illegal gaming activities and threatening harm to Laughlin and his family. He would serve time, but likely not more than sixty days. The Crooked Horse had burned to the ground. So any hopes he had of paying off his remaining debt to Eli had gone up in flames too.

But Riley didn't care about any of that. Screw them. Alex Laughlin was dead, and his wife and kids were in the breakroom with the captain right now. She could hear his wife's sobs.

"Riley, we should go home. Dan said it was okay." Jacob stood in front of her desk. "It's almost four in the morning. You must be tired after..."

"I am. I used everything I had to free those men and for what? So another would die? He warned me."

"Who warned you?" Jacob asked.

"Nothing. It doesn't matter. You know, through this entire fiasco, I thought it was you who was in danger. The terrible visions I had. But I had been deceived."

Jacob moved to sit in the chair next to her desk. "Riley, what you have is an incredible thing. Understanding why or how it works is a fruitless endeavor."

"No, it isn't. I can control it. I don't know why I saw those things. My own fear of losing you, I suppose. After Carl, well..." She trailed off.

Ethan emerged from the backroom with a coffee in his hand. "Captain says you should go home, Riley. Get some rest. Abrams and Decker just left too."

"What about you?" she asked.

"I'll hang here to make sure Laughlin's family gets settled in. I think Ward wants to take them back home."

"To their house?" Jacob asked. "If it was me, that's the last place I'd want to go. Too many memories."

He was right about that. Riley couldn't bear it if she was in the same position. Hell, she could hardly bear it now. Of course, Zoe Laughlin hadn't known she was behind her husband's death. "Fine, we'll go. But we're coming back in a few hours."

"Okay, then that's what we'll do." Jacob stood and took her hand to help Riley from her chair.

Ethan approached her. "I know you blame yourself, but none of this was your fault. You saved lives."

She didn't have the energy to counter his claim. "You should get some rest too." Riley walked toward him and wrapped her arms around his shoulders, pulling him close. His heart pounded. He loved her so much, she could feel it throughout his entire body. They'd been through a lot together. "I love you, Ethan."

He pushed her back gently and peered into her eyes. "If only," he whispered his reply.

Jacob gathered her things and waited by the door, seemingly unaware of their tender and quiet exchange.

Riley released her embrace and smiled. "I'll see you soon." She started toward Jacob and waited while he opened the door. A brief glance back and she saw something in Ethan again, except this was different. It was unknown. And then she recognized it. In the moments between their embrace and his final words to her, Ethan Pruitt had let her go.

"Are you ready?" Jacob said softly as he held the door for her.

She turned back. "I'm ready."

Riley waited on the other side of the door when Jack Thompson opened it. "Hi, Dad."

"Hi. Come in." He stepped aside. "Nate's in his room. He's expecting you."

"I'm sure he is." Riley started into the long corridor of a home she'd never been to before. A foreign place where her father lived with another family. She knocked on his door and slowly opened it. "Nate? Can I come in?"

He pulled off his headphones as he sat on his bed. "Hi, Riley. Yeah."

She walked inside and sat next to him. Neither said a word for a few minutes and it wasn't until Riley decided it should be her that she began. "So I hear you and I have a lot in common."

THE END

ABOUT THE AUTHOR

Bestselling author Robin Mahle lives in Virginia with her husband and two children. Her Kate Reid mysteries have drawn praise for grabbing hold of the reader and refusing to let go. And the intense, fast-paced style of storytelling led her to create another series, the Lacy Merrick thrillers, which readers have called "Believable, and ripped from today's headlines." Now with the Riley Thompson thrillers, readers will once again be taken on an incredible journey.

With powerful leading ladies and action-packed thrill rides, Robin hopes to continue taking readers on roller-coaster adventures that will leave them breathless.

If you enjoyed Ms. Mahle's work, please share your experience by leaving a review on Amazon.

Click here to visit Robin's Amazon Author Page.

ALSO BY ROBIN MAHLE

Force of Nature - A Riley Thompson Thriller (Book 0)

Behind Her Eyes - A Riley Thompson Thriller (Book 1)

All the Shiny Things - A Kate Reid Novel (Book 1)

Law of Five - A Kate Reid Novel (Book 2)

Gone Unnoticed – A Kate Reid Novel (Book 3)

Blackwaters – A Kate Reid Novel (Book 4)

Endangered - A Kate Reid Novel (Book 5)

The Pretty Ones - A Kate Reid Novel (Book 6)

The Last Word – A Kate Reid Novel (Book 7)

Deadly Reckoning - A Kate Reid Novel (Book 8)

To the Bone - A Kate Reid Novel (Book 9)

The Kill Season - A Kate Reid Novel (Book 10)

State of Denial - A Lacy Merrick Thriller (Book 1) - READ FOR FREE!

Shadow Rising – A Lacy Merrick Thriller (Book 2)

First Target – A Lacy Merrick Thriller (Book 3)

Ghost Nation - A Lacy Merrick Thriller (Book 4)

**Sign up to receive Robin's Newsletter so you can stay up to date on her new releases, events, contests and even exclusive new material!